CHARITY'S

GOLD RUSH

Cynthia Hickey

"For I know the plans I have for you," declares the Lord, "plans to prosper you and not to harm you, plans to give you hope and a future."

Jeremiah 29:11 (NIV)

1

"Tis no use talking when the harm is done, Lucas." Charity O'Connell slapped the wet shirt against the tin wash bucket. It was the tenth such proposal she'd received today, and Lucas had whiskey on his breath to boot. The man spent more time at the saloon than he did at his claim.

"I meant no harm, Miss Charity." The wizened old man grinned. He missed several teeth and the ones he still possessed were tobacco stained. "It's your beauty that makes me loco."

"You're as old as me dead uncle." Charity hung the clothes on a stretched piece of rope. Why couldn't she receive one offer from a strapping, good-looking young man and not one as old as the earth or as dirty as the bottom of a mud pit? She worked harder in America than she ever had in Ireland. If only the days were

1

longer and the amount of work shorter.

"You've a mean heart." Lucas spit a stream of tobacco in the dirt. "But I'll try again tomorrow."

Charity laughed. "Off with you. And leave that bag of clothes in your hand behind. I'll have them ready tomorrow."

When she'd hung the last pair of overalls on the line, she placed her hands on her hips and leaned back, popping the kinks from her spine. Backbreaking labor, that's what it was. But there were few ways for a girl to make a living in the mining town of Virginia City, Montana, and Charity refused to be a saloon girl. Da spoiled her for too many years when the gold was flowing.

She knocked the basin of dirty water over, letting the suds sink into the thirsty ground. With a laugh, she kicked off her shoes and sunk her toes deep into the wet softness. The squishy mud soothed away some of the aches of the day and left her feeling like a child again, if only for a moment.

Ah, silliness. She'd be better off taking stock of tomorrow's work and heading down the street for a bowl of stew than acting like a wee child. She glanced into the darkening sky. *Oh, Da, I miss you. We had such fun despite your gambling ways.*

She moved to a nearby horse trough and splashed her feet clear of the mud before slipping her shoes back on. With her stomach rumbling, eating needed to come first.

A restaurant, run by an elderly couple named

Connor, served the best stew in town. Ma and Pa's Kettle filled many a miner's belly. Charity pushed open the rickety door and stepped inside.

Immediately, the rumbles of at least twenty men ceased, greeting Charity with their stares and silence. She rolled her eyes. How many times did she have to eat there before they grew used to her presence and stopped gawking like she was a prize sheep on display? They all stood as one and waited to see which of them would have to give up their seat. Mrs. Connor insisted on manners in her restaurant and would harangue any man who didn't offer his chair to a lady.

Charity shook her head and motioned for them to sit. They followed her instruction, and she scooted into the curtained-off area that served as a kitchen. "I'm in no mood for a marriage proposal today. May I please eat in here?"

Mrs. Connor chuckled. "Suit yourself." She waved a sticky gravy ladle toward a lone chair. "I wouldn't mind the company. Mr. Connor is at the butcher. Still can't understand why you don't get hitched. A pretty gal like yourself ought not to be washing other men's unmentionables."

Fingering her faded calico dress, Charity sighed and sat, looping her feet around the chair legs. "Sure, it'd be nice, but a girl has to make a living and sitting on a brocade sofa acting like the queen of England ain't going to get it done. Besides, none of them makes my heart flutter." Silly or not, she wanted to feel something for the man she married. She picked at the frayed hem around her sleeve.

She needed to get to the mercantile for soap and thread. New fabric for a dress, too.

"Ah. Holding out for love." Mrs. Connor stirred the pot, then ladled a bowlful for Charity. "You wait. Love is waiting."

It'd been a mighty long corner. Charity sighed and dipped a biscuit into the thick broth of the stew before sticking a bite in her mouth. Beef and vegetables melded on her tongue and quieted her grumbling stomach.

Cooking and cleaning for one man sounded like a dream come true. But the right man. Not somebody she could smell coming up the road or old enough to be her da, with no teeth. Most were stained with tobacco. She popped the last of her biscuit into her mouth. And most of the men in town gambled away whatever gold they dug out of the ground. Just like her da. No, it looked like Charity O'Connell would be a spinster in a city full of men. A sad state of affairs, to be sure.

*

Gabriel Williams pulled his buckboard in front of the mercantile and set the brake. "Come on, young'uns."

"Ah, Pa. Can't we wait out here? There's more going on." Sam tugged the brim of his hat lower.

"Fine. If you're good, I'll buy you peppermints."

"Sure thing, Pa." Eight-year-old Sam leaned his dark head over the seat. Beside him, six-year-old Meg did the same. "We won't move a muscle."

Gabe grinned and climbed down. "See that you don't." He didn't like leaving the children alone on a rowdy street, but as a widower and a new Pa, he didn't have many options. They needed to learn responsibility sometime.

He stepped onto the sidewalk and opened the mercantile door as a woman waltzed out, her arms piled high with brown paper packages. Green eyes the color of a spring meadow peered over the top. The tantalizing scent of lilac soap teased his senses. Gabe tipped his hat. "Ma'am."

"Thank ye, kindly, sir." An Irish lilt sounded musical above the crude shouts of men.

The smell of pickles, tobacco, and wood stove smoke greeted Gabe as he stepped inside. He glanced back to see the woman make her way down the sidewalk, her dress swaying with each movement of her hips. He would've liked to have gotten a look at her face to see whether she was as pretty as she sounded.

He'd had his eyes open for a temporary ma for the children for a few months now and wondered whether the little gal was attached or not. Unlikely. Women were as scarce as an egg-laying rooster in Virginia City. A man had to get while the getting was good. And a pretty gal that smelled clean was definitely a prize.

"Howdy, Gabe. What can I get for you?" Mr. Miller, a spindly man with thinning hair leaned across his counter. "Don't see much of you anymore. Not since your Maggie passed on, God rest her soul."

5

"Lots of work to do." Gabe handed him his list. "This ought to hold me for a couple of months. Be back one more time before winter sets."

"Ought to get yourself another bride." Mr. Miller plunked a twenty-five pound sack of flour on the counter. "Winters won't seem so long then. Women are soft and warm on a cold night."

"Been thinking about it." A lot more than he wanted, to be honest. Especially since that stupid wager he placed against his, uh, Maggie's, land. Plumb loco, that's what he was.

Maybe he could put an ad in a newspaper for one of them mail-order brides. If he was quick, she'd get here before the snow hit and be a true help with the young'uns. Sam didn't always tell the truth, and Meg would follow along with whatever trouble her brother found. Somebody needed to keep an eye on them and it wasn't possible for him to be that someone.

But would a woman be content with a marriage that lasted a short while before getting annulled? Gabe couldn't be responsible for anyone longer than that. The frontier wasn't a safe place.

He glanced out the window at the empty wagon and clenched his teeth. If he didn't already have children, he doubted he'd plan on any. Not after their ma died. He'd stay a bachelor. The worry almost wasn't worth it, no matter how much he loved the rascals. Hadn't he proved that by keeping them? Nah, no woman in her right mind would agree to such a set-up. He'd have to continue to muddle through on his own.

"Here you go, Gabe." Mr. Miller slapped a box of nails on top of Gabe's growing pile of supplies. "Need help carrying it out?"

"Nope. Can make two trips, but I'm obliged." Gabe hoisted a sack on each shoulder and pushed through the door. He tossed the flour and sugar into the wagon bed and glanced around for his missing children. He should've known they wouldn't stay put. A flash of yellow caught his eye.

His heart sank to his toes at the sight of Meg rolled into a ball beneath a rearing horse.

*

A scream rent the air. Charity dropped her packages and whirled to face the street. A little girl cowered beneath the waving hooves of a reared horse. "God have mercy." Charity dashed into the street and hunched over the little girl. "Somebody help us!" She reached up with one hand and fumbled for the horse's flapping reins.

Charity gave the child a push. "Go stand by my packages. Hurry." The girl darted out of the street like a bullet. Charity rolled out of the way then leaped to her feet and grabbed the horse's bridle. "Shhh, beautiful. Shhh."

The horse snorted and tossed back its head. The rope set Charity's fingers on fire as it burnt its way along her palm. She hissed and let go.

"Are you loco!" A man shoved her out of the way and hurled himself at the wide-eyed animal. His hat fell at Charity's feet in a puff of dust.

7

Once Charity picked herself up out of the road, she gathered the crying little girl in her arms. The man, who towered over her by at least a foot, calmed the horse, and retied it to the closest hitching rail.

He turned and pierced her with eyes that appeared dark in the night. "I thank you for putting yourself in danger for the sake of my daughter, but ..." He bent and picked his hat up out of the dirt then slapped it against his leg. "That's the craziest thing I've ever seen."

The little girl wrenched free of Charity's grasp and flung her arms around her father's hips. Charity brushed the dust from her dress and gathered her packages. "You're welcome."

He put a hand on her arm, stopping her from leaving. "Please, let me carry those for you. It's the least I can do."

Peering at him over the stack in her arms, she couldn't help but feel small and insignificant next to his height and muscular build. My, but God was good to the man when He handed out looks. Charity's heart fluttered, and she smiled.

"Thank you." Charity was more than happy to relinquish her burden. As soon as her hands were free, the little girl slipped her small one into Charity's hand.

"I'm Meg. That's my pa, Gabriel Williams. My brother Sam is ..." She glanced up at her father.

"Where *is* your brother?" Mr. Williams said. His brows drew together.

"He made me promise not to tell." Meg ducked her head.

"Meg, I asked you a question."

Charity squirmed as much as the child next to her under the man's stern gaze. Must he be so mean? The child just endured a horrifying experience.

"He's at the saloon. Said he could sweep and make a few coins." Tears welled in Meg's eyes.

"Please show me to your home, Miss." A muscle twitched in Mr. Williams's jaw, alerting Charity to the fact he barely held his temper in check.

"Don't you want to fetch your son?" Charity frowned.

"Nobody in Virginia City will hurt him. Except me. I'll most likely tan his hide." His neck flushed crimson.

Charity fairly ran back to her tent. The sooner Mr. Williams delivered her purchases, the sooner he could take his stern attitude somewhere else.

They approached the place Charity called home, and she ran ahead to open the flap. "Just drop them on the table."

Mr. Williams set them down and held out a hand to Meg. "Come along, Meg. We need to fetch Sam and the rest of the supplies. Ma'am." He tipped his hat, turned, and was gone, making Charity's home bigger by his leaving.

Poor child. Such a furious man. What would his son have to endure at his hands for disobedience? Chills ran down Charity's spine, and she shook away the picture of violence from her mind. It was none of her business, and the lass had looked healthy enough. Most likely, the lad received a swat on the behind and little else.

9

She unwrapped yards of blue calico and another few yards of yellow. Doing laundry might be backbreaking work, but it paid well. Finding the time to sew the new dresses would be the hardest part. Keeping the fabric neatly folded, she placed it in a battered trunk with the rest of her precious belongings.

She'd hung up the last of her personal wash, donned her nightclothes, and sat on a three-legged stool, when a shadow loomed outside her door. Charity froze, her hand holding the brush suspended above her head.

"Ma'am? It's me, Gabriel Williams."

Heavens! Charity grabbed the quilt from her cot and wrapped it around her cotton nightgown. "Go away. I do not entertain men in my tent!"

"No, ma'am. I … uh, that is … please, could you step outside for a moment? My children are waiting in the wagon."

That should be safe enough and not do too much damage to her reputation. She wrapped the quilt tighter and stepped outside. A quarter moon cast deep shadows between the trees and tents. Charity squinted and peered under Mr. Williams's hat.

"Might I ask your name, ma'am?"

"It's Charity O'Connell."

He removed his hat and twisted the brim in his hands. "Miss O'Connell, I've come to ask you to be my bride."

2

2

His what?! Charity flushed and glanced around him. The children leaned over the seat staring in her direction. She transferred her attention to the strapping man in front of her. "Why?" After all, they'd barely met and from the looks of the supplies in the back of the wagon, the man was headed ... somewhere.

"Uh, well, I'm a widower and the young'uns need a ma. I've got a good ranch started half a day's ride from here. It's too difficult with two little ones and all the work I got to do. Place needs a woman, and Meg likes you." The words left his mouth in a rush of air.

The thrum of locusts filled the air, along with the occasional gun shot and whoop of a drunken miner. Not the most romantic proposal a girl ever received. Charity stepped closer and sniffed. No stench of alcohol or tobacco. She wasn't positive, but she thought he had all

11

his teeth. His son still looked in one piece, so maybe the man's bark was worse than his bite. She could definitely do worse. And given the caliber of men in the vicinity, worse was all she was likely to get.

She refocused her gaze on him and stepped closer. His lips trembled in an effort to smile. Charity sensed his nervousness, and her heart softened. Other men approached her with daring or drunkenness, not timidity.

Could she wed a stranger? Even a handsome one? Other men would leave her alone if she got hitched. The notion of having a man provide for her sounded good. No more mounds of laundry and marriage proposals from desperate men hankering for a wife. She gave a curt nod. "My answer is yes."

"Good." His shoulders relaxed. "I'll pick you up in the morning. If you need anything, me and the young 'uns will be bunking at the boarding house. Preacher is in town so we can get married right away." He clapped his hat back on his head and jogged to the wagon, climbed up, and once again, left Charity alone.

She shuffled back inside and sat on the cot. Despite the fact she'd marry in the morning, tears stung her eyes at the formality of his proposal. A girl wanted flowers and sweet words, not two children looking on from a wagon full of supplies, a horse snuffling over the prospected groom's shoulder, and a night too dark to see the man's face properly.

"Oh." Charity plopped back. She was a silly ninny, for sure. The man made her heart flutter. Isn't that what she told Mrs. Connor she wanted? But was it also wrong to want someone to love her?

Morning arrived with her still sprawled across the bed like a stranded seal. Charity untangled herself from the quilt and struggled to sit up. What would she wear that wouldn't have her looking like an impoverished immigrant? If only she'd had time to sew a new dress. Her yellow calico would have to do. Besides a small singed hole near the hem, it was the better of her two dresses and looked nice with her light red hair.

By the time she dressed and had her hair smoothed back and tied up with a ribbon, she heard the rumble of a wagon outside. Charity glanced around her home, noting the few items she'd take with her. The trunk of treasures, the quilt on the cot, the cot itself, a few blue tin plates with white speckles, and a shelf of books. That's it. All she had to her life. No matter. She was embarking on a new journey. With head held high and nerves strung tight, she strolled outside.

Mr. Williams stood beside the wagon, scuffing his boot in the dirt. When he saw her approaching, he whipped off his hat. "Ma'am."

"You might as well call me Charity, don't you think?" She gave him a shaky smile.

"And you can call me Gabriel, or Gabe. I answer to both." He held out his hand to help her into the seat. "I left the young'uns at the boarding house. Thought we could get hitched in private then pick them up on our way out." His gaze searched her face.

Charity swallowed past the boulder in her throat,

and turned her head. "Certainly." How could she do this? She didn't know the man. Maybe he was a scoundrel, or a gambler, or a secret drunk. Lord, help her. She twisted her hands in her lap.

Gabe clicked to the horses, and they moved toward a two-story, clapboard building at the end of the street. "I've got the preacher expecting us, and the innkeeper and his wife will stand in for our witnesses."

"That's fine." Her stomach rolled, and it took every ounce of willpower Charity possessed not to lose the stale biscuit she'd eaten for breakfast.

"There's something I ought to tell you." Gabe pulled the wagon in front of the building. "I'll understand if you change your mind."

Charity searched his face. Bright spots of color dotted his cheeks beneath his hat. "What is it, Mr. Williams?"

He faced her. "You seem a mite skittish. There's no reason to be, really. I plan on this being a marriage in name only."

"You plan on it being so?" The man had a lot of nerve. Didn't Charity's feelings count for anything?

"Well," he removed his hat and ran his hand through his hair. "I'm needing someone to watch my young'uns while I finish building the ranch. At the end of a year, next spring, actually, we'll get an annulment, and you'll be free to go along your way."

"And how will I benefit from this arrangement, Mr. Williams?" Charity blinked and ducked her head against the tears threatening to swell over. She should've known the man wouldn't want her for her sake alone. No, the only ones interested in Charity as a real wife were the ones she wouldn't touch with a ten-foot log. And all they wanted was someone to warm their beds.

Marriage to Mr. Williams would provide food on the table, a roof over her head, and, if she were lucky, a few snatched moments of peace once in a while to look for gold. There were worse things in the world than marriage to such a strapping man.

"Please call me Gabriel or Gabe. I'll compensate you well for your time. If nothing else, we can be friends."

"If that's what you want, Mr. Williams." Friends! Despite her willingness to wed the man, anger over his casual treatment of marriage replaced pain, and Charity clutched her reticule in order to keep herself from whacking the dolt upside the head.

Gabe climbed down and helped her off the seat. He ushered her through the parlor and upstairs where he knocked on a door. A portly, balding man opened the door, and Gabriel dragged Charity inside. If she ever got over her rattled nerves, she might have to work on her new husband's manners first thing.

"Reverend, we'd like to be married." Gabriel removed his black felt hat. "I know you're leaving town this morning, so we'd like to do it now."

"We'll need two witnesses." The Reverend removed a small black book from a nightstand.

Gabriel nodded. "I'll be right back." He dashed out the door, his heels pounding on the wooden floors.

She fiddled with her reticule. Not the wedding she'd imagined as a little girl. But, she'd said yes, and Charity Rose O'Connell did not go back on her word. Then why was her stomach in knots?

She avoided the eyes of the preacher who clutched his worn Bible in front of him like a shield. The room contained a cot, a wash basin, and a chipped night stand. Faded calico curtains fluttered like a wounded butterfly in a tepid breeze. Not exactly a fancy place to stay, but it looked clean.

She sagged with relief when Gabriel returned with the witnesses. Gabriel stood beside her, took her hand in his large callused one and stood rigid as the preacher read them their vows. That over, Gabe laid a chaste kiss on her cheek that left a heated mark as strong as a branding iron. Charity cupped her cheek.

Grabbing her arm, Gabe practically dragged her out of the room. So much for Charity's first kiss.

*

Gabe knew he had hurt Charity's feelings with his announcement of a name-only marriage. He supposed he should've mentioned it the night before when he asked her to marry him, but he plain didn't think about it. He'd already wasted two days in town and there was no one else to look after the stock but him. If only he hadn't made that stupid wager with Amos Jenkins. Nothing had gone right since. Gabe wasn't normally a gambling man. If Amos hadn't riled him, he probably wouldn't be dragging along a feisty Irish gal to be a mother to his children.

Oh, yeah. He hadn't missed the fire in her green eyes when he mentioned them being friends. She hadn't seemed too thrilled about the future annulment either. Well, they hardly knew each other. What did the woman think?

He glanced down at her set jaw and narrowed eyes. What'd he do? She was riled again, and they hadn't even left for home.

He only hoped life wouldn't be too interesting with the red-haired gal around. He had work to do and couldn't afford the distractions of a pretty face. Time was ticking, and every day presented Gabe with a new challenge of meeting the terms of Amos's stupid bet.

Gabe led his group to the wagon and headed toward home. Charity sat beside him like she had a pine trunk stuck down the back of her dress.

Gabe glanced at her out of the corner of his eye. "Something troubling you?"

"I'd like to collect my things, if it wouldn't be too much trouble," she said.

"Of course." Addlebrained! He should've known she'd want to stop for her things. Gabe eyed the sun rising in the sky. It'd be late afternoon before they got home at this rate.

"You needn't sigh. I don't have much." She clenched her fists in her lap.

"It's no problem." He stopped in front of her tent. "You want me to get everything?"

"Everything but the tent itself. That's rented." Charity allowed him to swing her from the seat. His

17

hands spanned her waist. Their gazes met for a minute, and Gabe tried desperately to work up moisture for his dry mouth.

A sprinkling of freckles dotted skin so pale he swore he could see the veins. Eyes that sparkled with gold flecks stared into his. Lips the color of pink roses trembled over a rounded chin and begged to be kissed. It'd been two years since a woman shared his roof. The thought slammed into Gabe like a bullet. The decision to marry might turn out worse than the wager against his land.

He released her and ducked inside the tent faster than a cat with its tail on fire. Hoisting her trunk on his shoulders, he headed back out and added her things to his own supplies. Several trips later, he stowed the last of her possessions.

"Gabriel Williams."

Gabe stiffened. Minutes away from escape. He turned with all the joy of a man led to a hanging.

Amos Jenkins sauntered up the road, mouth full with a chaw of tobacco. He spit, barely missing the toe of Gabe's boots. "Where you headed?"

"Ought not to be too hard to figure we're headed home." Gabe marched to the front of the wagon.

"Who's the woman?"

Gabe took a deep breath and turned to face him. "This is my wife."

Amos gave a wheezing laugh. "You got hitched? It won't do any good against our bet. I'll still own your land when the year is gone, unless you want to up our wager."

Charity whirled. Her face paled. "You're a gambling man?"

*

Her worst fear stared her in the face, then her new husband turned away, guilt marring his features. Seemed the man was more full of secrets than a politician's mistress.

Glancing around the group, she noted the curious faces of the children. Her heart wrenched. How could she protect them from the childhood she'd suffered? She sagged against the wagon. She could annul immediately, but she'd married Gabe knowing they'd part in a year. How could she go back on her word now? There was no way, in good conscience, she could leave the children to the same circumstances surrounding her own childhood.

Her gaze met Gabe's for a second before she turned away. She'd thought there might be something between them when he'd helped her from the wagon and his hands lingered at her waist. But there couldn't be. She wouldn't go through what her mama did before she died. Da promised repeatedly to stop gambling, to no avail. Charity vowed not to let the same thing happen to her.

It wasn't that Da didn't love her, he did. But he'd always told her that her sharp tongue would keep a man from wedding her, no matter how comely her face. That'd been the case until Virginia City. Then every mongrel within sight had come knocking. Now, she

19

found a man she could enjoy seeing across the breakfast table, and he turns out to be exactly like the others.

Taking a deep breath, she straightened. She'd make do for the time agreed upon. While Gabe worked the ranch, she'd take care of his home and children and dig for gold when she could. Somehow, someday, Charity would never have to rely on a man again and fulfill her Da's wish of striking gold at the same time.

"It's nice to meet you, sir, but I'm afraid we must be getting home." Charity hoisted her skirts and climbed into the wagon unassisted. "God's blessing on you."

Gabe looked taken aback but he didn't say anything. Instead, he launched himself beside her and headed them out of town.

Silence stretched as long as the road in front of them. Meg leaned across the seat and swiveled her head from Charity to Gabe to Charity again. What must be going through the child's mind?

"I need to go to the necessary, Pa."

"Can't you wait awhile longer? We're not even halfway yet." Gabe frowned.

"No. We were at Ma's place a long time."

Ma? Mercy. Charity had no idea how to be a mother. She should've thought things through a bit more. A gambling husband and two children and her not even married a full day yet. Her stomach threatened again.

Gabe stopped the wagon. At this rate, they'd travel

all day. "Charity, would you mind taking her into the bushes?"

"What?" Charity eyed the thick brush. Any manner of creature could be lurking in there. Give her the open land of Ireland any time. At least a person could see what was sneaking up on you.

"I don't like her going by herself." Gabe's tone left no room for argument. "Couldn't be helped before, but now she's got you."

Charity climbed unsteadily from the wagon and waited for Meg. Sam swung over the side and dashed out of sight. Meg followed. Well, why couldn't he have taken his sister? Charity lifted her dress high enough to keep from snagging it in the brambles and shuffled after them.

"Meg? Sam?" Bushes rustled and Charity jerked. "Where are you?"

Meg popped up. "Shhh. You make too much noise." She ducked back down behind a thick bush.

"What are you afraid of?" Sam appeared at Charity's elbow. "Pa told me how you saved Meg from a horse. Ain't nothing out here that big."

Charity clasped a hand to her throat. "Saints alive, child! You scared ten years off me. Besides, horses don't eat people."

"You're funny." Sam raced back to the wagon.

Meg finished her business and tucked her hand in Charity's. "I think I'm going to like you being my new ma, even if you do talk strange."

Charity's heart warmed at the little girl's words.

21

Hopefully, Charity was cut out to be a mother, strange words and all.

*

Amos leaned back in his leather chair and folded his ankles on top of his polished oak desk. He rolled an unlit cigarette between his fingers. So, Gabe got himself hitched again.

It wouldn't do him any good. He'd still lose his land, and most likely his new bride along with it. The man had already proved he couldn't keep a woman alive in Montana.

Amos tightened his fingers, snapping the cigarette. Growling, he tossed it in the waste receptacle at his feet. Amos had seen the pretty Irish gal around town, even thought once or twice about making her acquaintance. Pity she married Gabe. Doing so only put her in harm's way. Amos would have rather left her out of things.

He settled the chair back on all four legs and moved to the window where his ranch stretched out before him in a glorious display of green grass, wildflowers, and fat cattle. A successful ranch. The only thing lacking was a creek and a family. Both of which he intended to rectify within a year.

3

Charity clutched her stomach. What she'd originally thought was a lush green hill turned out to be her new home. It made her stone cottage in Ireland look like a mansion. A wooden door and a window with paper tacked over the opening comprised the front.

To her right sat a barn, glorious in comparison to the hovel Gabriel seemed so pleased about, judging by the grin on his face. A garden, surrounded by a split-rail fence, sat off to the east. She could imagine dipping her feet into a creek that bubbled about fifty yards away, and thanked the Lord she wouldn't have far to cart water. Trees dotted the landscape. A beautiful place, except for the hole in the ground that would be her home.

She accepted Gabriel's hand and allowed him to help her down, then pulled away as soon as possible. No sense dwelling on the heat of his skin against hers, or how safe his size made her. Her new husband made it quite clear they'd share a space for a year and no more.

Sam ran ahead and opened the door, Meg on his heels.

With head held high, Charity stepped inside her new home, and wilted. Little light came through the window. A wood stove occupied a corner of the one room. At least she wouldn't have to cook over an open fire. A wooden table with two benches took up the center of the space. Shelves with canned goods ran along the walls. Was that a bug scurrying across the packed dirt? Beneath the cans, clothing hung on hooks along walls covered with old newspapers. A tattered quilt separated two beds. Charity would bet her stockings that the mattresses were filled with straw. She'd give almost anything to sleep on goose feathers. Except, Charity didn't gamble. Mercy, she wasn't one to think above her lot in life, but she'd expected a bit more than this.

She stepped aside and let Gabe squeeze past with her trunk. He set it next to one of the beds. "I'll set up your cot and string another blanket. You and Meg can share this space, Sam and I will share the other."

"That'll be fine. Thank you." She opened the cedar chest and pulled out her best apron. A navy blue with ruffles along the hem. She'd get to work fixing supper. Tomorrow, she'd come up with a plan to spruce the place up a bit. Just because they lived in a hole like rabbits didn't mean they couldn't have a few nice things around them.

Once Gabe set the rest of things inside, he planted his hands on his hips. "Ain't much, but it's home. Figure you can add a woman's touch. Whatever you want is fine by me." He nodded, motioned for Sam to follow him, and ducked out the door.

"For sure, the man just hired a servant." What she wanted was a floor other than dirt and at least one glass window.

Charity yanked the tie behind her back into a bow. Why should the thought bother her? This way, there'd be no pawing when she was tired at the end of the day. She'd seen how her Mama barely tolerated Da's touch after a while. Of course, that could've been the whiskey on his breath. Still, Charity missed him. He'd loved his only child.

She stomped over to the shelf of canned goods. Most looked to be over a year old. Probably put up by his late wife. Charity sighed. She'd have to can, too, if they wanted to eat through the winter. No wonder the man wanted a wife.

By the time Gabe and Sam returned, Charity had set the table with her own tin blue dishes, biscuits wrapped in an embroidered towel nestled in a wooden bowl, and the luxury of a new candle stuck out of a jar. She ladled ham and beans onto each plate and stood back to see how the food was received.

"Sit, please." Gabe waved his fork. "No need to stand over our shoulders while we eat."

Charity raised her eyebrows. Da always wanted her

to wait a few minutes to see whether he wanted something else. Eating while the food was hot was a rare treat. "Thank you."

"Candle is a nice touch."

She speared him with a glance. "It is my wedding supper after all." The dolt.

He jerked and locked gazes with her.

Lifting her fork, Charity gave him the sweetest smile she could muster.

*

Gabe toed off his boots, unhooked his suspenders and let his pants fall, and then climbed beneath the blanket with Sam. His son immediately curled into him. Gabriel chuckled. No sense in fooling himself. He'd rather it were Charity beside him, thorns and all. But there wasn't any sense liking a gal that wouldn't be around long, or one with claws.

She'd seemed downright annoyed at supper. For the life of him, he couldn't figure out why. Seemed he'd been aggravating her all day. He'd been upfront with her about the marriage conditions. It couldn't be the fact they didn't share a bed that had her riled, could it? Maggie hadn't cared much for that part of marriage.

Lord, I'm a fool. But you promise to look out for the foolish, of which I'm king. Gabe cursed his impulsive nature. Should've left things alone. But the sight of emerald eyes over a stack of paper wrapped parcels had left him addled. Then, she'd darted into the road after Meg, and cinched the thought.

He'd loved Maggie, no denying it, but their love

hadn't been the heart-stampeding, word-stumbling emotion he might be able to feel around Charity. Obviously, he'd been without a wife too long. He shouldn't be having these feelings after only a day. But she shore was pretty, and her foot-stomping made him laugh inside.

He glanced at the divider between the two beds. If he were to have Sam sleep elsewhere and invite Charity over, they wouldn't be able to have an annulment. The last thing Gabe needed was the distraction of a woman. From now on, he'd make sure he spent all his time in the barn or with the cows. Maybe even have Meg bring his meals out to him.

Whatever it took not to have to look into those accusing green eyes.

*

Charity woke the next morning to a pair of black-eyed Susan eyes watching her sleep. "Good morning, Meg."

"Morning, Ma." The little girl bounced on her knees. "Pa and Sam ate the leftover biscuits and said they'd see us at dinner. Ain't you going to get up and do your chores?"

"In a moment." She glanced at the open front door. Sunlight spilled in, dust motes dancing on the beams. "Guess I overslept."

"Iffen we don't do our chores, Pa says he'll whoop us."

Heavens! "He hits you?" Charity'd like to see the man try to lift a hand against her. No man's bad temper could stand against a cast iron skillet against his skull.

"Nah. We always do our chores." Meg grinned, showing off dimples. "I suspect Pa's just teasing anyhow."

Charity threw off her quilt, shook it free of any bugs that might have landed during the night, and reached for the dress she'd worn yesterday. She felt silly for worrying about Sam's safety the day before. Obviously, Gabe cared deeply for his children. "Let me cook up some eggs, and we'll get started."

"Today's Monday, so it's wash and bread day."

Charity grimaced. "Who set those rules?"

"Ma did before she died. Since you're the new ma, you gotta follow 'em." Meg climbed from bed and dashed outside. Within minutes, she'd dragged a metal tub inside.

Charity shook her head. "Leave that outside. It'll turn the floor to mud. Gather up the dirty clothes while I fix breakfast." She'd be darned if she'd do all the work when there was another capable pair of hands around. Laundry! She would've liked a couple of days free considering that's all she seemed to do before.

The open door beckoned. Charity succumbed to its siren song and gazed out on a clear day. If she listened close, she could hear the breeze through the aspens and the gurgle of the brook. What a welcome change from the bustling town.

The sound of Gabe's voice and Sam's laugh reached her, and she turned toward the corral. Sam trotted around the enclosure on the back of a painted pony while Gabe shouted instructions. Didn't look to her like the two were getting much work done. Ah, well, that's the lot of women, wasn't it? Do the majority of the work while the men played?

She grabbed a bucket from beside the stoop and headed to the creek. Might as well get the water heating while she cooked. Mama always said a woman could do more than one thing at a time. As she strolled, she heard Gabe holler, "I bet you can't take him to a trot, Sam!"

Charity cringed. Did her new husband really bet again?

4

The sun's rays shone like jewels on the surface of the clear creek, kissing the crest of each gurgling ripple. A mockingbird warbled from an oak tree, lending its voice to the serenade of the wind's song through the branches.

What a contrast to dusty Virginia City, and a temptation Charity couldn't resist. She set the bucket on the bank and waded in. Icy water stung her ankles, and she gasped.

Charity laughed and, once her skin acclimated to the temperature, immersed herself. She stared up through the water at the distorted sun. What splendor! She rolled over and searched the creek bottom. Shiny gold flecks sparkled, and she almost gulped. Could that be gold?

Laundry and chores could wait. She'd worked from sunup to sundown for as long as she could remember. A few minutes rest wouldn't be the end of the world. Planting her legs on the creek bed, she pushed to the surface, determined to come back later when she was alone.

"Ma?" Meg stood beside the creek, tiny fists on her hips. "I thought you drowned."

"The water's wonderful. Come on in." Charity hiked her skirts and moved toward the bank until the water brushed the tops of her knees like liquid silk chilled from a cool breeze. Heaven. She shoved aside the temptation to strip down to her shift and have a longer swim, or better yet, spend time panning for the one thing that would make her life easier. There wasn't time. Not if she planned on doing the list of chores outlined by Meg.

"I love the water." She cupped her hands and splashed Meg as the little girl joined her.

The little girl shrieked and retaliated. Soon, Meg's clothes were as soaked as Charity's. Charity laughed. "I feel more like working now, don't you?"

"Yes!" Meg jumped up and down. "But the water's really cold."

"It is a bit of a chill, but I think maybe we'll come back to wash off the day's sweat when we're finished with our work. What do you say?" She patted Meg's head.

Meg nodded and pushed through the water until she reached the bank. Charity grinned. Despite Meg's blue-tinged lips she splashed and shrieked like she was having the time of her life. Maybe being a mother wasn't so hard after all. She grabbed the bucket she'd discarded, filled it, and began the first trek back to the waiting wash tub.

As they trudged past the corral, Gabriel and Sam turned and stared. "What happened?" Gabriel frowned and leaped the fence. His long strides carried him to their side. He followed them to the basin. "Did you fall in? Did something frighten you?"

"We played, Papa!" Meg clapped her hands. "And we're going back later to play again."

"Played?"

"Yes, Mr. Williams. We played." Charity narrowed her eyes. "Have you heard of it?"

Gabriel removed his hat and scratched his head. "Of course I have. There just doesn't seem to be a lot of time left for such foolishness once chores are done."

Charity dumped the water in the tub. "I intend to make time. Sometimes *before* beginning chores."

He crossed his arms. "I suppose that's all right, as long as the work gets done."

"You suppose?" Charity took a deep breath and bent to light a fire in the stack of wood piled for laundry. She'd keep her temper. After all, they'd have to live together for close to a year. There was no sense in causing waves. "That's kind of you. If you'll excuse me, I have more water to fetch. Today is wash day, after all."

"It's coming on lunch time."

Charity glanced at the sun. "So it is."

They'd played longer than she'd intended. She gritted her teeth. How could she tell him that ham and beans pretty much exhausted her cooking ability? That and scrambled eggs. She shrugged and headed back to the creek, leaving him standing with Meg. He'd figure out soon enough that the only things she knew how to do well were laundry and making soap.

By the time she'd filled the basin and shaved slivers of an astringent soap into the water, perspiration ran in rivulets down her back. So much for the relaxing swim. She groaned, remembering Meg's words about baking bread. However was she supposed to create time for all those things, especially when she had to cook meals three times a day and hadn't much of a clue how?

She glanced around for the men in the family. Nowhere in sight, but come the scent of food and they would stampede for the house.

She missed her mother. They could've sat down, and Charity could've asked all the questions swarming through her head. Or better yet, she would've learned these valuable skills while growing up. How to cook flavorful meals, and keep a house clean, sew clothes, raise children, can vegetables, and make a husband happy.

Gabriel was a fine looking husband. Better than Charity ever thought she'd find in the wilds of Montana. If she could learn how to be a proper wife, maybe he'd ask her to stay at the end of a year. She sagged against an oak tree and blinked away tears.

Ma died too young, and Charity's da paid for everything as long as there were funds to be made playing cards. When the money ran out, Charity learned

Cynthia Hickey

to do laundry, and ate her meals at the boarding house.

Ah, she was a failure at things most women took for granted. She straightened and grasped the wooden pole to swish clothes in the hot water. Well, life was like a cup of tea, it was all in how she made it. And Charity was determined to make the best of her new life. She'd work hard, and still find time to play a little each day.

"Meg, come stir this pot while I whip together something for lunch." Charity propped her hands on her hips and popped the kinks from her back.

She left the door open to the house in order to shed light on the shelves and surveyed what little was left. She needed to plant a garden immediately if she hoped to have any vegetables for the winter. If they cut another window in the wall, she could grow herbs inside year round on a plant shelf.

Today, it would be beans and day old rolls for lunch. She stuck her head out the door. "Meg, did your father happen to get a garden in by any chance?"

"He's got ground tilled behind the house."

"Seeds?"

"In jars behind the canned goods."

"Bless you." Meg was going to be invaluable, even as young as she was. The girl seemed much older than six. Charity grinned. She'd teach her new daughter how to be a child once she settled into a routine. With all the things filling her day, when would she have time to pan for gold?

*

Amos melted farther into the safety of the trees

34

and watched life progress on the Williams farm. No sane person could call it a ranch. Not with fifty head of cattle and a sod house. At least Amos didn't consider it much more than a homesteader's resting place.

What was Mrs. Williams doing inside the soddy? Such a lovely woman to be stuck in such a place. But then again, the Irish weren't used to much more than a hole in the ground. Still, her fair skinned and bright haired beauty alone warranted her worthy of more in Amos's eyes. Add in the fact that he'd spied through the open door earlier and noticed four beds instead of three. A marriage of convenience. He could give her more. Gabe didn't deserve her.

He'd laughed as Gabe replaced the fence railing earlier, then moved on to survey the house. Progress on the new place was moving faster than Amos liked. He would have to do something to slow things down.

*

Gabe fixed the fence post and stepped back to survey his work. The repair in the split-rail fence ought to work. Not many ranchers out here used fences, but then again, not many kept losing their cattle to the valleys farther up the mountain. "Ready to head back, Sam? Your new ma ought to have something fixed for us to eat by now." Although she had gotten a late start on the laundry. He hoped he hadn't married a sluggard. Playing in the creek! What would the woman think of next?

Maggie hadn't seemed to need such things as relaxation, other than their nightly winter Bible readings

and Sunday afternoons left to plan her chores for the
following week. She'd worked from sunup to sundown
with nary a complaint.

Gabe shook his head and headed for the house. He
stopped by the barn. Meg and Charity tugged the metal
washtub across the yard. What did they have up their
calico sleeves?

"Charity?"

"Thank the heavens!" Charity released her grip on
the handle. "Could you help me drag this to the creek
before your lunch burns?"

"Why?"

"So I can rinse the clothes." Charity spoke as if he
were slow-witted. "There's no sense in heating up
water when the day is beautiful and the creek is
running."

"But, that's not the way—"

She stuck up a finger. "I suggest you do not finish
that sentence. There is one thing we need to get
straight. I am not your former wife, nor will I do
everything the same way she did."

"But—"

The finger remained as rigid as a mountain pine.
"Enough, Mr. Williams. Will you help me or not?"

"Of course, I will." He wasn't a scoundrel. With a
grunt, he hefted the tub and marched to the creek. He
dropped it and turned. "Can we eat now?"

Charity narrowed her eyes and growled. "It's on
the stove. Help yourself."

Obviously he'd said something wrong again. But for

the life of him, Gabe had no idea what. When the little spitfire's eyes sparked like emeralds, and her brogue deepened, he knew he'd better change tactics, and change them fast. But she sure was pretty when she was spitting mad. "Aren't you going to eat?"

"When I'm finished with the laundry. Wouldn't want to jeopardize the day's schedule, would I?" Charity flounced around and stomped off.

Gabe glanced at his children. Meg shrugged, and Sam looked as clueless as Gabe felt. There wasn't anything left to do but go fill their plates.

*

Charity should have stayed and eaten lunch. Her stomach grumbled as she swished clothes in the clean water. She eyed the opposite bank. If she strung a rope, and securely attached the articles of clothing, she could let the water do the work while she panned for gold. Her gaze settled on the flecks in the sand. There was a lot of gold here, she just knew it. Buried beneath the surface like eggs laid in straw.

She plunged her hand into the sand and clutched a rock. Bringing it to the light, she almost shrieked at the gold strands weaving through the rock. It was easier than she'd expected. She'd be rich! She stilled. Half of whatever she found would belong to Gabe. It was his land after all, and he was her husband, even if in name only. She dropped the rock into her pocket. That meant she'd have to mine twice as much. She didn't mind sharing, as long as she got her fair share.

"Charity?"

She gasped and spun, nearly falling backward into the creek. Clutching her pocket, she took a deep breath. "Gabriel."

He held out a hand. "Please, come eat."

The offer was tempting, but she'd gone with only two meals a day for most of her life. "I really should finish here. This afternoon, I need to get the garden planted if we hope to eat during the winter."

"The children can help." He crossed his arms and leaned against the trunk of an aspen tree. A curl fell forward over one eye, giving him a rakish look.

Charity curled her fingers tighter around her treasure to prevent herself from reaching out and smoothing his hair away from his face. "That would be wonderful. Thank you."

He scratched his head. "Do you know how to cook anything other than beans?"

"Not really." She squared her shoulders. "Nor do I know how to sew, can, tend a garden or care for livestock."

"Well, that's a predicament." He ran both hands through his hair. "But one I can remedy easy enough. Our closest neighbor is a woman who has lived on these plains for quite some time. I'm sure she'd be glad to teach you what you need to know."

"That's very kind of you to think of a way to help me." Of course she knew for a fact that her learning would improve his life so they'd both benefit. She squatted next to the tub. "I'll be up in a little while."

"As you wish." His footsteps faded.

Charity closed her eyes. Should she have gone? What if she made him angry enough to sever their agreement early? She'd never strike it rich, then. She needed to tell him of her plans. Maybe he would help her. They could strike up a friendship. Become partners. She grinned and pushed to her feet. She'd show him the rock right away.

Fairly skipping to the house, she withdrew the rock, and burst into the house. "Gabriel, I have a wonderful plan that would benefit us both."

Her enthusiasm died at the sight of dirty dishes in the sink, a congealing pot of beans in the center of the table, and no family. Breathing sharply through her nose, she dropped the rock back in her pocket and rolled up her sleeves.

By the time the kitchen was in order, Charity's temper simmered like a pan over a slow burning fire. What could Gabriel possibly gain by taking the children off on an afternoon romp after lecturing her about no time for fun when there were chores to do?

With a snap of her apron, she draped it over a chair, and stormed outside and around the corner. There, poking holes in the dirt with a long stick, was Gabriel. The children followed along behind him, dropping seeds in the furrows of her garden.

5

Charity's throat stung from unshed tears. Gabriel cared enough about her workload to help her, and she'd done nothing but think evil thoughts while washing dishes. Oh, but she was a wretched woman of the worst kind.

"Surprise." Gabriel grinned. "I thought you were feeling overwhelmed with everything, so the children and I took this off your hands."

"Bless you." Charity blinked rapidly. "I have something to share with you, too." She pulled the stone from her pocket and, with a flourish, handed it to him. "We're going to be rich."

Gabriel's smile faded as he took the rock from her. "This is fool's gold. Worthless."

"No, 'tisn't." Charity shook her head. It couldn't be. "It's real, I'm sure of it."

He sighed. "I'd know if there were gold in my

creek, don't you think?"

"Have you searched?" There had to be gold. Miners used to come to Charity all the time, paying with dust or flakes, and there was very little of the precious stuff left in her trunk. Not enough to provide a life for herself, anyway.

"I'm sorry." He handed her the stick. "If you want to take over here, I'll head to the neighbors and set up a time for Mrs. Stoltz to help you. I'll be back by supper."

"Thank you." Charity dropped her 'gold' back in her pocket. Her heart thudded to her stomach same as the rock did in her pocket. She'd keep it as a reminder not to give up. There was a reason she was here, and the reason was gold. She knew it.

Sam and Meg stared at her with puppy dog eyes, leaving her feeling more foolish than the misbegotten excitement over striking it rich. She watched Gabriel disappear around the mound that was home. She needed a plan, and while she worked on one in her mind, she'd work on improving their living conditions. If not for herself, then for the children. No one should live on dirt floors with nothing over their heads but grass. Even back home, she'd had the luxury of a stone floor.

She glanced to the area north of the house where Gabriel had ropes strung, signifying the placement of rooms in the new place he wanted to build. A place that required time, money, and a temporary wife. All because of a bet!

Charity jammed the pointed end of the stick in the ground, burying a splinter in the palm of her hand. She hissed against the pain and stabbed the pole in the ground again. If no gold resided in the creek, then it lay somewhere else. Her gaze drifted across the plain. Were there caves hidden among the hills? Caves with veins of riches beyond her wildest dream?

She eyed Sam. Boys roamed the land, right? "Sam, do you know of any caves around here? Ones that run deep?"

He dropped seeds into a hole. "Sure I do, but Pa won't let me play in them. He says they're too dangerous."

"As I'm sure they are." What Charity needed was an excuse to explore one of these dangerous caves. Without the children, of course. She couldn't live with herself if something happened to one of them because of her negligence, and she was their mother, for now. Mothers did not put their children in danger.

A fine layer of grit covered her skin by the time they finished planting. Charity sighed and thought of the laundry she'd left beside the creek. With the children's help, she should be able to lug the tub back and hang the clothes to dry. Bread still waited to be made. Oh. Didn't bread have to rise? She slapped her forehead. She should've started that first thing in the morning. That's what she got for being a lazy goose and sleeping in. Charity O'Connell was never lazy. At least not until she got married and lost all ability to plan and schedule her day.

*

Gabe saddled Rogue, his horse, and headed toward

the Stoltz farm. He smiled. Gold in the creek. Silly woman. If nothing else, his new bride provided entertainment. He had to admit she was pleasant to look at, too, especially with that fiery hair spilling over her shoulders after her romp in the creek. Her soft snores from the other side of the hung blanket last night kept him from sleep, serving as a reminder that a desirable woman, his wife, at that, lay on the other side.

He wasn't lost to the fact that Meg didn't play like his sisters did when they were little. She had no dolls or play dishes. No friends her age. Best Gabe could figure, if Charity taught his daughter to be a little girl, if even for a short while, she'd be worth the time he spent teaching her to be a proper Montana wife. For another man.

Shoulders slumping, he spurred Rogue into a trot. After only one day, Gabe knew the homestead would be a lonely place without Charity's sparkle. He was a fool to broach the subject of a yearlong marriage. Neither of them had other prospects waiting and Charity had jumped at the offer of wedding him fast enough. In addition, she didn't seem thrilled about the marriage in name only. Gabe groaned. Yep, he was a darn fool.

The Stoltz farm was a modest place with a sod house, a barn, a handful of cattle, and a large garden. Pretty much like Gabe's own place. Except the Stoltz'es hadn't made a stupid gamble with a greedy man that he'd have a house built by a certain time or forfeit his land. They were content with their modest sod house that stayed cool in the summer and warm in the freezing winter.

"Hello, the house!" Gabe reined Rogue to a stop and dismounted, tossing the reins over a fence railing surrounded by grass for the horse to munch on.

"Mr. Williams." A portly Mrs. Stoltz smiled as she stepped out the door. "Mr. Stoltz is out in the west pasture. What brings you to our humble home?"

"I'm here to see you." Gabe removed his hat. "I got hitched to a woman who doesn't appear to know a thing about living out here. She can't cook, sew, or any of the other things a woman ought to know."

"And you want me to teach her." Mrs. Stoltz nodded. "Send her over first thing in the morning. Come on in, and enjoy some corn pone and milk."

"Much obliged." Gabe followed her into the dim recesses of a home filled with womanly touches. A doily decorated the center of the scarred wood table. Flowers graced the one windowsill beneath a lacy curtain, and a colorful quilt lay folded at the foot of a double wide bed.

"I'm figuring she'll have to stay a few days." Mrs. Stoltz reached on a shelf and pulled down a plate and a tin mug. "I've some recipes I can share, and we'll spend at least a day on cooking, another on sewing, and another on something fun like crochet or knitting. I can even get her started on a quilt. I have lots of extra squares to piece together." She clapped her hands. "It will be such fun to spend time with another woman."

"What about your husband?" He didn't want to

be the means of the other man suffering.

"He can manage for a few days without my undivided attention." She cut a wedge of corn pone and set it on the plate, before pouring the mug full of milk.

Gabe took a seat at the table. "She doesn't know anything."

"Why did you marry her then?" Mrs. Stoltz sat across from him. "Of course, you wouldn't be the first to marry because of a shapely body and a comely face."

He took a deep breath, and shoved his shame to the deepest part of him. "To save my farm from a man like Amos Jenkins." Her eyes widened as he filled her in on the biggest mistake of his life.

She shook her head when he finished. "I thought you were a wise man, Gabriel Williams."

"Not very, obviously." He bit into the corn pone, which stuck in his throat like a fat man squeezing through a skinny door.

"Does your bride know of this bet? What's her name?"

He nodded. "Charity O'Connell. We have a marriage in name only. Don't even sleep in the same bed."

"You don't deserve my corn pone." She yanked the plate away from him. "I've met little Miss Charity a while back at the mercantile. She doesn't deserve to be treated that way. Few women do." She narrowed her eyes. "Her pa gambled away every cent they had, or so folks say, forcing that little girl to make her way washing the clothes of dirty miners. For shame, Mr. Williams.

45

Your Maggie would never have stood for such behavior."

"Maggie was submissive enough to do as she was told." He reached for the plate.

Mrs. Stoltz held it out of his reach. "No disrespect for the dead, but Maggie had the personality of a bug, and you took advantage of her sweet nature plenty of times." She leaned back and placed the plate beside the wash sink, then straightened and crossed her arms. "Besides, she was born in Montana. Miss Charity wasn't. I hope you haven't been too heavy-handed with the girl."

Gabe chuckled. "She doesn't stand for it. Has the temper of a badger."

Mrs. Stoltz laughed. "I'm sure she does. How are you going to make this right? You need to apologize and let her make a decision on whether to stay. You need to do the Christian thing, Gabriel. Marriage is until death do you part. Not until it's consummated, or at least the vows ought to mean something."

"I don't know." What if Charity chose to leave immediately if given the chance? Gabe would lose everything. Without her taking over the regular chores and keeping track of the younguns, he'd never finish building on time.

His heart sank. He needed to do the right thing, ranch or not. Charity was a person, with feelings and a spirit. Gabe didn't want to be the one to break her with his bad choices. He'd spend some time dwelling on what to do. "We'll see what happens in a year. Can I have the plate back, please?"

*

By the time Charity finished hanging clothes, the sun hovered right above the mountains, casting the land in deep purple shadow. She glanced at the children's disappointed faces. "How about if we go on a treasure hunt?"

"You still looking for gold?" Sam's head jerked up. "I'd like some of that."

"No, I'm looking for things to make this house a home." Charity started for the barn. "You coming with me?"

"What are you going to find in the barn?" Sam trotted to her side, leaving Meg to trail behind.

"Surely your ma had some things, didn't she?"

"Yep, but Pa said he didn't want to have to care for them until he got the other house built. They're in the loft, and in her trunk in the house." Sam dashed ahead. "Ma's ma brought them over from Ireland."

Excitement bubbled up in Charity at the thought of things from her birth place. She didn't mind spreading around a few objects that once belonged to someone else. Meg should have her mother's things. She'd deal with Gabriel's wrath when the time came.

Sam scrabbled up the ladder to the loft. Straw rained down, catching in Charity and Meg's hair. "There's a mirror, a bureau, and some fancy dishes. Do you want them all?"

"Anything to place on the dirt floor?" They wouldn't be able to move furniture without Gabriel's

47

help, and Charity wasn't sure they'd get that. Not if he stored the items in the loft to keep them out of sight.

"There's a rug . . . and kittens!"

"Send down the rug. Sam?" When the boy didn't respond, Charity hitched her skirt and climbed the ladder.

Sam knelt beside a bed of straw. Three kittens looked up with wide eyes, and tried to scurry away when Charity appeared.

Charity leaped for a calico, and stirred up a cloud of dust. She sneezed. "Oh, aren't you a pretty wee thing. We could use a house cat." And Meg would love something cuddly to dress up in doll clothes and to love on.

Sam shook his head. "Pa won't allow an animal in the house, Ma. He's said it at least a hunnerd times. The house is too small. Besides, there's more than one here."

"Not for a bitty thing like a kitten. We'll have to talk him into it won't we? We can keep one and the other two can be barn cats." Charity nuzzled the ball of fur and sneezed again. "We'll call you Patches."

"Ma?" Meg's voice shrieked, raising the hair on Charity's arms. "Ma!"

Charity thrust the kitten into Sam's arms and scurried from the loft as fast as she could in a dress. Her feet tangled, and she lost her footing, sure she'd drop like a sack of potatoes to the hard ground. She kicked her legs, stirring up more dust, until she found the next rung of the ladder and wiped her streaming eyes on her sleeve.

Meg stood like a post, staring at the barn door. Charity rushed to her side. "What is it?"

Meg pointed. A snake coiled in the door's shadow. Charity's skin prickled. She had no experience with snakes, since Ireland had none. Were all snakes poisonous? She'd have to assume they were. Off with the serpent's head. That would be best. She whipped back and forth in search of something. There. She thrust Meg behind her, then grabbed a nearby hoe.

"Don't move, sweetie. I'll take care of it." Her heart threatened to burst free of its cage. Lord, have mercy! Charity raised the hoe and brought it down with all the force she had in her. The impact vibrated up her arms. The snake's head fell free, leaving its sinewy body to writhe in torment.

"Charity?" Gabe called from outside.

"In the barn. Be careful, there's—"

"Oh." Gabe stepped into the doorway. He glanced down. The color faded from his face. Before Charity could take a step toward him, he keeled over like a felled tree.

He'd died and left her a widow the second day of matrimony. Charity sagged to the ground in a heap of faded calico and covered her face with her hands. How could God be so cruel?

"Pa's afraid of snakes." Sam kicked the four-foot reptile away and knelt by his father's body. "He's not afraid of much, but always faints straight away when he sees a snake."

"He's not dead?" Charity crawled to Gabe's side. "Just fainted?"

"Yep. Dead away."

She bit her lip to prevent a giggle from escaping. Gabriel Williams, over six feet tall, and afraid of snakes to the point of losing unconsciousness. Despite her efforts, laughter escaped her.

"Don't. Laugh." Gabriel pushed to a sitting position. "Maggie died of snakebite. I can't stand the things."

"'Tis sorry I am, but it's naught but a wee serpent, and it's no longer alive." She would not admit her own fear. "I'll protect you whenever there's one around."

"I didn't know you had killed it." Gabriel glared at her. "I said not to laugh." His eyes narrowed at the cat. "What's that?"

"It's called a cat." Charity stood and brushed her skirt free of dirt and straw. She must look a fright with red eyes and nose. "We're taking it to the house."

"No, you're not." The color returning to his face, Gabriel got to his feet.

"It's the least you can do, on account of me saving your life." Charity grinned.

"The snake was already dead when I walked up."

"You wouldn't know it from your actions, now would you?" She took Patches from Sam's hands. "Come on, fearless husband. Let's see what I can scrounge up for supper."

"You're an evil woman, Charity O'Connell Williams." Gabe made a wide berth around the snake.

Charity Williams. She liked the sound of her new

name on his lips. The fact the man had a fear of snakes, endeared him, rather than showed a sign of weakness. She rather liked it. Now, how would he react when she requested his departed Maggie's belongings be carted back to the house?

6

"Is this a recent fear of snakes?" Charity jogged to keep up with Gabriel. She wanted to joke him out of his embarrassment, but didn't figure from the stony look on his face, that the idea would be well received. He was definitely one of the most prickly people she'd ever met.

"Nope. Been afraid all my life. I was bitten when I was a little guy and almost died." His jaw tightened. "Gave my ma a real fright. Then, after Maggie, well..."

"Do you have a scar? Can I see it?"

"It's on my upper thigh." He increased his pace, high spots of color on his cheeks. "You have an odd sense of curiosity."

"Oh." Charity put a hand over her mouth. Husband or not, that was an area of his body off limits for sure. When would she learn to think before speaking? She needed to get her mind onto something else. She should probably take care of the snake carcass before Gabriel needed to go back into the barn. What if he fainted and hit his head and no one was around to help?

He glanced sideways at her. "What are *you* afraid of?"

Things too numerous to mention. How could she tell him she was frightened of being alone or failing at the life she'd chosen to undertake? Or that the possibility of no one loving her just for who she was scared the daylights out of her? She straightened her shoulders. "Thunderstorms."

That was a lie. She loved the crackle of lightning and boom of thunder. She swallowed back the guilt and turned toward the barn. "I'll be in the house in a moment. Go relax and get to know Patches."

"I don't want a cat in the house."

Without looking over her shoulder, she said, "You're outnumbered, Mr. Williams."

Gabriel grabbed her upper arm and swung her around. "It's my home."

"And for the next twelve months, at least, it's mine, also." She yanked free and hitched her skirt in order to move quicker. "What do your children do in the long winter months?"

"They learn to read, do their sums, and I teach them Bible stories." He kept pace with her. "It's up to the parents to provide their children's religious training since we have no church this far out. Or a school for that matter. Occasionally, we'll make it into town for

53

shopping. Maybe twice a year."

"Do they have any toys?" She stopped and studied his face.

The man really did look confused. His brow lowered over hazel eyes that sparkled like the jewels she'd seen in a rich lady's ears once in London. Gabriel chewed the inside of his jaw, as if the word 'toy' wasn't in his vocabulary. Charity still had the simple linen doll her mother had made her when she was a wee child, the blue dress now faded. It was one of her most cherished possessions. "Simple things, like a carved horse or a rag doll? I didn't think so. The cat will keep away the mice and give the children a friend during the cold months."

"Do you ever ask permission for anything? Sam and Meg can occupy each other. They have before now."

"No. Now, unless you'd like to see the snake again, I suggest you go back with the children." Charity smiled. Asking permission only set a person up for heartbreak, or worse. It gave the opportunity for someone to take all that a person had and throw it away, leaving that person destitute and unable to provide a decent living for themselves.

She'd thought marriage would change that, until she discovered her new husband didn't want a true marriage. He wanted a wife as a means to win a gamble. Through a haze of unshed tears, she watched Gabriel rush back to the house. No matter. She'd make the most of the next year and worry about the days after when the time came.

By the time she had the carcass buried in a corner of the garden, the sun slept behind the mountain, and Gabriel had lit a lantern in the sod house's one window. Charity leaned on the shovel and stared inside as he tossed his head back in laughter. Meg threw her arms around her papa's neck while Sam watched from his seat at the table.

Charity swallowed against the lump in her throat. Such a pleasing picture they made. One she wasn't a part of. What would it feel like for Gabriel's strong arms to hold her or his lips to brush against hers? She closed her eyes, almost hearing his husky voice proclaim his love for her. Surely he cared. Otherwise he wouldn't have taken the time to till her garden, would he?

Wishful thinking and daydreams were a waste of time. And time seemed more precious than gold on the Montana prairie.

She leaned the shovel against the barn and shuffled inside to grab her own dinner.

"Evenin', Ma. We saved you a plate." Sam stood and pulled out her chair for her.

"Thank you." Charity moved to the washboard, washed her hands and face, and then turned to take her seat. Two pairs of dark eyes, and one pair that seemed to change shades of blue and green depending on his mood, stared at her.

She put a hand to her face. "Do I still have dirt?"

Gabriel shook his head. "The children were telling me how brave you were about killing—the, uh—snake." He shuddered. "I'm much obliged, Charity. You put their safety above your own."

"As any responsible adult would." His unwavering gaze made her uncomfortable. Charity busied herself sitting and arranging her napkin in her lap.

"Not everybody. I'd like to give thanks for not only our meal, but for you." Gabriel stretched his left arm across the table and waited for Charity to place her smaller hand in his. The children scrambled to their places and joined hands.

"Father, we ask that you bless this humble meal, and we thank you for using this brave woman to save my children and myself from certain death this night. Amen."

Certain death? Surely not. Charity fidgeted and drew her hand free. There hadn't been a lot of praying in the O'Connell home. Especially after her ma died, and Pa tossed everything else away on the card tables. Gabriel exaggerated the danger to his family. Instead of meeting his gaze, she dropped hers to a plate of milk and leftover corn pone. She really did need to learn how to cook.

*

"Mrs. Stoltz is more than willing to teach you a woman's place in Montana and how to do women's work." Gabe spooned a heaping spoonful of food into his mouth. "I'll take you over first thing in the morning. The children and I will do fine without you for a few days."

"Days?" Charity lifted her head. "You're sending

me away?"

"You'll know everything you need to by the time you get back." He grinned around his spoon.

She looked stricken rather than pleased. Would Gabe ever figure this woman out? All he wanted to do was make the next year as easy for her as possible. After all, the last thing he needed was for her to exhaust herself. Any fool could see she wasn't made of sturdy stock. Not with a waist as tiny as Meg's and her barely taller than Sam. But then again, she had Gabe beat in the bravery department. He set his spoon down with a clatter. "You don't want to go?"

"I just arrived." She still stared at her plate.

"I thought it would make things easier for you. You don't have to go, if it bothers you."

She took a deep breath. "No, you went to all the trouble. I'll pack my things before I go to sleep."

"Children, head to bed. Your ma and I need to talk." Gabe stood and cleared off his plate as Meg and Sam grumbled about going to bed early. Meg clutched the kitten her arms. "Charity, would you step outside, please? There's something I need to tell you."

Charity's eyes widened, and she gathered the children's plates along with her half-eaten dinner. After setting them into the washbasin, she brushed past him and outside.

Gabe rubbed the back of his neck, not knowing how to broach the subject of her feelings. He and Maggie had lived together like folks who'd never been apart, knowing what the other thought without having to say anything. Boring. Bland. Predictable. That's what his life had been like. Charity had been with them for two days and had already livened the place up more than he'd thought a person could. He stared toward where he planned to build the big house.

A gentle breeze carried the sweet scent of honeysuckle and teased the ends of Charity's curls. A coyote howled off in the distance. A beautiful mournful sound.

Gabe would make sure to build a couple of rocking chairs to set on the new porch. Wouldn't it be nice to pass a quiet evening listening to God's creation and watching the stars flicker to life each night? He glanced at Charity. If only all of God's creation was as easy to deal with as nature.

"After visiting with Mrs. Stoltz today," he began. He never did get to finish her corn pone. Charity's day old stuff hadn't been bad, just a bit dry. "It occurred to me that I might have brought you here under false pretenses."

"How so?" She crossed her arms and did not turn to look at him. If water could have frozen at her tone, the creek would have been hard enough for a team of horses to walk on.

"I don't think I was clear about my intentions when I asked you to marry me."

"You were more than clear, Mr. Williams."

He shook his head. She refused to call him by his first name when something had her riled. "Then is it the fact that it's a marriage in name only that bothers you? Because I would be willing to—"

She whirled too fast for him to back up before she punched him in the chest with her finger. "I am not a wanton woman, sir! I will not throw myself at a man, husband or no." Her brogue, which thickened when she was angry, made Gabe frown, straining to decipher her meaning.

"Of course, not. I just . . . uh," He didn't know what he meant. "Something is bothering you so just spit it out. I ain't a mind reader."

"You left out the very important fact that you are a gambler." She lifted her chin, and her eyes shimmered in the moonlight. "I would not have married you had I known. Now, you are also unhappy with my work and are sending me away before I've had a chance to prove myself." Her words caught on a sob, and she dashed toward the barn.

"No, you misunderstand." Gabe reached a hand toward her then let it fall, listening to her footsteps pound away. He wasn't a gambler. Not really. One stupid wager that he'd take back if he could. He'd insulted her and hurt her feelings. What could he possibly do to her next?

Sighing, he went back inside, leaving the door unlatched for Charity's return. He sat in his worn leather covered armchair beside the fireplace and toed off his boots. She called him a gambler, and he figured maybe she was right after all. A silly bet threatened everything he held dear, and because of it, he'd tricked a woman into marrying him.

He still stared into the fire's dying embers when Charity came in and latched the door behind her. "I will stick to my part of the bargain, Mr. Williams, have no fear. But I will not live in a hovel. By the time I return from my exile, I wish there to be a wooden floor and two glass windows, if you can manage."

"I can definitely manage the floor." How was he going to get the other house built if he had to keep putting work into this one? But, considering his deviousness, building her a floor for the winter was a small thing in comparison.

"There is also some furniture in the loft I would like brought down."

He shook his head. "You are welcome to anything in Maggie's trunk and the small stuff, but this sod house has no room for a bureau and mirror, or fancy dishes. Save them for the big house."

Charity locked her gaze on his. "Very well. Do the floor. I will do what I can to make this place more pleasant, and wait until my term of service is over." With a swish of her skirts, she disappeared behind the hanging quilt.

Despite the fact he'd made her angry, Gabe couldn't help but let a smile spread across his face. Montana needed more women with the backbone of Charity O'Connell Williams.

Fabric rustled. He glanced over to see her dress puddle to the floor where the quilt cleared the floor by a few inches. He swallowed against the dryness in his throat. For some reason he thought she would sleep fully clothed. Not in her underthings. His neck heated. He'd never get any sleep now. Not with the vision of pale skin and a waterfall of fiery hair running through his mind.

After shoving his feet back in his boots, he headed outside to the barn. There was always work to do to take a man's mind off most anything. His steps faltered at the barn door as he glanced around for the dead snake's buddies. Not seeing anything that didn't belong, he went inside and grabbed the rake. Mucking out Rogue's and the cow's stalls had always worked at taking away lustful wants when Maggie hadn't been in the mood.

Of course, this time, he might warrant a dunking in the icy creek.

7

Charity sat in the wagon, a tattered carpetbag at her feet, and blinked back tears. Sure, Gabriel thought he was doing the best thing, but Charity was just getting accustomed to living here, and now she had to leave for a few days. She took a deep breath and lifted her chin. She'd be the fastest learner any of these people had ever seen. Within a week, she'd be the finest prairie wife around. Somewhere, someday, she'd find that "someone" who valued her for who she was.

"Meg," she smiled down at the little girl. "Take care of the garden for me. Sam, help your father so he can make progress on the house."

Gabriel climbed up next to her. "This isn't forever, Charity. You'll be back by the week's end. I'm only trying to make things easier for you."

"But sending me away puts you farther behind in your goals." She shook her head. "Forget the floor. It is a selfish idea."

"The floor will only take me a day." He clicked to the horses. They snorted and plodded down the road. "You act like you're going to your death. Are the Irish always this dramatic?"

"Are you always forthright to the point of rudeness?" She crossed her arms. What a foolish infant she was. Of course, she'd be back. Why couldn't she let go of the fact that all this transpired because of his wager? It couldn't be undone, and he meant nothing personal toward her by having made the silly bet.

She glanced out the corner of her eye, noting the way Gabriel's forearms flexed when they worked the reins, and the way his hat shaded his eyes. She sighed. Why couldn't he have wanted her as a bride in every way? If she continued to act like a shrew, he'd never want her to stay.

His question from the night before sent heat coursing through her face. Obviously, the man would be more than willing to enjoy the blessings of a physical marriage. What man wouldn't? But what would it do to their agreement to part in a year's time? Charity wouldn't sell herself that way, not even for the hunger of feeling a strong man's arms around her. Divorce was not something she'd cotton to. Leaving things the way they were would allow them to have an annulment. She'd coped alone after her pa's death and could do so for as long as needed.

Since Gabriel seemed content to ride along in silence. Charity allowed her gaze to roam the countryside. Flowers in a rainbow of colors dotted the hills. Aspen, their white trunks shining in the sun, stood tall beside the creek they followed. The sky, bluer than anything she'd seen before her arrival in Montana two years ago, almost hurt her eyes with its brightness. In the distance, mountains rose, kissing the sky.

She lifted her face to the warm morning sun and closed her eyes. Maybe it was time she decided what she really wanted out of life. Gold or a family?

Why couldn't a girl have both? She glanced at Gabriel again and nodded. She'd be the best wife he could ever find. She'd strike it rich, and at the end of the year, he'd beg her to stay.

"Why do you keep staring at me?" Gabriel peered from under his hat brim. "I washed my face this morning."

"I wasn't staring." She turned back to the scenery, content with her backup plans for the future. If Gabriel followed through with sending her on her way, she would survive.

"I placed a paper pad and a pencil stub in your bag this morning so you can take notes at the Stoltzes'." He grinned, clearly pleased with himself. "You seem like a smart enough woman. I assume you can read?"

"Yes, thank you." The ninny. As if Charity was incapable of remembering anything.

She would love the opportunity to speak with his late wife. Had the man always been in the dark in regards to women as he appeared to be now? He meant well, but most of his comments were condescending.

Charity had a mind of her own and knew well how to use it, thanks to her parents who insisted she learn to write and do figures. She sighed. He would learn soon enough.

By the time the Stoltz farm came into view, a herd of buffalo stampeded through Charity's stomach. What if they didn't like her? What if she couldn't learn the things they taught her as well as she thought she could? Why hadn't her mother taught her these things instead of succumbing to Da's wishes in hiring help?

Money burned a hole in Da's pocket whenever he won at cards, and he had enjoyed nothing more than showering his "ladies" with finery, almost unheard of for the Irish.

Charity pressed a hand to her midsection. If she was a praying woman, she would have prayed for peace about the situation. Unfortunately, God had given up on the O'Connell's a while ago.

Gabriel pulled the wagon in front of a sod house that, at least on the outside, matched the home of the Williamses. He set the brake, hopped down, and then strolled to Charity's side. His large hands spanned her waist as he lowered her to the ground, doing nothing to calm her tumultuous stomach.

He smiled down at her and took her by the arm. "Relax. They're some of the most welcoming people you'll ever meet. My guess is, Mabel will become your best friend."

She allowed him to lead her to the door, which swung open before they could knock. A thickset woman with grey hair pulled Charity into a buxom hug that smelled of yeast and honey.

"You're the prettiest thing these parts have ever seen! I've seen you in town from a distance, passed a couple of times at the mercantile, and you are a darling. I'm Mabel Stoltz. You call me Mabel, and I'm very happy to meet you." Her grin revealed warm wrinkles around her eyes and settled Charity's nerves.

"Thank you for your offer of help." Charity took a step back before she suffocated in the woman's embrace.

"We'll have such fun." She turned to Gabriel, then glanced over his shoulder. "The young'uns?"

"Left at home." He tipped his hat. "I'd best get back to them. It's not a good thing to leave children alone for too long, and it's already been well over an hour."

"God speed, neighbor." Mabel nodded. "And make sure you bring them with you when you collect your bride on Saturday. I've a hankering for hugs from little ones."

Saturday? But today was only Monday! Charity gulped and stamped down the urge to climb back in the wagon. Other than doing folks's laundry, she tended to keep her mouth shut around people she didn't know, and with the way Mabel went on, talking was going to be an every minute occurrence.

"Come meet my groom, Hiram." Mabel practically shoved Charity through the door.

Wood floors! Doilies on every surface, paper on

the walls, and not an insect in sight. Charity's stomach began to relax. A woman's presence in a real home. She smiled for the first time since getting out of the wagon. "Your home is lovely."

"Thank you, dear. It ain't much, but it's all ours. Hiram, meet Gabriel's bride, Charity. If I'm not mistaken from her accent, we've an Irish gal here."

A man as thin as his wife was round, unfolded himself from a rocking chair in front of a stone fireplace. He smiled, nodded, and skedaddled out the door like a cat with cans tied to its tail.

Mabel laughed. "He's shy. Let's get lunch started and begin your first cooking lesson. What do you know how to make?"

"Beans and corn pone." Charity clutched the handle of her bag tighter. "And eggs. I make right fine biscuits, too."

"That's a wonderful start. We'll begin right away. There is a lot to do in the week you're here." Mabel bustled to an iron stove shoved in the corner she used as her cooking area. "I've got some chicken left over from last night's supper, so I'll teach you to make hash. You can do this with leftover beef, too. Set your bag next to those blankets over there." She pointed to the left of the fireplace. "That's your bed for the time you're here."

Charity set the bag on the floor and pulled out her paper and pencil. She'd thought she might have a moment to settle in before getting to work. With a deep breath, she clutched the precious pad to her chest and faced Mabel. "I'm ready."

"You can write? That's good. I can't even write my own name." Mabel chuckled. "We'll fill that pad with words in the days to come." She handed Charity a large kitchen knife. "Mince that chicken, over there. Not too fine, and make sure you remove all the bones."

Charity nodded and rushed to do her bidding. While Mabel chattered on like a flock of birds in the aspens, Charity chopped chicken, then onions, and added them with salt and butter to a waiting pan. She straightened. That wasn't too bad, but maybe Mabel started her on the easy things first.

*

Gabe kept the team at a fast trot on the way home, already missing Charity's presence. She was right. Sending her away would slow him down on building, but he honestly did not think he could eat beans and corn pone for the next year.

Remembering the pained look on her face when she'd brought up the subject of gambling, tore at Gabe's heart. Somebody hurt the woman deeply. Without regard to her feelings, Gabe had done the same thing. *Lord, forgive me. Somehow, I'll make things right.*

When he pulled into his yard, Sam and Meg pulled aside the oilcloth over the window and peered out. There really wasn't any way Sam could get a glass window installed in time, but he had extra lumber for a floor, and planks were definitely better than dirt come the frigid winter. He should have made such improvements before, for the sake of his children.

His shoulders sagged. He had been so focused on winning the bet, that he had allowed other important things, like his children, to fall to the wayside.

Meg and Sam raced outside, and Gabe noticed how short his daughter's dress was, rising several inches above tanned ankles. They would need to make a trip into town soon. If they were lucky, they would make two; one when Charity returned and one before the snow fell.

After pulling his handkerchief from his pocket, he wiped his brow free of sweat. The day promised to be a scorcher, and they hadn't had rain in weeks. Maybe laying a floor in the coolness of the sod house wouldn't be so bad after all.

He climbed from the wagon and unhitched the horses. "Come on young'uns. Let's get these horses put away and build your ma a floor."

By the noon hour, the three of them had carried or dragged enough lumber to cover the dirt. Once placed, Gabe would sand it, one section at a time. They ate cold ham and stale biscuits for lunch and supper.

By nightfall, Gabe stood back and looked with pride on a pine floor. Every muscle in his body ached, and the children had collapsed into bed over an hour ago, but the floor was finished. He hung his tools on a nail by the door and moved to his bed.

He'd never realized how quiet the place was before Charity came. He smiled, preferring her sharp comments over the silence. He shed his shirt and pants, draping them over a peg. Meg had certainly brightened with another female around the place. What would Charity say if Gabe asked her to be his wife in every sense, come what may? Even if he lost his land?

He shrugged and stretched out on the cornhusk mattress. She'd most likely scoff and say a deal was a deal. After less than a week as Mrs. Williams, she had no idea what kind of a man Gabe really was. He folded his arms behind his head. He had a year to convince her to stay, and what a year it promised to be.

*

Charity lay on her pallet beside the cold fireplace and stared through the dark at the ceiling. More tired than she could remember ever being, she willed her mind to slow. The day's activities, everything from cooking to gardening tips swirled through her mind like a dust devil she'd once seen. Already her pad of paper contained recipes, tips, and household advice from a woman who had been married most of her adult life.

From a few feet away, the Stoltzes murmured to each other that secret language between a husband and wife. Charity rolled to her side in an attempt to find a comfortable position on the hard wood floor and tune out their voices.

When Hiram had come in from working the fields, he'd gone straight to his wife and placed a tender kiss on her cheek. The memory caused tears to sting Charity's eyes. Her da had tried tender caresses with her mother, but Ma had always shrugged him off. Yet somehow, Charity had known that marriage could be a joyful thing and she'd kept an eye out for a husband of her own ever since.

No one had caught her fancy until Gabriel. Now, he wanted her only as a temporary solution to a problem. Charity sighed and rolled in the other direction. Da told her once that every human had another half. If they looked hard enough, they'd find the person who fulfilled them. Charity wasn't sure she ever would.

8

"Good morning." Mabel grinned down at Charity. "The sun is shining, God is in His heaven, and all is right with the world."

Charity blinked away the fog from sleep. How could she have overslept? What would Mabel think of her? She got groggily to her feet. "I'm so sorry."

"Don't worry. You worked hard yesterday." Mabel tied her apron around her ample waist. "After breakfast, I will teach you to make soap. I know you already do laundry well, but I'm guessing you bought your soap."

"Yes." Charity folded the blankets that formed her pallet and stacked them neatly in the corner. "I stayed too busy to learn anything else, and now there don't seem to be enough hours in the day." *Please, don't think me ungrateful.*

Mabel patted her shoulder. "Once you learn what

you need to know, and set up a schedule, you'll have time to simply be. You wait and see. There are many evenings when Hiram and I sit under that old oak tree and speak of the day's events." She laughed. "Not that a lot happens way out here, but it's nice to just rest together. You leave it all in God's hands. He'll see you through."

Not likely. Charity measured ingredients for buttermilk biscuits. The day before, Mabel had interspersed talk of God during their conversations, leaving Charity uncomfortable. It wasn't that she didn't believe in the Almighty, she just didn't have time to spend with someone who chose to take away everyone she cared about.

Gabriel seemed the same as the Stoltzes, bowing his head and giving thanks for the meals and thanks for Charity's care of the children, almost as if God were someone a mere human could speak with as they would a friend.

"You're faraway," Mabel said, scrambling eggs. "Missing Gabriel and the children?"

"Very much." Charity set the biscuits in the stove.

"He told me of the arrangement between the two of you."

Charity straightened so fast she hit her head on a low hanging shelf. Putting a hand to the sore spot, she turned.

"I gave him a good talking to." Mabel grinned. "Now, my Hiram, if he decided to be so devious, would receive a clunk on the head with my skillet."

Charity smiled. No condemnation reflected from the other woman's eyes. "I thought to finally have a family and home of my own."

"You do."

"For a time." Charity glanced at her fingers. Small flecks of blood dotted the pads. "Seems I've hurt myself."

"You poor thing!" Mabel set the pan of eggs aside and grabbed a rag, before helping Charity into a kitchen chair. "Sit and let me have a look." She parted Charity hair. "Just a scratch. You'll have a headache at the least." She dabbed at the cut. "Do you regret wedding Gabriel?"

Charity shrugged. "I don't think so. My worry is that it will be too difficult to leave when the time comes. Already Meg and Sam own my heart."

"And Gabriel too, I'll wager."

Charity cringed. Mabel was closer to the truth than she knew. Gabriel was claiming a piece of Charity's heart way faster than she liked.

"I see." Mabel sat across from her. "Why does the mention of gambling trouble you so? Or is it my mention of your husband?"

Charity twisted the rag in her hands. "Me Da made good money once upon a time, back in Ireland, running the stables for a wealthy Englishman. Mother and I had no idea he was gambling to add to his salary. Then, he got the idea of striking it rich in America. Ma died soon after we arrived. A little over two years ago now, Da lost everything, and Ma passed. I've been on me own ever since."

"Then Gabriel came along and promised you something more."

"It was never meant to be permanent." Charity pushed back from the table. "Let's finish breakfast and get to soap making, shall we?"

"Gabriel isn't your father, Charity." Mabel returned the eggs to the stove. "He made one mistake, but he's a good man. He'll do right by you. You trust in God and wait and see."

After they ate breakfast and washed the dishes, Mabel sent Charity around the corner of the barn to collect rainwater for the soap from a barrel stashed there. Charity eyed the small amount. Without rain for weeks, folks that didn't live near a creek would be hurting before long.

Filling two buckets, and depleting the amount to a drastically low level, Charity trudged back to the front yard. Mabel shouldn't have to give up precious stores of water because Charity didn't know how to do the simplest of chores.

"I've already collected the oak ash we need." Mabel poured the water carefully into a barrel. "The ash filters the lye. We'll be replacing and draining every day this week. On Saturday, we'll test it by floating an egg inside. I figure this will make both of us enough soap to last a while. Once you've gotten better at it, you can add some lavender or sunflower oil to make it smell pretty."

Charity studied the ash and rocks in the bottom

of the barrel. Purchasing one's soap was definitely easier and faster.

"This afternoon, we'll work on cutting out a pattern. We'll start with an easy project, like an apron. Tomorrow, I'll teach you about canning, then the next day something fun. We'll learn knitting and quilting." Mabel clapped her hands. "I feel as if the Lord has blessed me with a daughter after all these years."

"I have a little skill with a needle." She'd mended many ripped trousers and shirts for the miners in Virginia City. Her heart warmed at Mabel's words. Maybe she wouldn't be a total loss as a prairie wife, after all.

"Wonderful. The learning will go fast." Mabel wiped her hands on her apron. "I've some ham left. Let's fix some sandwiches for lunch and get started right away."

Was this what it was like to have a mother who took the time to teach her daughter valuable skills as she raised her? A mother who had a love for life and wanted to pass that same love on to her child? Charity's mother hadn't done much but sit and stare out the window since Charity turned six and Ma had lost a newborn baby girl.

It was Da's love that filled the empty spaces in her childhood. When he was sober and at home. Now, he had left her penniless and alone.

Charity glanced at the mountains rising behind the farm. "Are there any gold mines around here?"

"Hiram has found a few small nuggets in the

creek that sets aways back in those trees." Mabel tilted her head. "You aren't contemplating searching yourself, are you? Panning or mining is hard and dangerous work. Isn't that how your father died?"

Charity jerked. "How do you know that?"

"Bad news spreads through town like a plague. Even faster was the news that an eligible young woman was left without a protector." Mabel strolled into the house. "How you stayed unwed for this long remains a mystery."

"I do intend to be rich, Mabel." Charity marched to the stove. "One way or another, I will locate gold."

"Seems to be that you're driven by the wrong need, young lady." Mabel grabbed a knife and sliced into a fresh loaf of bread. "There's a hole in your heart that only God can fill. Not a husband, children, and definitely not gold."

"Please do not speak religion to me." Charity gripped the board that served as Mabel's counter and squeezed until her knuckles turned white. "Life is what I make it, and I choose to make it one where there is plenty of money. My Da used to say, 'May you live as long as you want, and never want as long as you live.' I intend to do just that."

"Oh, you poor child." Mabel folded her hands and brought them to her chest. "I will pray long and hard for you to find the truth."

"May I go outside for a moment? I have a need for some fresh air."

"Certainly."

Charity nodded and brushed past Mabel. Outside, she quickened her pace and marched past the barn and corral and into a stand of aspens. Once there, she collapsed with a flutter of her skirts and covered her face. Mabel could pray as long and as hard as she wanted, but Charity intended to only do what was required of her as Gabriel's wife. God might choose to help some people, but He didn't choose to help Charity.

*

Gabriel praised God he'd cut extra pine planks for flooring as he nailed the last one into place for his new house. Having the foresight to do so sped up the building process. With the foundation complete, he could start hammering boards into place for rooms. He'd spend as many days of the winter as he could in the barn building furniture. Things were finally heading in the direction he wanted them to go.

He glanced in the direction of the Stoltz farm, too far for him to see, yet he still searched for a woman with hair the color of ripe strawberries. It had been unsettling the last few nights, knowing she didn't sleep on her side of the quilt. No gentle snores or rustling of blankets. Sam and Meg did their chores, but without laughter. Even the kitten failed to elicit shouts of glee from them.

A dust devil rose, towering over the plains. If they didn't get rain soon, they'd lose their crops and some of the livestock. The creek was getting low, and the grass turning brown. Even the aspens looked as if they labored under the sun.

Sam handed him a dipper of water. "When's Ma coming home? You said she was away learning to cook, right? I'm tired of the same old thing every night."

Gabriel took a long drink then dumped the rest over his head. "We're picking her up in the morning."

"I'm going to go pick some wildflowers." Sam tore toward the creek.

Gabe smiled. If there were any flowers left, the creek would most likely be the only place around to find them.

"Pa?" Meg stopped in front of him, holding the kitten like it was a baby. Maybe Charity was right. The children needed a toy or two. It was something for Gabe to think about for Christmas instead of the usual fruit and nuts and the occasional new item of clothing.

"What do you need, Meg?"

"I miss Ma." Tears shimmered in her dark eyes. "I don't like being the only girl here."

"You were the only girl for a good long while." Gabe pocketed the last of his nails and stood, popping the kinks from his back.

"But not anymore!" Meg glowered up at him, squeezing the kitten hard enough to elicit a meow from the poor animal.

"Charity will be back in the morning." How would the children react when Charity left in the spring? One stupid wager left Gabe's life hanging upside down. An impulsive offer to a beautiful woman set it to spinning, and he had no idea how to set it right.

He stared at his daughter's face. Meg would never

forgive him. Tears ran down her cheeks in silent suffering. Gabe sighed. "Get your brother. We'll fetch your ma now."

*

Charity crossed her arms and stared over the prairie. The sun brushed the top of the mountains with indigo and purple. A slight breeze ruffled the dry grass and carried with it the faint scent of honeysuckle.

A cloud of dust hovered on the horizon. Most likely another infernal dust devil invited to stay by the lack of rain.

Mabel had stuffed Charity's head as full of womanly knowledge as she could in a week's time. Confident with the skills she'd learned, Charity would head home in the morning, ready to show Gabriel exactly what she was capable of.

The dust cloud moved closer. Charity squinted. Could it be? She poked her head into the house. "Gabriel's here." Early. What happened? Did something happen to one of the children? Charity hefted her skirts and took off down the road at a run.

She skidded to a halt at the surprised look on Gabriel's face. Behind him, Sam and Meg peered over his shoulder. "What's wrong?" Charity asked, a hand at her throat.

"The children missed you." Gabriel continued toward the house, calling over his shoulder, "We've come to take you home."

Home. What a wonderful word. Charity dashed back to the house and thundered inside, hurriedly gathering together her meager belongings and pad of paper. She grinned at Mabel. "They've come for me."

"Of course they have, child." Mabel pulled her into a hug. "You give that man time. Before you know it, he'll realize the treasure he has in front of him."

She hoped so, she really did, but Charity didn't count herself as much of a treasure. Once she found gold, then she'd have something of worth to give Gabriel. She returned Mabel's hug. "Thank you so much."

"We're family now," Mabel said. "Don't be a stranger. We're less than an hour's ride away. Once winter hits, you'll be snowed in. Let's get our visiting in while we can."

"Fourth of July." Charity stepped back. "Come for a picnic. I'll cook and show you my much improved skills."

"We'd be happy to." Mabel gave her a gentle shove toward the door. "Go. Your man is waiting."

If only her words were true.

9

Weeks passed with life settling into a routine of chores and stolen glances. Every time Charity's work took her outside, she made an effort to take Gabriel a drink of water or a bit to eat as he worked on the new house.

The frame stretched to the Montana sky, offering a glimpse of what the structure would someday look like. Two stories with a porch that stretched the length of the front. She tried to hope she would be around to live within its fine walls, but more often than not, Gabriel refused to meet her eye. Oh, but he did look her way. When he thought she didn't notice. The knowledge kept a spot warm at the bottom of her heart, a spark that needed but a bit of encouragement to flame.

Charity lifted her hair off her neck. This infernal drought! Tomorrow was the Fourth of July, and they were expecting the Stoltzes. She wanted to show Mabel the fine floor Gabe laid while she was gone, and have the other woman sample some of Charity's cooking.

She had forged ahead in a sweltering kitchen to bake apple pies, corn pone, and the ribs from a hog Gabriel obligingly slaughtered for the occasion. She'd even had time to fashion fabric from one of Maggie's old dresses into a new dress for Meg.

What she hadn't had time for was panning for that ever elusive gold. Sometimes, when Gabriel caught her staring out the door at the creek or mountains, she thought maybe he knew the thoughts that ran through her mind. Yet, he never said a word. Charity had moved the 'fool's' gold from her pocket to the mantel where she could lay eyes on it every day. Whenever she went to the creek for water, she scanned the bottom for a glint of something that might be real.

She reached out to check the laundry hanging on the line. Almost dry. It didn't take long in the hot summer, almost drying before she clipped them to the line.

From the open door of the sod house came the delectable scent of baking bread. She'd have to be careful not to burn it. The last thing she wanted to do was sit inside beside the sweltering stove and watch the bread bake. A sod house might be cooler than a log one, but with heat this intense, it didn't provide much relief.

Grabbing the bucket she used to carry drinking water, Charity strolled to the creek, filled it, and headed to where Gabriel and Sam mucked out the barn.

Gabe nodded and accepted the dipper of water.

"Thank you. I'm parched." After drinking his fill, he handed the dipper to Sam. "We haven't had a summer this hot in a long time."

Charity started. Was he actually talking to her? "Hmmm, guess not, but I'll be glad for cooler weather."

"Not once winter hits, and you're snowed in. Which doesn't happen all the time, from what I've heard, but enough to make folks cautious." He leaned against the rake, his gaze intense. "Sam, check on your sister, please."

"I can see her from here, Pa. She's playing with Patches."

"Do as I say, son."

Charity swallowed against the dryness in her throat, and reached for a drink. What had she done now?

Gabriel removed his hat. His hair was plastered to his skull with sweat, and he wiped his brow on the sleeve of his shirt. "I've been doing some thinking, Charity."

Uh-oh.

"Are you happy here?" he asked. "With me and the young'uns?"

"Well, if you'd talk to—"

"Hello, the house!"

Charity pulled herself away from Gabriel's gaze. Mr. Stoltz raced up the yard on the back of a brown mule.

"Fire! South of your house and moving fast. Me and the missus could see the smoke from our place. I got here as quick as I could."

Charity grabbed the bucket and ran for the house. "Sam! Meg! Gather up buckets and blankets." She'd seen a fire in town once and would never forget the sight of buildings burning, horses screaming, and people fleeing with what little they could carry.

"Charity!" Gabriel stopped her. "Have the children help you get everything you can inside the house. Sod doesn't burn. Then you stay put."

She whirled. "No, I can help you. Even Sam can—"

"It's too dangerous." He frowned.

"You can't fight a fire alone, Gabriel Williams." Charity put her hands on her hips. "We can argue about it or we can take action."

Mr. Stoltz slid from his mule's back and slapped the animal's rump to send it a safe distance away. "She's right. I'll stay and help, but it will be better with three."

"Look at her, Hiram. She's not much bigger than Sam."

"But I'm strong, Gabriel." She wouldn't hide in the house and worry about him. He couldn't ask her to. She dashed to the line of clean clothes and tossed them in the waiting basket.

"Meg, Sam, bring in whatever you can carry. Meg, put Patches inside." Charity hefted the basket, dropped it inside the door, and then started yanking blankets off the beds. She'd seen men beat at the flames before. She could do that. "Sam, when you've finished that, I need every bucket we have filled with water."

By the time she got back outside, Gabriel and

Hiram had started digging a trench around the immediate property. Charity stared at the newly framed house. Would all Gabriel's efforts have been in vain? She hoped not. If the house burned, his chances of having it built before his ridiculous deadline didn't look good.

Once they'd moved everything into the house small enough to carry, Charity and the children stood and watched the smoke move closer while the men continued to dig behind them. Maybe the flames wouldn't jump the creek. Charity's throat clogged at the thought of losing the small grove of aspen trees, and she glanced over her shoulder at the men. What would happen to them if everything burned?

"How did the fire start?" Gabriel shook his head. "No lightning that I know of."

Hiram shrugged. "I saw the silhouette of a man on a horse earlier, but only a darn fool would mess with fire in the middle of a drought."

"Could you see who it was? What did he look like?" Gabriel slapped his hat against his thigh.

"Can't say as I did get a clear look." Hiram clapped him on the shoulder. "We'll beat this thing, don't worry."

*

Gabe prayed so. He let his gaze roam over his family. Charity stood with her arms around the children, a tub of soaked blankets beside her. He shook his head. Silly woman, thinking she could beat off a brush fire with nothing but water and fabric.

When the crackling of flames filled the air and he could see the fire licking at the brush on the opposite side of the creek, he tightened his grip on his shovel as if he could hold the fire back by sheer will power. *Lord, don't let it jump the shallow creek.*

The fire ate its way up to the top of an aspen. With a crack, the tree fell, forming a fiery bridge, and enabling the flames to dance their way to the opposite side.

"Sam, Meg, I won't tell you again to get in the house." Gabriel rushed the flames and shoveled dirt on top of the burning tree. Hiram did the same.

Charity grabbed a blanket and beat at the smoldering grass. Her hairpins came loose, and her hair tumbled down her back, almost as red as the encroaching flames. Even as the fire continued to consume its way closer, she battled with the fierceness of a mother bear. Gabe wanted to grab her in his arms and praise her efforts.

"Sam!" She straightened. "We need more water."

"No." Gabe glared. "The children stay in the house."

"They can help. This is their home, too." Charity held her skirt above her ankles and stomped on an ember. "The fire isn't farther down the creek. They can fill the buckets there."

Gabe knew he'd lost the battle with her when she gathered all the blankets in her arms and tripped her way to the water. "Come on, Sam. Meg, you stay put."

The air filled with smoke, burning his throat and

stinging his eyes. Charity and Hiram must suffer the same, yet neither complained. The fire forced them back, foot-by-foot, as if its sole purpose was to devour the weeks of work Gabe spent in framing their new home. The fire wouldn't win. He wouldn't allow it. He didn't have time to cut more lumber, even if he had the funds to purchase more.

"We're losing it." Hiram beat at the flames with his shovel.

"No, we're not." Gabe hefted more dirt, working as feverishly as a dog digging up a bone for its last meal. Dust mingled in the air with the smoke, forcing him to pull the neckline of his shirt over his nose.

Charity coughed, tears streaming down soot-covered cheeks.

Hiram was right. The fire was winning. Gabe tossed down his shovel and dipped a bucket into the shallow creek, the heat searing the hair on his arms. He tossed bucket after bucket on the flames making their way to the house. "No!"

Charity thrust another bucket of water into his hands. "I'll fill, you toss. Hiram can beat with the blankets."

Gabe nodded. Charity O'Connell Williams was one of a kind, and he counted himself a lucky man to have her by his side.

The sun continued to set as they fought for everything they owned, until, finally, the flames died, petering out to black ash.

Charity sagged to the ground. "The trees. They're

gone."

Gabe plopped next to her. "They'll grow back. I owe you our home. You and Hiram."

She grunted. "It's my home, too, as you seem to so often forget." She glanced back at the house. "Meg, bring me the medical box, please."

"Why, are you injured?" Gabe ran his gaze over her.

"Just my leg. My dress caught fire, and I stuck my leg in the creek to put out the fire."

Without thinking, he shoved aside her dress, revealing blackened undergarments and a blistering calf. He scooped her in his arms and ran for the house. "Why didn't you say something you stubborn woman?"

"Because you would have stopped to take care of me, and there wasn't time." She laid her head on his shoulder. "It burns something fierce, though."

Hiram followed them, and stopped at the door. "I'm heading home now, Gabe. Want me to send the missus to look after Charity?"

Gabe maneuvered around farm equipment and clean laundry to set Charity on the bed and then turned, extending his hand. "We couldn't have done this without you, neighbor. I owe you more than I can say. If you hadn't warned us, we would've never got the trench dug." Not that it did a lot of good, but the fire hadn't reached the new house or the barn. "No, you keep your wife to home. I can care for Charity."

Hiram grinned through a blackened face. "You'd a done the same. You all right, Charity?"

"I'll be fine. No need to worry Mabel." She smiled, her teeth white through the soot.

As soon as Hiram had left, Gabe hurried back to Charity's side where Meg waited, a canister of salve in her hand.

Charity sighed and slapped his hand away. "Let me do it myself. It isn't proper."

"But, I'm your husband." Not proper? Had she inhaled too much smoke?

"Not in that way."

"It's blistering, Charity." He ripped her undergarments to above the knee. "Yours isn't the first woman's leg I've seen." Although it was quite shapely. He scooped some of the ointment in his fingers and spread it across the burn, trying not to dwell on how soft the underside of her leg had felt when he shoved up her skirts.

"Meg, honey, can you get me some clean water and a rag?" He smiled in his daughter's worried face.

"Is Ma going to be all right?" Meg's lip trembled.

"Right as rain." Gabe waved Sam over. "Keep an eye outside, all right? Let me know if any embers start back up."

"Sure, Pa." Sam skedaddled out the door.

When Meg returned with a bowl of water and a rag, Gabe dunked the square piece of flannel, wrung it out, and prepared to wipe Charity's face.

Her eyes widened, and she shoved his hands away again. She spoke slowly and distinctly. "You will not bathe me!"

"I'm just washing your face." She sure was standoffish for someone in pain.

"Please, Gabriel, go outside and see what work you can find. I'm sure there's plenty."

"Why? The fire's out." He scratched his head. "You worked as good as a man out there today. Let me take care of you now." And forever, if she'd let him. They still had a conversation to finish.

"I don't want you to." Tears welled in her eyes. "It's embarrassing. I need to change my clothes and clean up properly."

"But you're injured." Maybe he was dense, but he didn't understand the problem.

She closed her eyes for a moment, then gave him a stern look. "My dress is burned, my ... undergarments are ripped, thanks to you, and I'm filthy. I would really like to clean up. If you're that worried, Meg can help me."

Her Irish brogue deepened with each word, a clear sign her temper was about to flare as strong as the fire had burned outside. Planting his hands on his knees, he pushed to his feet. "All right. But if you need anything, call out."

"I will, and thank you." He shuffled to the door and stopped. "What if it gets infected?"

She pointed. "Out."

She sure was prickly. Gabe stepped outside, leaving the door open, and scanned the area around the house. Black aspen skeletons waved toward heaven. Equally dark patches of grass covered the ground, stopping twenty feet away from the barn. Gabe looked to heaven. *Thank you, Lord. We could have lost everything.*

Sam poked at the ground with a burned stick, his pants and shirt as filthy as Gabe felt he most likely was. "Come on, Son. Let's head down creek and wash this grime off." He slung an arm around Sam's shoulders. "I'm right proud of you. You did the work of a man out there."

Sam's face brightened, then saddened. "Is Ma going to be okay? I couldn't bear to lose another ma."

Gabe squeezed. "She'll be fine, but she's as grumpy as an old bear."

"Yep," Sam giggled. "Same as every other time she's around you. Why is that?"

Gabe wished he knew. "The relationship between a man and a woman is complicated. Only God truly understands it." And he sure wished the Almighty would see fit to share the knowledge.

10

The next morning, Charity limped outside. Her burned leg screeched with pain. Every time she recalled Gabriel ripping the leg of her under drawers, her face flamed, and she broke out into a sweat. Married or not, the gesture had been too intimate, not to mention it was the only pair of bloomers she owned. No amount of mending would make them look nice. When would she find time to sew a new pair?

Today was the fourth of July, and everything in front of her held the lovely, festive color of scorched grey. Oh, well. It was freedom they celebrated, and whether the Stoltzes still arrived as planned or not, Charity intended to have that picnic she'd worked so hard cooking for.

She made her way slowly to the barn. They'd need something for a makeshift table. She found planks for the top, barrels for the legs, and crates for seats. One by one she dragged them outside and sent Meg for the Irish lace tablecloth in her trunk—one of the few possessions Charity's mother had left her.

In the center of the table, she set an apple pie, a pan of cornpone, and her blue speckled tin plates and matching mugs. Flowers would have been nice, but the fire destroyed them all, unless she wanted to take a hike upstream, which she didn't. There wasn't time, and her injured leg would never forgive her.

Once the table was set for company, Charity headed back to the stove to baste the ribs again. The smell of homemade sauce and mouthwatering, beef cooked overnight filled the sod house.

"Who set up the table outside?" Gabriel stood in the doorway, arms crossed.

Charity turned. "I did, why?"

"I thought I told you to take it easy on your leg."

"I'm not an invalid, Gabriel. I'm perfectly capable of carrying on with my work." She replaced the lid on the ribs. Her leg did pain her, but she'd planned this day for weeks and didn't intend to let anything happen to keep it from being as wonderful a day as she had planned it to be.

Gabriel pulled a leather book from the mantel and plopped into his chair with a huff. The sound of rustling paper competed with the song of Sam's and Meg's laughter drifting from outside.

Did the man really have time to read? Charity loved reading, but this wasn't the time. She could think of plenty of work if he didn't have anything to do. "What are you doing?"

"Looking for a Bible verse on freedom," he said without glancing up. "I'd like to read a couple at supper."

"What does the Bible have to do with the Fourth of July?" She recalled him saying the family read a lot of Bible stories on winter evenings, but this was the middle of the summer.

"You'd be surprised. Try to rest your leg, even if for a little while. You'll regret it if you don't." Gabriel flashed a grin, which set Charity's heart fluttering, and took his Bible outside.

Charity was glad Mabel had taught her to knit and quilt. It would give her something to do besides sit and listen to stories from a book once the heavy snows fell. Her mother had believed in God and the Bible. Look where it got her. Dead from poverty and a broken heart. Religion wasn't for Charity. Gabriel could teach his children, but she'd mind her own business and keep her opinion to herself.

Sounds of a wagon pulling into the yard drew her away from the stove and outside. The Stoltzes pulled up to the barn, Mabel's arms loaded down with a basket. She waved and waited for Hiram to help her down.

Charity grinned and limped as fast as she could to greet them. She might have grumbled at first about spending a week with Mabel learning skills she needed, but now she was thankful for the knowledge and the right to call the other woman 'friend'.

Mabel set her basket on the wagon seat and pulled

Charity into a hug. "A month is too long, my friend."

"It is." Charity waved the children forward, proud of the yellow calico Meg wore.

"Did you make this?" Mabel fingered Meg's sleeve.

"I did, out of one of Maggie's old dresses."

"You do me proud. You are a real fast learner." Mabel retrieved her basket. "I've brought a few jars of wild plum jam and some mashed potatoes. I know you said not to bring anything, but this jam is a gift. There will be some left to enjoy in the winter."

"Thank you." Tears stung Charity's eyes. When was the last time someone gave her something without expecting anything in return? "I will save it for special occasions."

"How's your leg?" Mabel strolled beside her as they headed for the table. "Hiram told me how brave you were during the fire. I would have fallen to pieces."

"It's sore, but I'll survive." Charity took a jar of jam from the basket and set the rest under what used to be her favorite aspen tree. "It's the loss of trees and flowers that pains me more."

"All those things will grow back. A life won't." Mabel swept her skirt aside and took a seat on one of the crates. "It's a miserably hot day. Looks like rain."

"Rain would be welcome." Even more so if it would have arrived a couple of days earlier. Charity's burn throbbed, and she sat opposite Mabel, keeping her face composed so her friend wouldn't guess her discomfort.

"Hiram found something in regards to yesterday's fire." Mabel lowered her voice and leaned closer.

"Won't tell me what, but I'm sure he's telling Gabe right this minute."

Charity glanced toward the new house where the men strolled, heads together. "Do folks around here usually set fires on each other?"

"Not usually. Land and homes are too precious." Mabel frowned. "Might be Indians, I suppose. Sometimes they get a bee in their bonnet about the white folks infringing on what they think is theirs, but as far as I know, Gabe gets along with most of them. Has even taught some of them the Good Word."

Charity's heart hitched. Indians! Living in Virginia City, she hadn't given them much thought. She scanned the landscape for feather adorned savages.

"How are you Gabe getting along since your return?" Mabel's question pulled Charity from her frightened thoughts.

"What?"

Mabel chuckled. "You and Gabe?" She waved a hand. "It's none of my business."

"It's fine." Charity looked back at the men. Gabe kicked a rock and crossed his arms. "He's not very talkative. It almost seems as if he avoids me. I think I make him uncomfortable."

"Probably." Mabel shrugged. "I doubt he's met anyone like you. You're as different from his late wife as summer is from winter. Speaking of winter, he won't be able to avoid you then."

"Maybe not, but come late spring, he'll still send me away. If I've learned anything, it's that Gabriel

Willliams is a man of his word."

*

"A tobacco tin, you say?" Gabe clenched his fists. He knew who carried one of those. A lot of men, but he'd bet his money on just one. "Does it happen to be gold with black lettering?"

"Yep." Hiram pulled a scorched tin from his pocket. "Mean anything to you."

"It might." Gabe took it and folded his fist around it. "Amos Jenkins. The man's trying to run me off my land. Since I got married and I'm making progress, he thinks he can burn me out." He patted one of the house's timbers. "But I'm ahead of schedule. Once I get the outside finished, I can work on the inside when the snows hit. I'm winning that bet, no matter what." He wouldn't let some lowlife scoundrel take away all that was important to him.

"Careful you don't let that desire affect other more important things." Hiram nodded toward the makeshift table where the women sat. Sam and Meg bounded across the yard, Patches scampering behind them, and joined the women.

Gabe should get them a dog. A dog would be a good warning signal, and a better playmate than a cat. But dogs needed companionship and food. A cat could hunt for mice. "Nothing is more important than my children." Or Charity for that matter, but he'd worked too hard on developing his land to let a wager made in a fit of anger ruin everything.

"Sounds to me like you need to have a serious

conversation with God. Have you ever stopped to ask Him what He wants for your life? Maybe you aren't meant to stay here."

"Of course I am. This is what I've worked my whole life for. It's what Maggie wanted." How could Hiram suggest such a thing?

"Maybe so. At least think about it." Hiram rubbed his belly. "We going to eat soon? My stomach thinks my throat's been cut."

"Sure. Let's keep our suspicions about the fire between us, all right? I don't want the women to worry." Or Charity to think she needed to go investigating. The woman seemed to have more curiosity than that kitten she found.

By the time they joined the women, Charity was limping out from the soddie, loaded down with the pan of ribs. Gabe rushed to her side and relieved her of the heavy burden. Why wouldn't she listen to reason and take it easy on her leg?

"Don't scowl at me," she warned. "You were busy, and I wasn't going to ask our company to fetch it. 'T'wouldn't be proper. "

"Then you should have called for me." He shifted the pan in order to get a more comfortable grip.

"You were deep in conversation." She planted her fists on her hips and tilted her head to scowl at him. "Was it about the fire? Mabel thinks Indians might be the culprits."

"It wasn't Indians, and you women don't need to worry yourselves." Gabe marched to the table and set

99

the pan in the center. Dishes of mashed potatoes, cornpone, and an apple pie filled the rest of the space.

"No, of course not. We should only concern ourselves with the house and children."

"Exactly."

Mabel frowned, Hiram paled, and the children's eyes widened. What was wrong with everyone? Why was it that Charity took offense at everything Gabe said? For centuries men and women had defined roles in the household. It's how God ordained thing, right? Yet Charity acted as if it were all new. Something he made up. His Ma had seemed content in her role. Weren't all women the same? Maybe he needed to rethink things.

He stormed to the barn and grabbed his Bible from the work bench he had left it on. They could all use a little of God's word. He took his seat at the end of the table and laid the worn leather book on the wood planks. "I thought we'd celebrate today with verses explaining what freedom really means to us."

Charity plopped into her seat at the other end of the table and focused on her hands. The rest of them stared expectantly at Gabe. One day, he'd ask Charity what she had against God. He opened the Bible.

"Psalm 119:45 says I will walk at liberty, for I seek your precepts. Isaiah 61:1 says He has sent me to heal the brokenhearted, to proclaim liberty to the captives and the opening of the prison to those who are bound. Romans 8:21 because the creation itself also will be delivered from the bondage of corruption into the glorious liberty of the children of God." He glanced at those listening.

"I believe that, although America earned her freedom from England, we have more freedom through Christ than we could ever obtain from a bullet shot into an enemy. It's the blood of God's son that gives us the freedom we celebrate today."

"You ever thought of taking up preaching?" Hiram asked. "You've a knack for it, even if you are a mite short-winded. Those are the exact reasons we ought to be celebrating today."

Gabe shook his head. "God hasn't called me to minister to any other than my own family." And one red-headed woman who still hadn't looked up from her clenched hands. Maybe she pondered his words and would, in time, ask God to release her from the chains that bound her. "Let's eat. Hiram, would you say the blessing?" Gabe held out his hands, and they joined in a circle.

"Lord we ask for your blessing on this food and on the hands that prepared it. May we enjoy a day of fellowship as we celebrate freedom earned through your Son and through the men who won our victory over England's tyranny. Amen."

*

Charity plunged her hands into the washbasin, thankful the water was hot enough to blame for the flush on her face. Freedom, indeed! A woman wasn't free in today's world. They were left to the whim and supposed protection of men. The only way Charity could really be free from her troubles was to strike it rich.

Her shoulders sagged. As if that was going to happen. Two months living where the gold was within reach, she just knew it, and she had yet to find time to pan for it.

"What's got you all in a dither?" Mabel set a stack of plates next to the basin.

"Gabriel's Bible verses."

"Ah." Mabel grabbed a dishtowel. "You don't agree."

"Nope. A bunch of foolishness." Charity scrubbed a pot hard enough to splash water and soak the front of her dress. Maybe a wet front would cool her down.

"As soon as I saw the Bible in his hand, I wondered how you were going to respond." Mabel dried the pan Charity had washed. "Gabe is a God-fearing man, Charity. Whether you share his beliefs or not might be the deciding factor as to what happens come springtime."

She was well aware of that fact, but she couldn't accept a loving God for no one. It wasn't that she didn't believe, but rather she didn't believe God cared for her. Some people were not good enough for God. No matter how hard she tried, Charity would not be considered one of the good ones. She was too hot-tempered and un-submissive.

"People are allowed to believe what they want. What I want to know is what the two men were conversing about."

"Hiram still won't say." Mabel reached for another plate. "I'm thinking Gabe won't say either?"

"Not a word. Told me it wasn't something women needed to worry about."

"And that sat with you like a tick, didn't it?" Mabel chuckled. "As life goes on, you'll learn to let some things slide. Pick your battles, I always say. You'll figure out your man's secrets soon enough."

"Gabriel isn't my man." Charity washed the last plate and handed it over. She would like him to be her husband as a man should, but didn't think there was a man out there for her.

She glanced out the window. Hiram and Gabriel stood in close conversation again, studying something in Gabriel's hand. "You're one of the lucky ones, Mabel. Not every man can be like your Hiram. You can tell he loves you more than the air he breathes. It's in his eyes."

Mabel clapped her on the shoulder. "That is the truth, my dear. But God made a man for every woman. Give it time." She bustled outside, leaving Charity to ponder her words.

11

Amos grinned as he knocked the rail from the posts. After mounting his horse, he cracked his whip over the cattle's heads and urged them out of the valley and into the next. He wasn't stealing them. Amos knew the penalty for thievery. He just wanted to set Gabe back a bit on achieving his goal. Lay claim to this lush land Maggie once slaved over. Land that should have been Amos's after she died. Prime land with hills and valleys and a creek that never ran dry.

One of the cows balked, and Amos flicked the whip across its back. If Gabe took advantage of the free range, he might not know for a day or two that his cattle was missing. Ever since Amos destroyed part of the fence a year ago, Gabe had kept them penned. Now, Amos had to sneak a little closer. If Gabe ever got a dog, he'd have to find another way to antagonize and slow the man down.

Once his marriage of convenience was over, Amos would rub salt in the wound by courting the newest Mrs. Williams. Then, he'd find a way to lay claim to Maggie's children, and his family would be complete. Gabe Williams would be where Amos is now. Alone and bitter.

He had thought the fire would take care of things. With the loss of his tobacco tin, it didn't take an overly smart man to figure out who had set the blaze. Proving it, though. That was another thing. Let Gabe come confront him. He'd welcome the challenge.

Maybe revenge would heal the ache in Amos's heart over losing Maggie.

*

"Cattle's gone." Gabriel grabbed his rifle from the over the fireplace. "I'll be gone most of the day. Keep the young'uns close to home."

Charity glanced up from her mending, her heart skittering. "Do you need help?"

"Can you ride?" He paused by the door, glancing over his shoulder, eyebrows raised.

She shook her head.

"Then you're best suited to stay here minding Meg and Sam." He slapped his hat on his head and stormed out.

Charity needed to add learning to ride to her never-ending list of things she needed to accomplish. She poked the needle through the knee of Sam's britches hard and jabbed her finger. She hissed and stuck the injured appendage in her mouth, then paused.

With Gabriel gone, she could take the children panning for gold!

"Come on children, we're going for a walk." Charity glanced outside to make sure they heard her, then moved to gather the makings of a simple lunch. What else would she need? Water, a pan, a sifter. She gathered everything in a blanket and hoisted the pack over her shoulder before heading outside.

"Where we going?" Sam sat Patches in the house and closed the door.

"To find some gold."

"Yippee!" Meg clapped her hands.

"Pa said there ain't any." Sam cocked his head. "He's going to be mad at you."

What else was new? "We'll be home before he is." It wasn't like they were being devious, exactly. Gabriel had never come right out and said Charity couldn't look for gold. He'd told her to watch the children. She could do both.

"Now, we'll follow the creek aways upstream and start there. We'll have fun."

"Why do you want to do this, anyway?" Sam took the blanket pack from her. "Pa buys everything we need."

Charity bit her tongue to keep from blurting out the fact she wouldn't be with them by this time next year and needed to provide a living for herself. She really did not want to do laundry anymore and fend off the unwanted advances from dirty men. "More money always helps."

They trudged through the ash and burned grass until they left the area around the house. Slowly, black became brown as evidence from the fire faded from view to be replaced by signs of the drought. The dry grass rasped against the hem of Charity's dress and poked at her legs. The aspens upstream drooped from lack of water.

Clouds overhead promised rain in the near future, leaving the air heavy with humidity. Charity picked up the pace and sloshed across a creek that almost reached Meg's waist. It must have already been raining in the mountains for the creek to be so high.

The clouds had been there since yesterday and still hadn't dropped their load in the valley. Who was to say it would happen on that particular day? Other than her ill luck. From their weight and the grey curtain in the distance, the rain poured higher in the mountains, refreshing the thirsty land. They would need to be careful crossing the creeks.

Charity and the children walked for an hour before Charity's leg throbbed, and she figured they had gone far enough. The creek they stopped at bubbled clear and strong from a fissure under some rocks. Underground brooks were known to hold gold—she thought she had heard that somewhere, maybe from miners talking around the table at the diner.

After Sam dropped the pack, she dug out the simple sandwiches. They would need to eat so they would have the strength to pan. "I'll work here with this tin plate. You two work at stirring up the bottom."

107

"How are we supposed to do that?" Sam wanted to know.

"Take off your shoes and splash around."

"We'll get wet."

Charity sighed. "It's hot enough that you'll be all right." The boy was just like his father, having no idea how to have fun. Life had to be more than hard work, surely, even on the prairie.

Leaving her shoes on the bank, Charity tucked her skirt up into the waist of her apron and waded into the frigid water. Pinpricks of ice shot through her feet and calves and numbed the burn on her leg. Panning was going to be hard work.

She scooped the fine silt from the bottom of the creek into her pan and swirled it, losing everything in the current. The next time, she slowed down and repeated the process, letting the water slop out gradually over the rim of the pan. The silt washed away with the water, but heavier bits settled in the bottom, and at last fine particles of yellow showed. She knew there was gold! "Look, you two."

Sam and Meg clustered around her. "Wow," Sam said. "We're rich."

Charity giggled. "Not yet, but it's promising."

Thunder rumbled. No! It couldn't rain. Not today. They needed to hurry.

She glanced to where Sam and Meg laughed and splashed each other with cupped hands. They kicked, sending water flying into the air. She should have brought them here days ago.

As more flakes appeared in her plate, Charity's spirits rose, even as her back ached from the strain of bending. Finally, life was letting her have the upper hand. Now that she knew where to find the shiny stuff, she would head here at every opportunity. When she could find no more gold in the creek, she'd search for those caves Sam mentioned.

The thunder rumbled louder, clearly closer.

Less than an hour later, with very little gold wrapped in a cloth, Charity lifted her face to the first of the raindrops. Fat plops hit the creek water, splashing as if the rain came from below as well as from above them. Lightning cut across the sky with a crack.

Meg screamed.

"Come on." Charity rushed to the bank and slipped on her shoes. "We'd best hurry home." She didn't want them caught in a downpour. What if the creek rose further? It wouldn't get deep enough to warrant swimming, would it? Charity couldn't swim.

The children rushed to do her bidding. Despite hurrying, the three of them were soon drenched as the clouds finally released their burden of rain. Charity's shoulders slumped. Gabriel was going to kill her.

The section of creek that had been deep enough on the way to the gold, had rose, and now ran swift. Charity and the children stopped at the bank. It couldn't be over Meg's waist. They should be all right. If they hurried.

Sam splashed across, holding the blanket pack over his head, and soon made his way up the opposite bank.

Charity placed her hands on Meg's shoulders and steered her into the water.

The water continued to rise. Charity's heart threatened to burst free. A rush of water hit her in the chest. She glanced upstream to see a wall of water rushing toward her. Meg would never make it! With all the strength she could dredge up, Charity lifted the child and tossed her to the muddy creek bank. Meg fell with a sharp cry, her hands scrabbling on the steep bank for a handhold. Sam reached down and pulled her up.

Charity's skirts tangled around her legs. She couldn't move. She locked eyes with Sam as another wall hit her, sweeping her feet from under her.

*

Gabe found his fifty head of cattle in a meadow two hours ride from the house. It didn't take a smart man to figure out who had removed the boards. With a yell and a crack of his whip, he steered the herd back toward home as lightning crashed overhead.

He needed to cut the drive short by speeding them toward home. With the fire-ravished land and ground hard from no rain, a storm could cause the creek to rise to a disastrous level, not to mention the danger of land erosion. Charity most likely wouldn't know what to do or where he kept the sandbags.

The cattle bellowed as thunder ripped the sky. Gabe urged them faster. Building the sod house so near the creek might not have been his best idea, but he was planning for the future, intending to use the modest structure to prevent rising waters from getting to the new place. He'd filled sandbags and stacked them in the barn, just in case, and had only needed them once before. When the rising creek flooded the rattlers from their hiding places, thus resulting in Maggie's death, he'd sworn never to be caught unawares again. Yet, here he was, away from home, and a killer storm rolling through.

"Yah!" He cracked his whip over the back of the nearest steer and kicked Rogue into a gallop.

By the time he herded the cattle back into the enclosure and temporarily fixed the fence, the rain poured from his hat like a curtain. He shivered against the rivulets running down the back of his collar. Sitting by a warm fire, surrounded by Charity and the children, sounded mighty good. Most likely Charity would have a fine stew simmering on the stove. He turned Rogue toward the barn.

After rubbing the horse down, Gabe dashed across the muddy yard and burst into an empty house. No fire. No children. No Charity. Where in the world could she have taken them on a day like today? He turned and squinted outside, peering through the downpour.

Sam and Meg raced toward him. Gabe ran to meet them, scooped Meg into his arms and ushered Sam into the house. "Where's Charity?"

"The creek took her, Pa." Sam swiped his forearm across his dripping brow. Water pooled on the floor under his feet.

"I don't understand." Took her? Did Sam mean she was gone? "Where did you three go?"

"Looking for gold," Meg informed him. "We found some too."

"Get some towels, sweetie." Gabe brushed her wet hair out of her face, then turned back to Sam. "Explain quickly, son."

"We went on a picnic and looked for gold. Ma found some. Then it started to thunder, and she said we had to get home. When we crossed where the creek bends and widens, Ma was swept down river." Tears poured down his face. "We were all crossing together, then we heard a loud noise. Ma picked Meg up and threw her onto the bank. When we looked back, she was gone. I tried to find her, Pa, I did."

Gabe pulled him into his arms. "You did what you could. I'll find her. What I'd like for you to do now, is pile sand bags in front of the house. If the water gets too far, take your sister to the top of the sod roof. Can you do that? If I'm not back by morning, ride your pony to Hiram and Mabel. They'll watch out for you."

Sam nodded.

"Good boy." Gabe dashed back into the rain and to the barn to fetch Rogue. *Lord, let me find her—alive, please.* His heart lay as cold as the clothes on his back. Maybe he wasn't meant to be married out here. Montana seemed determined to claim everything he considered his.

With his horse resaddled Gabe raced in the direction he believed Charity and the children had gone. Rain continued to unleash from heavy clouds, making visibility difficult. Rogue plundered heavily across rivulets and mud.

When they reached the bend Sam had described, Gabe slid from Rogue and scanned the bank. "Charity!" He'd never hear her over the pounding rain.

*

Water closed over her head as Charity lost her footing again. The icy water numbed her legs, making it impossible to stand. Her back slammed against a boulder. She fought her way to the surface, gulped air, and grasped at anything she passed on the bank that might slow her down. It wasn't that the water was deep, but rather too swift for her to gain a footing.

Why hadn't she learned to swim? She pushed to the surface again and grabbed for a low-hanging willow branch. Her legs ached from the frigid water. Gabriel would come for her. She just needed to hold on long enough. A log rammed into her, knocking her loose with a bruising thud. All she had to do was keep her head above water long enough to be rescued.

Maybe the current would sweep her past the homestead, where Gabriel and the children could watch her as she was swept out of reach. Umph. She rolled into a space between a rock and tree. Her skirt tangled. She tried to keep her nose and mouth clear of the water while wrapping her arms around the tree trunk. She laid her head back and closed her eyes.

*

Gabe caught a glimpse of her right before she submerged again. He raced down the bank, his eyes scanning for something long enough to hold out to her.

113

"Charity!"

His feet slipped, sending him crashing to the ground, knocking the breath from him. Get up! He pushed to his feet and followed her bobbing form. Every time she disappeared from sight, his heart stopped, only to thunder like buffalo when he spotted her again.

Behind him, Rogue trotted like an obedient dog, for which Gabe was thankful. He didn't want to hunt up the horse once he dragged Charity to safety. Precious time he'd need to get her in front of a warm fire and out of wet clothes. The day might be hot, but the mountain runoff could be like ice.

She lodged against the bank, and Gabe almost cried with relief. Then her eyes closed. No, no, no, no. He jumped into the creek and gasped at the knife-cutting cold. "Charity!"

She opened her eyes and turned her head. "You came." Her grip loosened, and she went under.

"Of course, I did." Gabe grabbed her under the arms and fought the current, dragging her with him, until he lay panting in the mud. Keeping his arms tight around her, he willed what body heat was left in him to her. Shudders shook both their bodies.

"Come on, sweetheart. Work with me. We've got to get on the horse." He sat up, keeping her against his chest.

"Can't."

"Yes, you can."

"I lost the gold."

"That's all right." He got to his feet and pulled her up, propping her against Rogue. "Stay like that until I'm in the saddle."

She nodded and slid to the ground. He refused to lose another wife because he was incapable of saving her. He jumped down and hauled her into his arms. With what strength he had left, Gabe hefted her over the horse, facedown, and climbed on behind her. He clicked to Rogue and kept him at a pace that he hoped wouldn't be too uncomfortable for Charity.

"Come on, sweetheart. It's not far now." Please, God.

12

Charity's teeth chattered so hard she bit her tongue. She closed her eyes against the pain and taste of rusted metal.

After depositing her in front of the fire and wrapping a quilt around her, Gabriel had ordered Meg to help her undress. Then he'd darted back outside, muttering something about sandbags. Charity shuddered, wanting nothing more than to curl up and get warm.

He needed to stay near the fire as much as she did. She hated to think of what could have happened if he hadn't found her. An icy watery grave. She shivered.

Meg pushed the quilt aside and unfastened the buttons at the top of Charity's dress. Charity stood and let the sodden mess fall to the floor, followed by her underwear. She still hadn't replaced the ripped pair and stared down at it in embarrassment.

She grabbed her nightgown from the rocking chair, donned it, and wrapped up again in the quilt as tight as a caterpillar in its cocoon. She would never be warm again. She stretched her bare feet closer to the fire. The log popped, sending crimson embers up the fireplace and a blast of heat to Charity's face.

Meg whimpered. Charity craned her neck. "What's wrong?"

"I don't want to lose another ma." She sniffed.

"Come here." Charity held the blanket open. "You can help me get warm."

Meg launched herself on Charity's lap. "I can help." She snuggled close. "I won't let you die."

Charity chuckled, breathing in the smell of little girl and wet hair. "I'm Irish. We don't die easy. We're much too stubborn."

"Really?" Meg lifted her tear-stained face.

"Really." Using the corner of the quilt, Charity tenderly wiped her cheeks. "Now close your eyes. We'll both rest until the men get back."

She smiled at calling Sam a man, but the young boy acted far older than his eight years. More often than not, he knew more about living on the prairie then Charity did. How was she going to walk away in a few months and leave these little ones behind—not to mention their father? He might fuss and grumble, but when one of them was in danger, he thrust himself into harm's way to rescue them.

Tears dripped down her face, warming her skin. She had a family. Her arms tightened around Meg. One she didn't want to let go of. Her gaze dropped to her sodden dress with its ripped pocket. And she'd lost the gold, the one thing she had that might have swayed Gabriel's favor in her direction. It hadn't been much, but it was a start.

Her toes burned as they warmed, sending prickles up and down legs that hurt more now than they had in the cold water. Her head pounded, and her nose ran. She wouldn't be sick. Not in the normally hot month of July. She wouldn't allow it. Closing her eyes, she laid her head back against the rocking chair's headrest.

*

The rain stopped by the time Gabe and Sam finished placing the sandbags. Gabe glanced at the mountains. The sun set behind lavender gray clouds that were pregnant with the promise of more moisture. The air felt heavy enough that a person could grab hold and wring out the water.

If the rain quit up in the mountains too, they ought to be able to escape flooding down here. He laid a hand on Sam's head. "You did the work of a man today, son. I'm mighty proud of you." Sam worked too hard for a child. Maybe Charity was right by stating the children needed to play more, but life was hard on the prairie. Everyone needed to do his or her share and then some.

"Do you think this ma's going to die like the last one?" Sam frowned, his eyes worried. "Because if she does, I don't think you should find another one."

"I don't think so, but we'll head in now, dry off, and get some coffee going to warm everyone up. What do you think about that?" It bothered Gabe that Sam didn't seem to miss Maggie much. She hadn't been the most affectionate of women, but she'd loved her children, and he was old enough to remember her.

"She looked really bad when you brung her home." Sam didn't appear to be mollified easily. "Real white. I like her. She's funny and gives me lots of hugs."

Gabe clamped his lips tight. How could he reassure his son when worries of his own threatened to swamp him? Maybe he should have stayed in the house instead of rushing outside to check for flooding. But Meg would have come running if Charity needed him, right?

He wasn't used to playing doctor. Sam and Meg were rarely sick, or hurt, for that matter. God had certainly blessed them all with good health, but Charity looked frail. Pale as a cloud and thin as a flower stalk. He sighed. And as beautiful as a summer day.

"Come on, son. Let's go in."

He froze in the doorway at the sight of Charity and Meg, asleep, cuddled together in the rocking chair. If he was a drawing man, he would have put pencil to paper and sketched the image to keep it with him always. Something to pull out and look at, even after Charity left.

The fire set her in shadows, highlighting her hair with scarlet and gold. The quilt draped off one shapely shoulder, showing the thin nightgown she wore and setting his imagination into overdrive. Gabe tore his gaze away. It wouldn't do him any good to dwell on her assets or what could be. Although she was good to the children, Charity didn't show any signs of wanting to stay. Her goal was to find gold and skedaddle to the nearest city. Gabe had no idea what he would tell the children when the time came. More and more he second-guessed his motives, and wisdom, for marrying Charity. Not the wisest decision he'd ever made, especially since he didn't seem capable of keeping wives alive.

Gabe moved as quietly as he could while wearing boots on a wood floor, and set a pot on the stove for coffee. "Sam, I think there's a little cocoa left in that tin. Hand it here, and I'll make some hot chocolate for you and your sister. Then you go change into dry clothes."

"What about you?" Charity stirred, pulling the quilt back into place, her voice raspy from sleep. "You must be chilled."

Gabe hurried across the room to take Meg from her lap. His hand brushed Charity's hip and caused his pulse to soar. "How are you feeling?"

"Better. Meg helped warm me." She smoothed an errant curl from Meg's face. "I'm hungry, too."

Gabe laid Meg on the bed. He would wake her when the chocolate was finished. "I can heat up some leftover biscuits."

"With some of Mabel's jam, please." Charity stood, her toes peeking from under the hem of her nightgown, and shuffled to the table.

Gabe's heart lodged in his throat. "I should change." He slipped behind the privacy quilt.

How would he make it through a long winter in

close proximity to Charity? Maybe he could request that she keep her hair. Then he wouldn't be tempted to bury his face in the silky strands, or run his fingers through the length of it. Those mesmerizing green eyes were temptation enough. He would insist she keep shoes or socks on her feet, and wear a thicker nightgown. A man could only stand so much.

In dry clothes, he returned to the stove. Charity ran the tip of her finger along a groove in the table, seemingly deep in thought. What ran through her pretty head? Was she counting down the days until she was "free"?

"I'm sorry."

He had to strain to hear her. "For what?"

"Endangering the children." She lifted shimmering eyes. "I'd already checked our creek for gold and thought we could have an afternoon of fun farther upstream. I didn't realize the danger of rain in the mountains."

Gabe measured the coffee, struggling to keep his emotions in check. Her and that infernal gold! "Why are you so interested in finding gold? If there's something you need, I'll—"

"I won't always be here." Her voice trembled.

He took a deep breath. "I won't let you leave empty handed. Besides—" he swallowed past the boulder in his throat. "You saved Meg's life today, from what Sam says. I owe you."

She jerked. "You want to pay me for saving Meg? What kind of woman do you take me for? What kind of

121

person?" She stood, her knuckles white where she gripped the blanket. "Drink the coffee alone. I'm warm enough now, and I'm going to bed."

No, he didn't want to pay her for saving his daughter. Although it was becoming a common occurrence, it seemed, with the horse on the day they met and now the flood. No longer in the mood for coffee, he covered the pot and glanced toward the children's beds. Fast asleep. He removed the water from the stove.

*

Hot tears stung Charity's eyes. She turned her head to gaze on Meg's sleeping face, barely discernible through the deepening dark in the house. How could Gabriel suggest she wanted money for caring for Meg? Her daughter? At least for a time.

He'd said many careless things over the weeks they had been wed, but this one hurt the most. Even more so when she realized he had no idea that what he'd said hurt her. Dense man.

She heard him ready for bed on the other side of the hanging blanket. A shiver skipped down her spine, reminding her of the day's events. How would it feel to snuggle against Gabriel? He gave off heat when he stood next to her. Sleeping would only make his body heat increase. Charity rolled tighter in her blankets.

He had pulled her from the creek as if she weighed no more than Meg. Charity had felt safe in his arms, and discovered she liked the feeling. For once, she wished she had learned the practice of flirtation while growing up. Surely, Gabriel hungered for a woman's presence in his bed. They were married, after all. It wouldn't be immoral. If Charity were a devious woman, she could easily make it so that an annulment was impossible.

Sighing, she rolled to face the wall, the scent of damp dirt filling her nostrils. She couldn't deceive him that way. Not with the way her heart softened toward him more each day. She blinked against the escaping tears. She'd lost the meager amount of gold panned that day and would have to start again. One obstacle after another reared in front of her, preventing her from achieving a sense of peace or accomplishing her goal.

Wait, Mabel said. But for how long? How could Charity manage being cooped in a one-room house with Gabriel through the winter? She was no stranger to Montana's brutal snow storms. They could be snowed in for days, weeks even. With nothing to do but stare at each other.

13

Charity gathered the blankets off the bed and dragged them outside to be washed. She still didn't follow the schedule set in place by Gabriel's late wife, instead choosing to do chores as they needed to be done, but the work never ended.

She smiled. Why didn't that bother her? After all, she'd married Gabriel hoping for an easier life. Instead, work had increased if that were possible. Cooking and cleaning for a family was far more satisfying than cleaning for strangers, and there were hugs to be had at the end of the day, even if they weren't from her husband. After two years of solitary living, a family filled an empty spot in her heart and gave Charity purpose.

Hammering filled the air, drawing her attention to the new house. Gabriel knelt on freshly placed decking boards and laid shingles. She looked away before she dropped the blankets. How could he sit so high off the ground? What if he lost his balance? She'd become a widow before she really became a wife. She would need to keep a close eye on Gabriel to keep him safe.

She dropped her bundle into the hot water and shaved off some soap. The children's voices came from the barn, happy while they worked on their chores. A peaceful day. Charity lifted her face to the sun. After her chilly dunking in the creek a few days ago, she'd never complain about the sun's heat again.

Opening her eyes, she headed back to the house for more laundry. As she stooped to gather Sam's and Meg's clothing from the floor beside their beds, a shadow blocked the door. She straightened and turned. An Indian ducked under the door frame, staring at her with black expressionless eyes.

Charity choked back a scream and dashed around the table. She grabbed a knife from the counter and clutched it in her sweaty hand. "Go away! I'll cut you. I mean it."

The Indian placed a hand on his bare chest. "I Red Feather."

"I don't care who you are. Go away." Her voice rose to a shriek as her gaze traveled over buckskin britches, a bronzed chest, and up to long braided hair adorned with a single eagle's feather with a red painted tip.

Would he scalp her? Charity put her free hand to her hair. She liked her hair. It was her one glorious feature. Her crowning glory as her mother used to say.

"I friend." Red Feather scowled.

"Not my friend." She stepped back. He had an odd sense of friendship, coming up behind someone and scaring them half to death. She excused his ignorance to his being a savage. Perhaps he didn't know proper social skills, but she still didn't want him in her house.

How much damage could she actually do with a kitchen knife? The man towered over her, almost as tall as Gabriel, with bulging muscles and a rank scent. Was it bear grease? Didn't she read in a dime novel that Indians plastered themselves with it?

What did he want with her? Was he alone? She craned to see around him.

"I brought horse."

Mercy! "I'm not going anywhere with you." He was going to take her away. Maybe make her one of his squaws. Her legs trembled, and she placed a hand on the table to steady herself. She should have stayed in the city! Indians didn't roam the city streets, unless they were a hired scout.

Where were the children? She straightened her shoulders. If going with Red Feather insured their safety, then go with him she would. "Okay, I'll go with you."

He scratched his head, which most likely crawled with lice, Charity shuddered at the thought, and he stared at her for a moment, before bursting into laughter. "Pale woman with fire hair funny." He crooked his finger. "Come with me. We find Gabriel."

Gabriel? "What did you do to my husband?" She advanced with the knife held out in front of her. She'd never made another person bleed but thought she could, if she had to.

His grin faded. "You come with me. Gabriel explain Red Feather is friend."

Now, she'd made him angry. Why couldn't she keep her mouth shut? Most likely he'd lure her outside, ravish her, then scalp her and leave as crow food.

He motioned her forward again. "Come."

*

Gabe stepped inside the house. His eyes widened at the sight of Charity in a stare contest, knife in hand, with Red Feather. "What's going on?"

"Your squaw wants to kill me." Red Feather turned and grasped Gabe's forearm in greeting. "She brave woman."

"Yes, she is." He grinned. "Put the knife down, Charity. Red Feather is my friend."

"I brought pony," Red Feather said.

"Wonderful. Come on, Charity. We have a gift for you." Gabe waved Red Feather out ahead of him. What did Charity think she could do with a little pig sticker like the knife in her hand? She sure was cute standing in a defensive pose with her face all red and her hair coming loose from its bun. He wanted to grab her close and hug her tight. Instead, he opted for taking the knife from her hand and setting it on the table.

Keeping a wary eye on Red Feather, Charity bustled outside then stuck like a burr under a saddle to Gabe's side as they approached the back of the house. He couldn't wait for her to see what Red Feather brought.

They rounded the corner, and Charity gasped. A cinnamon-colored mare with a black mane and tail ripped at a few blades of unburned grass, her reins looped over a fence. Charity cast shimmering eyes on Gabe. "For me?"

"Isn't she a beauty?" Just like her mistress. Gabe scratched behind the horse's ears. "I traded Red Feather a milk cow for her."

"She's gorgeous. I'm going to call her Ruby." Charity rubbed her hand over the horse's muzzle. "But I can't ride."

"I'll teach you." Gabe leaned against the fence. "It's a skill everyone should know out here."

Her look grew pensive. "There's so much to know out here."

"It's only been a couple of months. You're doing great." He turned to Red Feather. "Thank you, my friend."

"If you tire of your woman, I will give you back the cow for her," Red Feather offered.

"Tempting, but no thanks." Gabriel patted her head, eliciting a squawk of protest from Charity. "But I think we'll keep her around for a while."

Red Feather nodded and loped away.

"Keep me around for a while?" Charity planted fists on her hips.

"I had to say something. It wouldn't seem strange to him to trade you."

"Couldn't you have just said no?"

"Most likely, but my way was more fun. Would you

like to start learning to ride now?" Gabe itched to shove back the loose strands of hair from Charity's face. When had he begun to feel as if she were more than just someone to watch over his children? He didn't want to love another woman, not that that was how he felt at the moment. He couldn't allow himself to love again. Already, Charity's life had been endangered twice. His heart couldn't take another loss like he'd suffered with Maggie.

"All right." Charity took a deep breath. "What do I do first?"

"There's a stump by the corral that will be perfect as a mounting block." He unlooped Ruby's reins and led the horse to the stump. "Step on this, insert your left foot in the stirrup, and swing your right leg over."

She glanced skeptically at him, then hitched her skirts and took her place on the sawed off block of wood. Grasping the saddle horn, she swung her leg high and . . . fell backward.

Gabe caught her and rolled, shielding her from the brunt of the hard landing. As he lay catching his breath, he couldn't help but notice how soft Charity felt lying on his chest. His arms tightened. What if he kissed her? Would she slap him? Their gazes locked. She smelled like soap and sunshine. He closed his eyes, breathing deeply, and prepared to see what her lips tasted like.

"Are you all right?" Charity shifted against his hold. "Did I hurt you?"

Did the woman have to talk so much? Gabe groaned inwardly. "I'm fine." He released his hold and waited while she got to her feet before getting to his. "Don't swing your leg so high. Just up and over."

"I told you I didn't know how to ride." She flounced back to the stump. "But I'm determined to learn."

Of that, Gabe had no doubt. She had conquered every task she had undertaken so far.

The next time she went to throw her leg over the saddle, Gabe was prepared. He placed his hands on her waist and kept her steady. She glanced over her shoulder and glared, eliciting a laugh from him. She sure was fun to rile.

Sam and Meg had claimed seats on the corral fence and clapped as Charity trotted the horse into the pen, her hair coming fully out of her bun by the jostling.

"Tighten your grip with your thighs, but don't squeeze, and keep your feet in the stirrups." Gabe crossed his arms and leaned against the top rail. "Feel the horse move."

"How do I tighten without squeezing?" She shrieked as Ruby increased her pace. "I need a pillow for the saddle, I feel her moving so much. 'Tis a very hard saddle."

Gabe laughed and vaulted over the fence. He grabbed the reins. "I'll lead her. You concentrate on getting a feel for the horse. Close your eyes, and let your other senses take over."

She sighed and did as he said. "I smell horse, burned grass, and cattle."

"Feel, Charity." He jogged around the perimeter of the corral. By the time he was winded, she wasn't bouncing quite so much and had a smile on her face. "Good job. I think that's enough for today."

"Thank heaven."

"Wait." Gabe dropped the reins and tried to catch Charity before she hit the ground. Too late. She landed in a pile of green calico and petticoats. "Your legs aren't ready for you to dismount by yourself."

"Really?" Her eyes sparked. "Guess I figured that one out." She held out a hand for him to pull her to her feet. "Me legs are wobbly. I'm going to rinse the laundry. Something I do know how to do."

He loved how her brogue deepened when she was angry. It was almost like she tried to squelch her accent the rest of the time. As if she were ashamed to be Irish. It was a pity, but he had heard stories of how the Irish were treated back east. Obviously, her family had gotten a taste of the bigotry.

"Meg rides better than you, Ma." Sam hopped from the fence. Gabe shot him a "hush" look, but the boy kept talking. "How is it that a full-grown woman can't ride a horse? Didn't you have horses where you came from?"

"Where I came from?" Charity scowled.

"I'm guessing you're from across the ocean. You talk funny most of the time."

Charity increased her pace to the house. Sam kept up with her, with Gabe chuckling behind them, holding Meg's hand.

"I suppose I could help you learn in between my chores. Pa's too busy to spend a lot of time on a greenhorn." Sam halted. "But I can't give you a boost like Pa did. You'll have to learn to get on by yourself."

Charity practically ran into the house and slammed the door.

"What did I say?" Sam turned.

"She did the best she could, son. It sounded like you were giving her a hard time for struggling so." Gabe clapped him on the shoulder as he strolled by.

Sam jogged next to him. "I wasn't, I swear. Why are womenfolk so touchy?"

"You'll have to ask God that someday, son."

*

After weeks of daily riding lessons, Charity's muscles complained less, and she bounced less in the saddle, resulting in less sore places on her body. Meg and Sam cheered the first time Ruby trotted around the corral without Charity falling off. She might not be an expert, but at least she could stay on the horse's back. The sense of accomplishment at mastering the skill kept her skipping through the day.

She couldn't believe Gabe had gone to the trouble of getting her a horse. And he gave up a prized cow in order to do so! Charity was a blessed woman indeed. She hoped she could take the gentle mare with her when she left in a few months and wondered whether that would be proper, considering the horse was a gift to help her station as Gabriel's wife.

She slipped into the barn and pulled a carrot from the pocket of her apron. She'd taken to visiting Ruby each afternoon, after chores and before supper preparations. Something about the gentle nickering and nuzzles helped fill the empty spaces in Charity's heart that ached to be filled with affection. Between the pets and the children, the loneliness dropped away more each day.

She held the carrot out to the horse and rubbed a hand up and down Ruby's muzzle while the horse munched. "Funny, how a four-legged creature has become my best friend. Thought it might be Patches, but then you came along and stole me heart." Charity laid her forehead against Ruby's.

If only Gabriel seemed as happy to spend time with her as Ruby did. Or the children. Or the cat. The man wolfed down breakfast each morning and dashed out the door, not to be seen again until suppertime. If Charity wanted to see him, it was up to her to find a way, mostly in the form of taking water or food to him.

Charity gave Ruby a pat then moved to look out the barn door. Bits of green poked through the blackened dirt. The creek had returned to its normal depth, and birds to the branches of the skeletal aspens. She glanced upstream. Dare she make another attempt at the gold? Who knew when Gabriel would leave the homestead again for hours at a time? Lately, he'd stuck around like glue on a shoe, hanging from the roof of the new house, or working around the barn. She loved seeing him around, but winter would arrive soon and put an end to any opportunity of gold panning.

Winter. Shut inside with her husband. He'd almost kissed her that first day of learning to ride, she knew it.

But she'd gotten scared and jumped off him as if he would bite her. Foolishness. If she wanted him to ask her to stay, she would have to win him with womanly ways. That would more than likely involve kissing, something Charity had no skill at either, having never been kissed. A miner tried once, and she'd smacked him with her broom until he ran for the hills.

She glanced to the back of the house where Gabriel cut hay with a scythe. He swung the tool, muscles rippling. She definitely wanted him to try kissing her again, and the next time she'd let him.

14

Charity lay in bed and listened to the wind howl. Heavens, it sounded as if it would rip the door off its hinges. She pulled the quilt higher and turned her head to check on Meg who slept despite the noise. Charity shivered. The air felt mighty cold for an August morning.

The last thing she wanted to do was get up and cook breakfast. But, being a married woman and a mother, she couldn't consider her time her own. She tossed aside the blankets and hurriedly dressed, donning a tattered sweater over her green work dress. After hurriedly twisting her hair into a bun, she was ready to begin her day.

"Good morning," she told Gabriel, who started a fire in the fireplace. "It's cold."

"Unusual weather for August, but not entirely unheard of." He straightened and reached for his coat. "Cattle are out again. I'll be gone most of the day." He speared her with a glance. "This time, keep the children close to home. It might snow."

"Snow?" She sped to the window. Heavy slate-colored clouds covered the sky. The aspen trees danced as if to fast fiddler music. "But we haven't gone to town for our winter supplies." How would they make it through the winter? Not to mention she was nowhere near ready to be confined to the cabin with Gabriel for months.

"If it does snow, it won't last. We'll have to go to town as soon as it melts."

"Do you want me to pack you a meal?" Charity grabbed her shawl from the back of the rocking chair and draped it over her shoulders. Despite the fire, the outer edges of the room carried a definite chill.

"I grabbed some jerked venison and the canteen. I'll be fine." He slapped his hat on his head and wrenched open the door. The wind ripped it from his hand and slammed it back into the wall.

He wouldn't have to worry about Charity and the children venturing out in such fierce weather. They'd occupy themselves inside with schooling and the kitten. It might not officially be winter yet, but schooling was a good idea any time. "Will Ruby be all right in the barn?"

"Ruby and Sam's pony will be fine." He stepped outside and pulled the door closed.

The wind continued to howl, ebbing and increasing in volume until Charity wanted to join in with screams of her own. The children continued to sleep, and she allowed them to rest as long as they wanted. With them out of her hair, she could work on sewing their Christmas clothes from a green velvet cloak she'd found in their mother's trunk.

Fetching the item, she carried it to the rocker, and sat, rubbing her hand over the soft fabric. She would love to keep it for herself, never having owned something so fine, but the cloak belonged to their mother. She had no right to keep it. It would make a lovely vest for Sam and a dress for Meg.

She had nothing to wear herself for the holiday, nor fabric to make Gabriel a shirt. She thought of the money in the pouch stashed in her own trunk from her laundering days. There would be more than enough for fabric and Christmas gifts. She grinned, envisioning the toys she would purchase. She could replenish the gold when the weather cleared. Especially since she now knew where to pan.

While the wind continued to batter their home, and the children snored softly, Charity cut out the needed pieces from the fabric and giggled as Patches played with the scraps. The fire eventually warmed the inside of the soddy, and Charity could almost forget about Gabriel out in the storm. Almost.

With each rattle of the door, her heart stopped. With each roar of the wind, her blood chilled. The clock on the mantle continued to tick tock its way to daylight.

When the children began to wake, Charity shoved her work back into the chest and bustled to the stove. Cooked oats would warm them and keep them satisfied for a while.

She mixed the oats with heated milk while the children grumbled about the cold and layered their clothing. Charity shook her head. August, and it was freezing! She had lived in Virginia City for two years and never experienced this. Of course, here they lived half a day's ride up the mountain, and in a valley to boot.

She spooned the oatmeal into tin bowls and sprinkled a little brown sugar on top. "Breakfast!"

"It's snowing!" Meg passed the table and sprinted to the window. She threw open the shutters. "Look, Ma. It's Christmas!"

"Not yet, it isn't." Charity joined her. The white flakes failed to bring Charity joy. Her worry over Gabriel overshadowed the beauty of the moment. At least the wind had died down. She put an arm around Meg. "Come eat."

Who kept letting Gabriel's cattle loose? No wonder her husband didn't take advantage of free range. She'd wondered why he insisted on keeping his cattle in a fenced valley. If someone kept sabotaging his work, he'd be broke in a week. There'd been no more mention of the wager he'd spoken of on their wedding day, but something drove the man almost to the breaking point in finishing the new house.

Sooner or later, Charity intended to sit him down and talk about the situation. The more she got to know her husband, the more difficult it was to believe him to be a gambling man. Yet, he wasn't a liar. His actions had spoken for their selves.

*

Gabe pulled the collar of his coat higher on his neck and hunched his shoulders against the biting wind. Every time someone let his cattle out, they seemed to drift to the same valley. If not for that, he'd be at his wits end. As it was, he knew exactly where to begin searching in the blowing snow. Already, an inch of white powder obscured any tracks.

Although he had no proof Amos was behind the happenings on his homestead, Gabe intended to visit the sheriff when they made their trip to town. He still had the tobacco tin hidden in the barn.

Having vied with Gabe for Maggie's hand didn't give the man the right to sabotage their agreement. It needed to be a fair fight. Gabe would die before he willingly let the land go to Amos. He'd make the improvements agreed on before the deadline. If not, where would he and Maggie's young'uns go?

The thought had occurred to him that Amos might even try taking the children, considering he was a distant cousin of Maggie's, but so far, other than wanting the land, the man hadn't said anything. Still, to be on the safe side, Gabe would do everything in his power to meet the other man's terms drawn up in that ridiculous contract between Amos and Maggie. He refused to lose his land or the children he loved as his own.

Snow continued to fall. The stillness surrounded Gabe, making him feel as if he were the only person left on the mountain. He shivered. The snow would melt in a day or two, and summer would return, but right now it felt as though he'd never be warm again.

He caught a glimpse of brown among the white and steered Rogue in that direction. Sure enough, his cattle stood, heads hanging, in the same valley he'd found them in the last time. Gabe unfurled his whip and cracked it over their heads to start them home.

A boom came from the tree line behind him. A searing pain shot through his side. Holding on to the horn, he struggled to stay in the saddle. Wetness that had nothing to do with the snow spread across his ribcage.

*

Amos lowered his rifle. Desperation spread through him when Gabe kicked his horse into a trot. He'd missed making the shot that would have changed the course of his life. He never thought he would put a man through the sight of his rifle, but tamer actions haven't worked. Drastic measures needed to be taken.

How had he sunk so low as to contemplate killing a man? What would Maggie say if she were alive? She'd chosen Gabe. Why couldn't Amos resign himself to that? If she were here, she would gaze upon him with a sorrowful expression in those dark eyes of hers until he wanted nothing more than to disappear into the dirt.

He holstered his gun and turned his horse toward home. Maybe the snow had frozen his heart into a hard unfeeling mass. Or maybe Gabe's failure to keep the woman he loved safe had done that two years ago.

Lord, what have I become? That I would so desperately want a man dead in order to possess what he had?

If Gabe ended up dying from his wounds, and if word got out that Amos shot Gabe Williams, his new widow wouldn't marry him if he were the last man on earth. She most likely didn't know his name, much less his face. Amos had already spent too much time in a fairy-tale world of his own making. It was time to let past hurts go and move on with his life.

Plenty of women would want to be the wife of a successful rancher. A man who stood to gain a lot more if fate were on his side.

But if Amos stepped back, Gabe wouldn't suffer. He wasn't sure he could allow that.

*

Charity opened the door and peeked outside, blinking against the stinging wind that chapped her cheeks and glued snowflakes to her eyelashes. Gabe should have been back hours ago. What little bit of weak sunlight they'd had all day was quickly disappearing. She shivered and closed the door.

She needed to go look for him, but she had no idea how to saddle Ruby, nor was she familiar with the surrounding landscape. No help for it. Gabriel might need her. Squaring her shoulders, she grabbed her heavy wool coat. "Sam, Meg, you stay here. I'm going to look for your pa."

"On foot?" Sam glanced up from his bowl of ham and beans.

"Yes, I'll take the lantern. Which direction does he usually head?"

"North."

Charity raised her eyebrows.

"That way." Sam pointed to the back of the soddy. "There's a path up the mountain. It's steep, but you can't miss the valley on the other side." Sam stood. "Maybe I should go with you."

"No, you stay with your sister." Charity eyed the rifle over the mantel, then disregarded the idea. She couldn't load or shoot. She grabbed the lantern and lit it with a piece of kindling.

The wind stole her breath the instant she stepped outside. Sam had told her it would warm up again, but with a day like the one this one, Charity had a hard time believing it. She lifted the lantern and trudged in the direction Sam mentioned.

Before long, her legs trembled from the strain of making her way up the mountainside. Her foot slipped on a patch of ice, and she fell to her knees. The lantern shattered on a rock. The night pushed in on her with all its fearsome darkness. Her breath hitched.

She knew without looking that she sported skinned knees from slipping and falling on the hard ground, and she had yet to spot a single cow or her husband. Of course, should she find the four-legged animals, she wouldn't have a clue what to do with them.

She tugged her coat closer around her and continued, blocking her mind from the pain in her feet and nose. What if she walked past Gabriel in the storm? He could be lying behind any rock or bush. There was some visibility, but with her head down against the wind, she might miss him. What if he died out here? Then what would she do? She could always move back to Virginia City, but what about Sam and Meg? As their stepmother, was she their legal guardian?

What about her growing feelings for Gabriel? The thought of him lying dead, alone, in the snow, chilled her more than the storm.

"Charity O'Connell Williams you're a ninny." The wind whipped away her words. Thinking the worst, as always. Most likely she traveled on a fool's journey, and Gabriel was already on his way home. She turned to head back. A whinny came from her right, and Rogue stepped from the bushes with Gabriel hunched low on his horse's back.

"Gabriel!" Charity rushed to him. "What happened?"

"Fool woman. We're in a snow storm." He groaned. "Where are the children?"

"They're safe at home—where we should be." She ran her hands over his leg and side, then pulled them away sticky. "You're bleeding!"

"Someone shot me. Rogue was on his way home. You've put yourself in danger coming out here."

Charity stared at the horse and her injured husband. She needed to mount behind Gabriel. Grasping Rogue's reins, she led the horse to a nearby boulder and climbed up behind her husband. They could share body warmth. She dug in her heels and urged the horse to head home fast.

Someone shot Gabriel. Who could hate him that

much? Charity swallowed and glanced over her shoulder. Was the shooter still out there, or had he run away like the coward he was? She clicked to Rogue again and tensed, expecting a bullet in the back at any moment.

Gabriel slumped forward. Charity wrapped her arm around his waist and did her best to hold him in the saddle. Not an easy task considering the difference in their sizes. She wasn't sure how she'd get him off the horse and into the house, but Ma always told her she could do anything she put her mind to. She hoped that included an abundance of strength when she needed it.

Gabriel's blood began to soak through her coat. Her stomach churned. What kind of damage had the shooter done? Would she have to dig a bullet out of her husband? She kept her lips clamped tight against the acid rising in her throat. She'd need God's help, if He felt so inclined this once, to help Gabriel.

15

Gabriel still had the strength to assist Charity with getting him into the house. Although he leaned heavily on her shoulders, they managed to bang open the door and stumble over the threshold, landing in a pile of torn petticoats and groans.

Tears welled in Meg's eyes at the sight of them, and Sam bolted the door shut behind them. Charity breathed a sigh of relief once she struggled to her feet, and Gabriel collapsed on his bed.

She stared at the widening blood stain on his coat. Squeamish or not, the coat, and the shirt, needed to come off immediately. "Sam, remove your pa's boots, then take care of Rogue, please. Meg, put some water on the stove to heat." Charity knelt beside her trunk and dug until she located her medicine box. *Please, don't let Gabriel need the bullet removed*. The thought of doing so churned her stomach. She wasn't used to the sight of blood and torn flesh.

The silence behind her alerted her to the fact the children had yet to follow her instructions. Charity turned with a scowl that quickly faded. Sam and Meg held hands as Sam quietly prayed for their pa's recovery. Charity swallowed against the boulder in her throat. Hadn't her ma once said something about a childlike faith? She'd like to have that indulgence, she really would, but once again God threatened to take away someone important to her. She refused to let Him as long as she had breath in her body.

She choked back a sob and began tugging off Gabriel's coat. It wasn't easy with him lying injured and unconscious. "I'll need that water soon, Meg." She hated interrupting their prayer, since God might actually listen to children, but she couldn't stop Gabriel's bleeding if she had to take the time to heat water. "Sam, fetch me clean cloths before you head out to the horse." Blood seeped into the blanket under Gabriel's inert body.

Sam thrust a clean dishtowel into her hands and watched as Charity pressed it against Gabriel's wound.

"Hurry, son, and take care of the horse. I'm going to need your help." Maybe she ought to let Rogue wait, but her husband loved that horse and wouldn't appreciate it being left out in the weather. Charity didn't want him to worry about anything when he woke.

After several moments of pressing the cloths against his side, Charity unbuttoned Gabe's shirt. She chose not to think about what she would see as she removed it. Besides the wound, she'd see her husband's unclothed chest for the first time. She had never seen any man unclothed for that matter. Red Feather didn't count, and Charity had done everything possible not to dwell on the Indian's lack of dress. She had never even seen her Da without a shirt on.

The sides of Gabriel's shirt fell away, revealing a deep gash through the fleshy area at his waist. Charity smiled nervously. No entrance or exit hole, thus no bullet to dig out. Just a deep gash to stitch. She supposed she ought to thank God for the small favor. She pressed another towel against her husband's wound and waited for Sam to come back. Where was that boy?

He burst through the door along with a rush of cold air. "What do you need me to do?"

"Hold this against your pa's wound while I sterilize my needle. We don't need to dig the bullet out. Just clean and stitch." Charity moved back and let Sam take over. While she worked on sterilization, Meg poured hot water over more clean cloths.

Charity scrubbed her hands with lye soap and threaded her sharpest needle. She took a deep breath, knowing she would need a steady hand. Her hands shook as if she had the palsy.

Squinting, she took another deep breath, held it, and guided the thread through the eye of the needle. After retrieving the small bottle of spirits she kept in her medicine box, she was ready to work. Gabriel groaned when she poured the liquor across his wound, but didn't wake. The guttural sound he made tore at Charity's heart. She didn't want to do this. But if not her, then who? Certainly not one of the children, and the Stoltzes lived too far away to fetch for help.

She exhaled sharply through her nose, then jabbed the needle through his skin and tried to do her best stitching. Not being a seamstress, she worried about the neatness of the stitches. No help for it. She needed to get the wound closed.

By the time Gabriel was stitched and bandaged, Charity's head throbbed and the fire had begun to die down. She glanced at the children, their eyes shimmering as they stared down at their father. Her heart faltered. She'd been so focused on Gabriel, she'd lost all thought of them until that moment.

Charity couldn't remember the last time she had been so tired. She convinced the children their pa would be okay and encouraged them to go to bed. She ducked behind her curtain.

Her limbs trembled as she shed her soiled dress and donned her flannel nightgown. She dragged the rocking chair close to Gabriel's bed, placed more wood on the fire, wrapped her shawl around her shoulders, and then settled in for a long night of watching over him.

The flames flickered, highlighting his bare chest. What would it feel like to lay her head there? Have his arms wrap around her in love?

She crossed her arms. She could have become a

widow that day, and there were still the cattle to bring home. How did women and children survive life on the prairie without a man? Did they pack up and move to the nearest town, finding whatever job they could? The selfish thoughts running through her mind left her empty. She didn't want to go back to the unmarried life. Real marriage or not, Charity was content with the life she had now. Mostly.

Gabriel's brow furrowed. Charity reached out and smoothed the frown away. When would she admit to herself she was falling in love with her husband?

It would do her no good. He had made it clear from the beginning where his thoughts and heart lay. She'd thought she had hers under control, as well. Obviously not. Tears burned her eyes. She swiped them away and blamed them on the stress of the day.

Gabriel thrashed, and Charity laid a calming hand on his shoulder, his skin warm beneath her palm. When he settled, she grabbed a quilt from the foot of the bed and pulled it over him. Her gaze landed on the rifle over the mantel.

As soon as Gabriel was able, she'd ask him to teach her to shoot. If a no-good scoundrel came sniffing around, she'd need to be able to defend the home. And if it happened to be the man who shot her husband, she would gladly pay him back with a bullet of her own.

*

Fire burned through Gabe's side and silk tickled his hand. He turned his head. Charity lay stretched out on the bed beside him, her hair loose and flowing across

149

the pillow. He'd wondered what it would be like to have her sleep beside him, but hadn't planned on it being because he was injured. He moved to wrap an arm around her and draw her close, but stopped as his side screamed.

He would die for a drink of water, but he definitely did not want to wake his sleeping wife. Not while he had a rare opportunity to study her. She rolled over and faced him. If he wanted to, Gabe swore he could count all the amber freckles that dotted her nose. Her lashes, dark for a woman with red hair, rested on her cheeks, hiding eyes the color of a summer meadow. He tried to conjure up a picture of Maggie's hair, and failed. He seemed to recall it being the color of straw, and her eyes as dark as his children's. Next to the vibrancy of Charity, Maggie had been a tame sparrow.

Sure she had had gumption. After all, the trek across the continent after the war couldn't have been easy, but Maggie did everything in a quiet manner, often melting into the background. Charity would also be noticed wherever she went.

His gaze wandered over the curves of her shoulder and hip and back to her face. He caught just a glimpse of a rounded freckled cheek and brushed aside the urge to caress her face and wake her with a kiss.

Gabe tore his gaze away and laid his arm over his eyes. He was nuts comparing the two women. They were as different as night and day. He groaned at his foolish thoughts.

"Oh." Charity bolted from the bed, jostling the

mattress. "I must have fallen asleep." She put hands to her cheeks. "How do you feel? May I fetch something for you?" She placed the back of her hand against his forehead. "No fever. That's good. How long did I sleep? Gracious."

"Charity, stop." Gabe held out a hand. "Sit. Please, don't be embarrassed on my account."

"Embarrassed for what?" She perched on the edge of the rocking chair and twisted her hands in her nightgown.

"There's nothing wrong with the two of us sharing a bed. We're married." She was adorable with her cheeks flushed and hair wild about her head.

"Not in … that way."

"You were only sleeping, Charity." He grinned. Maybe when he healed and was on his feet, they could do more than sleep.

"Yes, well." She leaped to her feet. "Let me fix you some coffee."

"Water will be fine. I'm going to drowse back off in a moment." The pain in his side was fierce enough that all he wanted to do was grit his teeth and hide away until he healed. And feel Charity's soothing cool touch on his face.

Before she returned with his drink, his eyes closed.

Charity could not believe she allowed Gabe to wake before she did. What was the matter with her? Oh, she was a wanton woman. Married or not, a woman did not lie with her husband without invitation, did she?

Oh, but the bed had looked so inviting, and she had been so tired. She'd meant to be awake before him and he none the wiser.

She leaned both hands on the counter beside the wash basin and lowered her head. What must he think of her?

She took a mug from the upper shelf and poured water from the pitcher. How easy it would be to slip and ruin all of her plans for the future. She could so easily succumb to the benefits of a physical marriage, and thus, be unable to receive an annulment. Although Ma always looked at intimacy has another chore, when Charity looked into Gabriel's eyes, she felt flutters that told her physical love could be something more than an obligation. She could look for gold whether married or not, but how would Gabriel feel if he fell prey to a moment of temptation? He'd most likely hate her forever.

With a sigh, Charity moved to the bed and gazed at her sleeping husband. She set the cup on the table, and settled back into the rocking chair. Maybe she ought to go to her own cot in order not to climb back beside Gabriel. If she did, she'd get no sleep for worrying about him waking up and staring at her again.

Her head nodded, her chin rested on her chest, and her eyes closed.

"Ma?" Sam patted her shoulder.

Charity opened her eyes to the sight of both children staring at her. "What's wrong? Did he take a turn for the worse?" She cupped Gabriel's cheek. His skin was as hot as an ember. "Bring me cool water. Quickly." She tore the blankets off him and glanced outside. Of course, it would stop snowing. "Get the water from the creek, and try to find me some unburned bark from an aspen tree."

The children rushed outside to do her bidding, leaving coats and cloaks behind. If they weren't careful, Charity would be treating them for fever too.

Again, she dug through her medicine chest and pulled out a tin of dehydrated aspen bark. She had enough for a few days of treatment, but figured with winter still a couple of months away, she had time to harvest and prepare more. Obviously, that wasn't the case.

Please, God, spare Gabriel. If He did, Charity promised to pay close attention to the scriptures Gabriel read from the Bible during the winter months. If God could show His mercy this time, she would give Him another chance to show her He loved her.

16

"Hello, the house!"

Charity tossed down the spoon she'd been using to stir the stew for the day's meal and rushed to the door. Hiram and Red Feather strolled toward her from the direction of the creek. Tears welled in her eyes as she threw open the door. "Come in, please!" Her knees weakened from the prospect of help.

"Howdy, Charity." Hiram whipped off his hat. "Is your husband home? Red Feather saw a few of his cows wandering so we figured it might warrant coming to see if something is amiss. I wondered why he didn't come straight here, but Red Feather said he was led to go to my place."

Charity sniffed. "Gabriel went out day before yesterday to search for the cattle. This is the second time someone let them loose. He was shot. I've been caring for him and haven't had the opportunity to go

154

looking for them myself."

"Shot?" Hiram glanced at Red Feather.

"A flesh wound, but he ran a fever all day yesterday and through the night." Charity stepped aside and let the men enter. "I've been cooling him with creek water and aspen bark tea. I think it's working, but I've been dreadful worried, all the same."

Red Feather knelt beside the bed and peered under Gabriel's bandages. His face remained impassive. Planting his hands on his thighs, he stood. "No infection. Gabriel will live. I go find cows."

"Thank you so much! I'm mighty grateful." Charity almost hugged him, but then, remembering the way the Indian appraised her on their first meeting, stepped back and held out her hand instead.

Red Feather stared at her hand before shaking. "Old man will stay with you until I return."

"Old man," Hiram sputtered. "Savage." His eyes twinkled, belying the harshness of his words. "You be careful. If there's someone out there with a vengeance, you don't want to be the next victim."

"Red Feather move like the smoke. I be back before sundown or I not be back."

With the way he scooted out the door, Charity had no doubt he'd scout around just as he said, invisible. "Hiram, can I get you some coffee?"

"Much obliged." He removed his hat, hung it on a nail, then sat at the table. "Has Gabriel said anything about who he thinks might have done this?"

Charity shook her head. "I think he has his

suspicions, but hasn't discussed them with me."
Nothing a woman should concern herself with, he'd say.
She lifted the pot off the stove and poured the fragrant
brew into two cups. She'd earned one for herself.

Hiram glanced around the soddy. "Where's the
young'uns?"

"Chores. With me nursing Gabriel, I don't have a
lot of time for the livestock." She glanced out the still
open door. The day before yesterday's blast of
unseasonably cold weather had left as quickly as it had
arrived. Although the day was still cooler than normal,
the sun glistened off what was left of the snowfall piled
against buildings. Tomorrow, all signs of an early winter
would be gone and the last days of summer would
linger for a while.

Hiram sipped his coffee. "I'll take this out to the
barn and see what I can do to help. Don't want to leave
you until Red Feather gets back."

"What are you not telling me?" He and Red
Feather had never worried before. Of course, Gabriel
was always here, but surely they realized he would be
gone for a full day sometimes. Had they somehow
known Gabriel was wounded? Were she and the
children in danger?

Hiram swallowed, his Adam's apple bobbing.
"Gabriel will have my head if I tell you."

"I'll have your head if you don't." She put her fists
on her hips.

Hiram turned his coffee cup in his hands. "Don't
get your Irish dander up with me, missy. Red Feather

was out hunting. Came across a couple of Gabe's cows. He followed the tracks, which happened to go close to my land. He fetched me, and we backtracked. Wasn't hard to see blood drops on the rocks, so we hightailed it here."

"And, you thought to tell me a falsehood as to why you came?" She cast a glance to where Gabriel's blankets rustled. "Don't get me wrong. I am grateful you are here."

He lowered his head. "We're figuring it's the same scalawag that started the fire."

"You have a big mouth." Gabriel panted as he tried to sit up.

"The fire wasn't an accident?" Charity rushed to Gabriel's side and propped pillows under him. A quick touch to his face showed her his fever had ebbed. "Why didn't you tell me?"

"It's a man's place to protect his family." Gabriel reached for the cup of water on a crate Charity had moved close to the bed.

"Women can help." She narrowed her eyes. "Once you're on your feet. I want you to teach me how to shoot."

"Why?"

"What if something really does happen to you? I'll need to fend for meself and the children."

"That's why women remarry out here. For the protection."

"Heaven save me from a stubborn fool." Charity whirled and stormed outside. Her husband would teach

157

her to shoot, of that she had no doubt. All she needed to do was badger him enough and show him the logic in the idea. Most likely Maggie had known, so why the hesitation in Charity's case? Gabriel Williams was the most infuriating man!

She plopped on a stump outside the barn and rested her chin in her hands. Maybe she was fatigued and small things bothered her more than they should. Gabriel's distrust in allowing her to be his partner in all things was another sign of his plans to eventually send her away. Why did she keep hoping things might be different?

"Ma?" Sam stepped out of the barn. "Is Pa dead?" His chin trembled.

Charity held out her arms. Sam, followed by his sister, launched into her lap. "Your father will be fine." Cranky as ever.

"Then why are you sad?" Meg asked.

"I'm tired, 'tis all." Charity smoothed chocolate-colored hair away from her daughter's face. "You look so much like your father."

"He ain't our real pa." Sam pulled away and leaned against her knee. "But we love him like he is."

"Not your real pa?" Her heart thudded to her stomach as her hand fluttered around her throat. Another secret Gabriel kept from her? Did she know anything about her husband?

"Nah, our pa died in the war, then Ma remarried this pa. But, they talk like they used to know each other when they were young'uns. When she died, he kept us."

Something else that ate at Gabriel like a starving hound? Did his desire to keep the children have anything to do with his wager against the land? Charity held the children tight. They had no blood relatives left. Gabriel needed to take care of himself so he would be around to raise these children. Somehow, Charity needed to convince him to let her stay on past the agreed date. If she was no longer around, and Gabriel died, who would care for these angels? She needed to have a serious conversation with her husband.

She set her chin. She'd refuse to go, simple as that. "Your father is awake. Why don't the two of you go in and check on him? He could use some kisses and hugs."

They dashed away, leaving Charity to dwell in her thoughts. Her gaze roamed past the burned aspens to the creek, then over to the barn and the frame of the new house. She'd grown attached to the land, despite the difficulty of each day's work, and she loved the stubborn man lying wounded on the bed. She straightened. She had all winter to convince Gabriel to keep her, not to mention Thanksgiving and Christmas. Two days she would make very special.

Gabriel came slowly out of the sod house, leaning on Hiram's shoulder. Charity gasped. Fully dressed with his rifle in hand! "Are you crazy?" She rushed to his side. "I wonder about your mental state sometimes. You should be in bed."

"Red Feather is out looking for *my* cattle. A man looks out for his own."

"Sometimes friends help!"

Charity glared at Hiram, who shrugged. "He wouldn't stay down. Short of shooting him again, there wasn't much I could do."

"Now, what? You're going to get on your horse?" Charity stomped her foot. "I didn't climb on that monster of a horse and keep you from falling off so you could go back out and finish what someone else started!"

*

"What are you talking about?" Gabe nodded toward the barn. "Hiram, help me get Rogue ready."

"You can't even saddle your horse." Charity flitted around him like an annoying gnat. When had she gotten so bossy? Tears welled in her eyes, giving his heart a lurch.

"Are you crying?" He hadn't been in her company for five minutes. How could he have said something to hurt her feelings?

"That's my cue to vamoose." Hiram tipped his hat and sauntered to the horse he left to graze in the corral.

Charity sniffed. "I'm not crying."

"Yes, you are." Gabe sagged against the barn. Maybe he wasn't ready to get back on the horse. His side burned like all get out. "What did I say this time?"

"Nothing. Get yourself killed if you want to." She gathered her skirts and sprinted for the house.

Could she possibly be fearful for his safety? The thought warmed him and lent him strength. Not enough to actually go looking for the cattle like he wanted, but enough to sit outside and wait for Red Feather.

Life had gotten as unpredictable as a tornado. Maybe they should start their nightly Bible readings before winter set in. Who said they could only read during the months they were snowed in?

God wasn't a seasonable God. Most likely. More Bible reading would do them all good and help solve whatever problems Charity carted around that made her as flighty as a squirrel. It might even help Gabe know how to deal with the unknown person stealing his cattle. Well, not stealing actually. More like relocating.

He gnawed his lip. Why would someone let the cattle loose, but not keep them, and then try to kill Gabe? What would he do when he found the culprit?

Instinct made him want to shoot the culprit. His heart told him that wasn't the answer. Did he really want to shoot Amos? Maggie would most likely come down from heaven and give him a slap alongside the head if he killed her cousin, distant relation and scoundrel that the man was.

A commotion near the corral drew his head up. Red Feather galloped up, and dismounted. "Cows back in pasture. I set plank back in fence. Why not move them closer to home until you handle this trouble?"

Gabe braced a hand against the barn and pushed to his feet. "I've been thinking on it. Been thinking about a dog, too."

"Red Feather have pup. I bring it and its mother. She good watchdog."

"I'm obliged. The young'uns will love the puppy.

What breed?"

Red Feather shrugged. "Big. Wolf, maybe. Found after white people drove wagons across land. Dog and pups were left. Only one survived."

Gabe rubbed his chin. A wolf for the children? "Is it tame?"

"Like a baby wolf." Red Feather grinned. "No worry. She won't eat your young. I fetch. I kept for to celebrate your white man's Christmas. As a gift for you. They're in the woods." He nodded and rode away, leaving Gabe second-guessing his decision about a dog.

Within fifteen minutes, Red Feather returned leading the largest dog Gabe had ever seen. The dog's back almost came to his waist. Wiry hair, brindled grey and black, and a lolling tongue. A fearsome looking beast, yet almost regal. "That thing's a horse!"

"No." Charity sprinted toward them. "It's an Irish Wolfhound." She dropped to her knees and wrapped her arms around the adult's neck. "My you're a beauty. Is she ours? And the pup?"

Red Feather nodded before Gabe could change his mind.

"Where are we going to keep something that size? Not in the house." Definitely not. They already had a cat.

"Yes, we are." Charity stood, keeping a hand on the dog's head. The dog gazed at her with soulful eyes. "They aren't staying outside in a Montana winter. We'll manage. Come on, Lady. You too, Prince."

Lady? Prince? Gabe shook his head. What had he

gotten himself into this time? "Thank you very much, Red Feather."

His friend clapped him on the shoulder and laughed. "You very welcome, my white brother."

Sam and Meg ran from the house squealing. Meg gathered the pup in her arms, the young things legs dragging the ground. "Is it Christmas?"

"Might as well be." Gabe slumped back on his stump. The bullet might not have killed him, but living with Charity very well could.

A few minutes later, he sighed and slowly made his way to the house. He opened the door and stepped into a din that most likely rivaled the wailing of an asylum.

Lady barked, deep and throaty. Prince yipped and raced around the table, Meg in hot pursuit. Patches launched herself, claws extended at Gabe's leg and scurried up and around to his back. He added his own yell to the mix and whirled to unlatch the menace shredding his skin. "Get this infernal animal off me."

Charity giggled and grabbed the cat by the scruff of the neck. "She's only frightened."

"She isn't the only one." Gabe clutched his side and tottered to his leather chair. After carefully lowering himself, he closed his eyes and laid his head back. Yep, the woman would definitely be the death of him.

What in the world would they feed two dogs the size of small ponies? He hadn't realized Red Feather had such a wicked sense of humor. No wonder he was so quick to give them up. What could he get the man as a gift that would rival the one Gabe had received?

Payback would be a real pleasure. Maybe he should give him Charity after all.

He opened one eye and watched as Charity nuzzled the cat, then bent over to let Lady and Patches get acquainted with the kitten. Her face lit with pleasure, her fiery hair slipping free of its restraints. He fought a smile. Send her away and miss all this?

Hiram poked his head in the door, took a look around, and backed out. Smart man. Now, he could return to his pleasant quiet home. Maybe Gabe could go with him. He chuckled and closed his eye again. Nope. He might complain, but he'd lived more in the couple of months since he'd married Charity then he had in all the years before.

The new house couldn't get built fast enough. This little one was busting at the seams. A laugh escaped him, then another. Soon, he wrapped his arms around his waist and howled. Charity gave him a perplexed look which only made him laugh harder. The house quieted, all its occupants staring as he lost himself in joy.

Thank you Lord, for the full life you've given me.

17

A week later, Gabe loaded his family, minus the pets, into the wagon and headed for Virginia City. They'd spend the night in the same hotel in which he'd married Charity. What had seemed like a spur of the moment, desperate action, turned out to be the best decision he'd ever made. He couldn't imagine the homestead without her.

The afternoon and next morning would give them time to purchase winter supplies and Christmas gifts, although he knew Charity had been working on a few things in the rare moments she had the house to herself. It had been fun to see her scamper every time he or one of the children walked in the door.

He wanted to get her something special and wracked his brain trying to decide what. He was a fair whittler, so something to that effect was an option. Maybe a nativity? Her trunk contained a few frilly things like tablecloths and doilies, so maybe a nice mantel clock other than the plain one that sat there now? Something that would look nice in the new house? He made a note to purchase yarn to occupy her hands during the winter months.

Sam and Meg said the dogs were all they wanted as presents but Gabe knew come Christmas morning, their tone would change. Every child wanted a present. Gabe didn't have a lot of money, but he had enough to make this year's holiday one Charity would never forget. Come spring, leaving would be the last thing on her mind.

"You should've let us bring Prince, at least." Sam leaned over the seat. "He's just a pup. He'll miss us."

"He has his mother," Gabe replied. "They're fine in the barn for one night."

"I bet he digs out and gets lost."

"No betting, please." Charity frowned. "Must everything be a bet between you two?"

"It's harmless talk," Gabe assured her.

"To some." Charity stared at the road in front of them. Her bottom lip quivered. "To others, it's a wasted life."

They definitely needed to have a talk about Gabe's wager. Charity deserved to know the circumstances that led to his moment of foolishness. Winter would give them plenty of opportunity for long heart-to-heart talks once the children were in bed. Maybe, then, she would tell him what plagued her so.

"Can I have a peppermint stick from the

mercantile, Pa?" Meg joined her brother at leaning over the seat. "It's been such a long time."

"You can have two." Gabe flicked the reins to encourage Rogue and Ruby to move faster. Charity's horse hadn't liked the harness at first, but she'd adapted nicely. "You'll also have fabric for new clothes. Charity, there's a list in the pocket of my jacket. Feel free to add to it anything you need."

"Sugar, flour, salt, coffee?"

"All there."

"Wicks for candles?"

"Whatever you need."

She smiled and nodded.

"I'll take care of feed for the animals while you take the children to the mercantile. Then we'll meet at the diner for supper. If we place our orders today, we can pick them up in the morning after breakfast." No need to rush the biannual trip to town. They wouldn't be back again until the snows melted.

The children settled down until the first houses appeared, then even Charity sat straighter at that point. Gabe had always regretted the thought of more people settling the area, but maybe it wasn't such a bad thing. Women seemed to need folks around once in a while. Charity sure was teaching him a lot about women.

Maybe if he'd known some of the things he knew now, Maggie would have been happier. Then, she wouldn't have felt the need for long solitary walks in the afternoon and wouldn't have stumbled across that snake.

He set the wagon brake in front of the mercantile. "I'll meet you back here in an hour for supper." He jumped down and helped Charity out then reached for Meg. Sam wasted no time in leaping over the back. "You two young'uns stay close to your ma. No wandering off."

Gabe set a fast pace straight for the Sheriff's office. Sheriff Bill Spraggins, a man whose lanky frame reminded Gabe of a crow, reclined behind a battered wood desk. The toes of his cowboy boots, propped on the scarred surface, faced the door. A black Stetson sat low over his eyes. Gabe slammed the door.

Sheriff Spraggins grunted and let his chair fall back into place with a thud. "Gabe Williams. Didn't see you come in."

"Maybe 'cause you were sleeping." Gabe grinned. The sheriff must have had a rough night. The two didn't always see eye-to-eye, considering Gabe rarely came to town and often had a beef with Amos when he did, but he figured a positive attitude might help the sheriff be more willing to listen to what he had to say.

"What brings you in, Gabe?" The sheriff leaned his elbows on the desk. "Haven't seen your face in months."

Gabe pulled the tobacco tin from his pocket and tossed it in front of the sheriff. It clattered to a stop on the desk. "First of all, found this on my land right after a fire that almost destroyed everything I've worked for. On two separate occasions, someone lets my cows loose. The last time, the culprit shot me."

"Loose? It's free range out here."

"Not for me. I keep them fenced in a pretty little valley not far from my house. I haven't used free range since a year ago. Not since things started happening." Gabe didn't wait to be asked. He swung a cane bottom chair around and straddled it. "If I lose my house or my cattle, I'm done for."

Sheriff Spraggins picked up the tin. "Any idea who this belongs to?"

"I'm guessing Amos Jenkins."

"Guessing." Spraggins dropped the tin into a desk drawer. "I'll look into it Gabe, but without proof, there isn't a lot I can do. You can't go around accusing law-abiding people without proof of some kind."

"I know it's Amos, and so do you." Gabe frowned, crossing his arms on the back of the chair. "He's wanted my land ever since I married Maggie."

"You mean he's wanted Maggie's land. He is co-signer."

"Not if I meet the stipulations set in place." Gabe stood forcibly enough to send the chair crashing to the floor. "And I intend to do just that."

"What kind of stipulations?"

Gabe took a deep breath and closed his eyes. He still didn't understand Maggie's motivation. "The land had to be developed in five years. If Maggie died while married, the same terms applied to her spouse. And by developed, the terms state a wood framed house." He glared at the sheriff. "Seems silly to me, but who knows why she made such a deal. Amos must have got her

169

dander up good. A house is a house, but if I want to keep what I've sweated over, I'm up against a wall."

"Don't step outside the law, Gabe." Spraggins used his index finger to push his hat back. "Jenkins has a lot of stock in this town. Folks'll side with him easy enough."

"I noticed you didn't comment on the fact I was shot, so it's easy to see whose side you're on."

"A sheriff only takes sides between law-abiding and law-breaking. 'Sides, you're still breathing so no real harm done."

"I hope you do choose the right side." Gabe spun and stormed outside before he said something that would get him into trouble or locked behind bars. He didn't care how much money Amos had or how many influential friends. What he wanted was to be left alone to farm his homestead and raise his family.

He headed to the feed store. As he turned the corner by the bank, Amos strolled from the saloon, his arm around a pretty gal. Gabe froze and locked gazes with his nemesis. "Jenkins."

Amos's eyes widened, then narrowed as his lips curved into a cold, thin smile. "Williams." He ruffled the girl's hair, then let his hand trail down her bare arm. "See you later, sweetheart."

Gabe grimaced. "Bet you're surprised to see me, you back-shooting, cow stealing, scoundrel."

"Such words from a Christian man. Having problems?" Amos took a shiny tobacco tin from his pocket and rolled a cigarette. "If it's too much for you, I have a solution to your predicament."

"Nothing you say will change my mind." Gabe crossed his arms, fairly certain the tin shoved back into Amos's pocket was a new one to replace the one the sheriff now had. "But shooting a man in the back? That's low, even for you."

Amos lit his cigarette and took a slow drag, then blew the smoke in Gabe's face. "I don't know what you're talking about."

Gabe squinted and stepped closer, putting his face inches from the other man. "Watch yourself, Amos. I won't be so easily taken the next time."

*

Charity strolled into the mercantile. A bell tinkled over her head, and she breathed deeply of pickles, tobacco, and wood smoke. Immediately the children ran to the counter and perused the candy, standing on tip toes to peer into jars. Charity dug the shopping list from her reticule and approached the portly man behind the counter. He wore a spotless starched apron and a wide smile.

"Charity! Haven't seen you in a month of Sundays."

"Mr. Harper." She held out her hand. "It's good to see you again, too."

"Haven't heard of anyone's laundry business doing quite as well as yours did. I don't sell as much soap, that's for sure. Of course, a Chinee man moved in with his wife. Heard tell they were starting up a laundry, but they ain't as pretty as you." He clapped his hands on the polished wood. "How may I help you?"

Charity handed him her list. "I'd like to browse a bit, see if I want to add to this, and pick up my purchases in the morning. Will that be all right?"

"Whatever you want. It's nice to see your face again. These your children?"

"Yes. I married into a ready-made family."

"Yep, heard tell you married Gabriel Williams. He's a good man. You couldn't have done much better." Mr. Harper stuck her list under his statement book. The bell tinkled over the door, and he frowned over Charity's shoulder.

She turned as Amos Jenkins sauntered inside. The man acted as if he owned the place. He flicked what was left of a cigarette at the spittoon and missed. With a grind of his boot, he crushed the burning end into the floor. Charity stuck her nose in the air and moved to the yard goods. Amos followed.

"Mrs. Williams, if I remember correctly. "

"The children give away the fact of who I am." Charity fingered a bolt of yellow calico which would make a fine new dress for Meg. "Seeing as how you know their father."

He sidestepped in front of her. "We ought to get better acquainted, Mrs. Williams. We're practically kin."

"How so?" Had Gabriel withheld another secret from her? Wasn't this the man he placed his silly wager with? Every time Charity turned around she learned another nugget of information her husband neglected to tell her. Pain stabbed her heart. When would Gabe trust her with all his secrets?

"I'm his late wife's cousin. Which means, those young'uns are more mine than they are his And it isn't often I forget a pretty face. Why, I remember when you used to do my laundry. You've moved up in the world."

Charity moved quickly to the counter and pulled the children close to her. Absolutely no way would she allow him to touch one hair on their heads. She remembered him, too. Tight fisted with his money, and quick to complain about the service.

"Gabriel married their mother. That counts for something." It had to. Life in the wilds of Montana didn't guarantee anyone would live to an old age. If it weren't certain Gabe could keep the children, then Charity definitely couldn't if she were widowed.

Meg pressed against her leg. "We don't know you, mister."

"That's enough, Amos." Mr. Harper came from around the counter. "Best you leave Charity and these little ones alone. I'm sure a man as important as you think you are has better things to do than harass my customers."

Amos narrowed his eyes. "Careful, Harper. I can make things difficult for you."

"I don't cotton to threats. If you ain't buying, skedaddle." Harper crossed his arms over his round paunch.

Amos tipped his hat in Charity's direction. "Ma'am. Until we meet again."

She gave him a cool nod and watched him leave. "Thank you, Mr. Harper. I'm not sure why he felt the need to accost me."

"Amos thinks he owns this town. Guess he might have enough money to at that, yet it never seems to be enough. Anyway, most folks are afraid of riling him." Mr. Harper moved back behind the counter. "I wouldn't fret. The feud between him and your husband has been going on for years. It's harmless enough. While you continue to browse, I'll start filling your order."

It didn't seem harmless. Gabriel may not have said anything, but Charity began to suspect that the wager was behind the disappearing cattle and the fire. The afternoon of shopping lost its luster. If not for the expectant looks on the children's faces, she'd leave the store and wait in the buckboard for Gabriel. As it was, she made a mental note of the things she wanted to purchase for Christmas, then wrote them on the list Mr. Harper had.

"Can we have a peppermint now?" Meg tugged on her sleeve. "And I want to buy Pa a new shirt for Christmas. Do we have enough money?"

Gabriel hadn't given her a spending limit, but there was nothing wrong with being frugal. "How about the fabric for a new shirt? You can help me sew it."

"What about me?" Sam said. "I can't sew a shirt, nor darn socks."

"How about a pair of store bought socks, then." Mr. Harper showed Sam a thick pair of grey wool socks. "Ought to keep him warm doing winter chores."

"We'll take them," Charity said. "Do you have any books?"

"Got *Great Expectations* by Charles Dickens in trade for some mining supplies."

"I'll take it, too." It ought to give Gabriel something to read when the sun set and the snows fell. Something other than Bible verses every night. Maybe he read the Bible because he had nothing else to read.

Probably not. Gabriel believed every word he read between the leather. Each time he read, Charity found something else to do, but the look in his eyes when she did tugged at her conscience. She'd have to make a better effort to listen to what he read.

Gabriel might not think books a worthy expense, but Charity did. There was never enough to read. Nor the time for that matter, except in winter. "In fact, I'll take whatever books you have." She could use them to teach the children to read.

She pulled out her pouch of gold. This would be a Christmas Gabriel would never forget.

*

What a pretty lady. Amos lit a cigarette and melted into the shadows beside the livery. Especially when her eyes flashed as they had when he'd made his comment about the children. He hadn't really appreciate her looks when she'd washed his shirts.

He'd need to tread lightly. That she-cat wouldn't step aside easily if she thought her loved ones were in danger.

Gabe stepped from the sheriff's office and tugged his hat brim before turning toward the mercantile. Amos watched with an ache in his gut as Charity exited

the store and linked arms with her husband. The
children skipped around them. Gabe bent his head to
hear something Charity said, then threw his head back
in laughter.

A slow-burning fire rose in Amos's stomach. He
followed, ducking behind corners when one of them
looked back, until they entered the diner. They sat at a
table beside the window, Charity and the little girl on
one side, Gabe and his son on the other.

That should be Amos's family enjoying a meal out.
Amos's beautiful wife smiling up at him. His wife whose
lovely lips touched the water glass. He dropped his
cigarette and ground it into the dirt, imagining he
smashed Gabe's face.

Somehow, someway, Gabe Williams would pay for
depriving Amos of the life he deserved. And Amos had
all winter to work on that plan.

18

Charity rolled her glass between her hands, barely listening to the excited chattering of the children as they relayed to Gabriel all the good things available at the mercantile, and how the packages had stacked up on the counter. Instead, her mind raced with the implications Amos had spoken of.

Finding out he was a blood relation to the children could change everything if something happened to Gabriel. Somehow, Charity had to keep her husband safe. Not only for the children's sakes, but for hers. She didn't want to lose any of them. In a few short months, they had become her family and filled some empty spots in her heart.

She studied the line of Gabriel's strong jaw and the width of his shoulders as he laughed at something Sam said. Gabriel still held himself a little stiff as if his stitches pulled, but otherwise, no one would be able to tell a bullet cut a crease in his side. He'd recovered quickly and nicely, laying Charity's and the children's fears to rest. At least for now.

The waitress brought their meals of stew and biscuits, then retreated to wait on other customers. The tantalizing aroma of meat broth teased Charity's stomach. She dipped her spoon into it and pulled her gaze away from Gabe's chiseled face.

The sun set behind the mountains. Gas lights flickered on inside the restaurant. Charity didn't want to be anywhere but where she was—sitting across from a handsome man she called husband and watching the lamplight flicker in his eyes when he glanced at her.

How much did she really want, or need, gold? With winter fast approaching, her chances of actually striking it rich were diminishing by the day. But if not gold, what else did she have of value to offer Gabriel to entice him to let her stay? If he sent her away, she would definitely need riches in order to survive, or go back to doing laundry. Only the former appealed to her.

"You seem deep in thought this evening." Gabriel smiled at her over the rim of his glass.

"Just thinking of the shopping I did today." Charity gripped her spoon tighter to keep her hands from shaking. She had never been a good liar. "The children enjoyed themselves so much picking out Christmas presents."

"Did you enjoy yourself?"

Oh, how easily the falsehoods leaped to her tongue. "Very much." She didn't dare tell him about

Amos accosting her. There would be no telling how Gabriel would react.

She forced an answering smile. "Did you accomplish everything you wished to?"

"Mostly. I'll need to stop at the mercantile myself in the morning. The livery should have the feed loaded early enough we can be home by supper."

"That will be wonderful." Charity bit into a piece of venison soaked in stew juices. She tasted onions and pepper and made a mental note to add some to her own pot when she cooked. Home by supper. It really did sound wonderful, although the thought of being cooped up in a sod house for months wasn't any more appealing than it had been a month ago.

What if Gabriel decided he didn't like her after having nothing but her company all day? She wasn't skilled in social graces or flirtation. She was plain, simple, Charity. After a while, she couldn't even use the children as a buffer. She didn't go to sleep as early as they did, either. She was doomed for failure and felt her heart break a bit at the thought.

Well, O'Connell's never gave up. Neither would she. She kept the smile forced on her face and focused on Gabriel. The Irish were full of blarney, and Charity's da had been the best teacher a girl could have. Certainly, she had learned some of his charming ways.

She lifted her glass. "Here's to a prosperous winter."

*

Gabe grinned and returned Charity's toast.

179

Something was on her pretty little mind, but he wouldn't force her to tell him until she was ready. Hopefully, it had nothing to do with fears about spending the winter with him. He was actually looking forward to some alone time with her. Getting to know the real Charity O'Connell Williams.

He glanced out the window to full dark. Supper had been pleasant enough to make him forget the passing of time. "We should head to the hotel." He dug the cost of the meal out of his pocket and tossed it on the table.

With the children ahead of them, Gabe placed his hand on the curve of Charity's back, and steered her outside. Her flesh warmed his palm through the thin calico dress, alerting him to her womanly softness. He would like to wrap his arm securely around her, but didn't relish getting punched. Her feistiness was one of the things he loved about her.

His steps faltered. Loved about her? Heaven help him. Had attraction deepened to something much stronger?

Charity peered up at him. "Are you all right?"

"Sure, just tripped over something." His crazy thoughts.

An orange glow like the end of a burning cigarette showed by the livery, then fell and was snuffed out. Gabe narrowed his eyes to see through the night. A light flickered on in a nearby window and illuminated the man's face. Amos? "Charity, take the children back to the hotel. There's one more thing I need to check on."

"Now?" Charity frowned. "Nothing is open except for saloons. You aren't going gambling, are you?"

"Pa?" Sam tapped his shoulder and pointed. "I think that's the man we saw at the mercantile today. He said he was our cousin and was bothering Ma."

Amos sauntered across the street. The strike of a match glowed on his face as he lit another cigarette.

Gabe turned to Charity. "Why didn't you tell me he bothered you today?"

"It was nothing, Gabriel. Really. Mr. Harper ran him off." She laid a hand on his arm. "Please don't go after him."

"He shouldn't be allowed to bother my family." Heat rose up Gabe's neck and into his face. "Now, do as I've asked."

She stiffened. "Come along, children. The master has spoken." She took them by the hand and marched down the sidewalk, heels clicking, skirts swaying, toward the hotel.

He hadn't intended to make her mad, but he sure seemed to do that a lot. Gabe tugged his hat more firmly on his head and jogged in the direction in which Amos had disappeared. He wasn't sure what he'd do once he caught the man. He knew what he wanted to do, and acting on that want would land Gabe in jail, not to mention give him one more thing to repent of. Something he definitely did not want.

Amos looked Gabe's way, then dashed around the corner to the saloon and raced inside. Gabe followed, pushing through the swinging doors into a smoke-filled room. Immediately a heavily painted woman in a scarlet dress sashayed his way displaying more of the female form than should be showed to men not her husband. Gabe shook his head and studied the crowd for Amos.

There he was, beside the bar, with a whiskey already in hand. Gabe bellied up next to him. "Got a concern with my missus, Amos?"

"Can't say as I do." Amos tossed the drink back and waved for another. "Just getting acquainted since she's mothering my cousins."

"Distant cousins."

"Still blood. More than you can say." Amos turned and leaned against the bar, elbows propped on the polished oak. "Kind of funny how you think getting hitched is going to save your land. I wonder if your lovely wife knows how you're using her."

"My wife knows everything." Gabe jabbed his index finger into Amos's chest. "Stay away from my land, my wife, my children."

"Or what?"

"I'll take the law into my own hands." Gabe gave him one more hard jab then stormed back outside. He paced up and down the street, allowing the night air to cool his anger before heading to his room.

He shouldn't have allowed Amos to rile him. But just looking at the man-made Gabe want to punch him in the nose. And now, he'd threatened him in front of witnesses. Did he even use the brain God gave him?

*

Charity rushed the children to the hotel. Asked,

Gabe had said. Ordered was more like it! Gabriel Williams rarely asked for anything. Most likely she'd have to bail him out of jail come morning. Maybe. She might leave him there to rot!

"Come on, you two. Time for bed." She unlocked the door to their room and smiled at the sight of two beds. Thank goodness she wouldn't have to sleep next to Gabriel. She wasn't ready for such intimacy. Not unless he professed to love her and asked her to stay past their agreed upon date. Otherwise, he could stay on his side of the room and she would stay on hers.

Once Meg and Sam were tucked into bed, Charity blew out the lamp and toed off her boots. She pulled the room's only chair, a straight-backed one made of oak, to the window, and sat down to wait.

Amos wandered past the hotel and glanced up at the window as if he knew which room was theirs. Charity ducked behind the curtain. A moment later, she made out Gabriel's form headed her way. Amos ducked into a nearby alley. What was that evil man planning? Was he lying in ambush for Gabriel?

Charity leaped up and tried to open the window. Nailed shut. She needed to warn her husband. He possibly headed toward the hotel and danger.

She grabbed her boots and slipped her feet into them. Her boot caught in the hem of her dress, and she stumbled, banging her shin on the bed frame. She hissed against the pain.

After checking to make sure the children slept, she dropped the room key into her pocket and slipped out of the room, closing the door behind her.

Hitching her skirt above her ankles, she thundered down the stairs with an odd jerking gait after hitting her leg, past a startled elderly couple, and into the street. Gabriel came her way with his head down. She thought of calling out to him, but didn't want to alert Amos that she knew he was close by. Instead, she took a deep breath and walked, or rather limped, toward her husband as if she didn't have a care in the world.

A hand grabbed her arm and jerked her into the alley. Before she could scream, her captor clamped a hand over her mouth and an arm wrapped around her waist, lifting her off her feet.

She kicked, connecting with his shin, and heard a grunt. She bit the fleshy part of her attacker's palm. He released his grip. She stomped hard on his foot. When he let go of her, she dashed into the street and collided with Gabriel.

"Charity? What's wrong? What happened?" He gripped her shoulders.

She pointed to the alley. "Someone grabbed me. I didn't get a look at his face."

"You didn't see him?" He stared intently at her. "Are you hurt?"

"I'm not hurt." A little bruised maybe. And scared. "I saw no one but Amos a few minutes ago, but this man felt bigger."

"That could be the fear talking." Gabriel released her and clenched his fists. "I'll kill him."

She grabbed his sleeve. "I'm not positive it was

Amos. I fought and got away. Please don't accuse someone without proof."

He shook free. "What if he would have … hurt you? Done … despicable things?"

She placed a hand on her churning stomach. "He didn't. He wouldn't." Everyone in Virginia City knew her. No one would hurt her, would they? Of course, someone new could have drifted to town and taken advantage of a foolish woman going out at night alone.

Gabriel glanced down the alley then took Charity by the elbow and pulled her back to the hotel. He stopped in the shadows at the corner. "What are you doing outside alone?"

"I was waiting for you by the window, and—a" She yanked free. "I saw Amos duck into the alley and thought he was lying in wait for you. I came out to warn you."

"As much as I appreciate the thought, you could have been killed, or worse." He bent to make his eyes even with hers. "I never took you for a simple woman." He knocked on her head. "I thought God gave you more sense."

"Simple?" She planted her fists on her hips, wanting nothing more than to hit him. Forget about how scared she had been. "See if I worry about your safety again, you ungrateful lout!"

Gabriel's eyes narrowed. "You are an infuriating woman."

He pulled her close. Twisting his fingers in her hair, he bent and claimed her lips with a ferocity that matched the anger burning in her chest. She planted her hands against him, prepared to shove him away, then relented, melting against him. Her hands drifted up his muscled back and around his neck. His arms lowered, wrapping around her. Charity closed her eyes and drifted with the sensation.

*

Tears burned Amos's eyes as he watched Gabe kiss his bride. His fingers twitched over the six-shooter on his hip. It would be so easy to aim and pull the trigger. But if he missed, he'd hit Charity, and killing a woman was something he could not live with. He had not sunk that low.

What were they thinking kissing in public? Had they no shame? Maybe Charity wasn't as virtuous as Maggie had been after all.

Amos wiped his eyes on his shirt sleeve. He had almost laughed out loud when Gabe confronted him in the saloon. The man was itching for a fight. One that Amos was more than ready to give him. But if he were to kill Gabe, it needed to look like an accident.

The children and Charity would suffer no matter how he died, but they would want nothing to do with Amos if they knew he took away their father and husband. Amos wanted nothing more than to *be* a husband and a father. And he would do almost anything to obtain what he considered his right.

19

If Gabe pulled Charity any closer they would meld into one being. He'd never tasted anything so sweet; felt his blood rush quite so fast; felt hair as silky soft as hers when it cascaded over his fingers. It wasn't until a drunken man staggered by, throwing out obscene suggestions that Gabe realized he'd kissed Charity on the street corner like a common thug. A disorderly cowpoke in town for a bit of frivolity.

With as much cheer as a child sent to the woodshed, he set her away. "I'm sorry. I shouldn't have behaved that way."

But when he realized how close she had come to danger, maybe even death, he had lost all capacity for reason.

In spite of the urge to pull her in for another kiss, Gabe turned Charity toward the hotel. "Go on. I'll be up in a few minutes."

Her eyes searched his face before she touched her lips, nodded, and whirled to run inside. Her skirts blew, offering him a glimpse of a lace-trimmed petticoat. Oh, but she had felt good in his arms. Her curves fit his planes as if God made them to fit together. Kissing Maggie had been pleasant, but she'd been nowhere near as passionate as Charity.

Gabe rubbed his hands down his face. How would he survive the night sleeping in the same room as his fiery wife? Sure, they'd be in separate beds, but he'd hear her move, hear her snores. He wanted his husbandly rights with Charity. He could no longer contemplate allowing her to leave come spring. *Lord, make her feel the same way about me. Let our winter Bible readings touch her heart so she loves You and me.*

Their kiss hadn't left her unaffected. Only a man with no emotion or feeling in his body would think so. He was definitely a man with feeling. Gabe grinned, remembering the feel of her melting in his arms. The ardor of her kiss. Whistling, he pushed open the hotel door and made his way to their room.

The lamp's wick had been turned down low. Charity's red hair fanned across the pillow in the bed beside Meg. Sam snorted and rolled over in the bed Gabe would share with his son. He glanced at Charity's back. Given the choice, he'd snuggle with her. Not that he had that option.

He laid his shirt and britches across the back of the chair, then pulled back the thin blanket and climbed into bed beside Sam. He crossed his arms behind his head and stared through the dim light at the rough planks across the ceiling. He needed to think of something other than Charity.

What was he going to do about Amos? Now that his fondness for Charity had leaped into love, he wanted to explore the feelings, not dwell on a loco man out to get land that once belonged to Maggie. He grunted. So much for not thinking about his wife. Her face overshadowed his every thought. He exhaled hard enough to ruffle his bangs and pulled his attention to something else.

He needed to finish the house. Short of shooting Amos, that was the only way to get the man to leave them alone. Again, he wanted to kick himself for giving in to a moment of anger and making that stupid wager.

What was he thinking that night? He knew gambling was wrong. Anger was wrong. But Amos knew just where his weak spots were. Now, the man threatened to take the children. What could he possibly want with them?

Gabe rolled to his side. If Charity left, and Amos took custody of Meg and Sam, Gabe would be alone. He'd have no one to provide for, to protect. He might as well quit living.

*

Charity lay as still as possible, focusing on keeping her breathing steady, as Gabriel readied for bed. She inched her hand toward her face and brushed her fingers across her still tingling lips. She never imagined a kiss could make a person lose all reason or go as limp as

189

a rag doll. She wanted another one and another.

What would Gabriel do if she climbed out of bed, moved Sam to lie beside his sister, and Charity took the little boy's place? Would Gabriel kick her out? Act outraged? Or would he gather her in his arms and make her feel like a proper wife? Would he be upset if she ruined his plans of an annulment?

Tears stung her eyes. She blinked to clear them, not wanting Gabriel to know she wasn't asleep. She couldn't be the reason for his plans not succeeding.

She had no idea how to make him want her. No idea what made a good wife. Her heart ached. She saw her future, and it looked as grim and drab as the dreariest winter day. God would again take away the person most important to her. She sniffed. Unless she figured out a way to keep him.

She'd thought gold was the answer, but time was running out. "I love you, Gabriel Williams," she whispered. "Someday, you'll love me, too."

The next morning, Charity avoided Gabriel's eyes as if his glance would turn her into wood. Her cheeks flushed at each thought of their kiss. The drive home loomed before them like an eternity. She trembled as he helped her into the wagon after breakfast, his strong hands burning her skin through the calico fabric of her dress.

"Are you angry with me?" Gabriel tilted her face until she looked at him.

"No." Heaven help her. "It was a heated moment. A kiss out of fear for my safety." If only it could have been from more than that. She busied herself getting Meg situated in the back with a quilt.

Gabriel sighed and climbed beside her. After a stop at the mercantile, where he loaded their packages in back with the children, he set the horses for home, and Charity sat ramrod straight against the bench back. If she fell against him, he might think she was being forward, and she already suffered enough embarrassment from succumbing to his kisses the way she had.

She ran her pointer finger over her lips and cast a sideways glance at Gabriel who was grinning. "What is so funny?" She dropped her hand in her lap and twisted a handful of the blue flowered fabric.

"Nothing." He flicked the reins to urge the horses faster.

"Are you laughing at me?" Had kissing her been so horrible that he thought it a laughing matter?

"No." He glanced over his shoulder. "You young'uns grab a peppermint stick out of that bag." He turned his attention back to Charity. "I'm glad to know that you weren't unaffected by the kiss."

"Unaffected?" She wrapped her shawl tighter around her, more as protection than against the morning chill. "I have never kissed another man besides you."

"Ever?" He raised his brows.

"Lots of marriage proposals, no kisses." She still thought he poked fun at her. What seemed so strange about her not having kissed a lot of men? She doubted

191

most women had. It wasn't comely or proper.

Her shoulders slumped. He *did* think her a woman of loose morals. She wanted to disappear.

"I consider it a privilege that I was your first."

A privilege? The man toyed with her affections. She put her hands on her cheeks in an effort to cool them. What should be her response? "Thank you?" The wagon wheel hit a rut in the road, and her thanks came out as more of a hiccup.

He tossed his head back and guffawed, the sound ringing through the trees. Despite her discomfort at the topic, Charity joined in with his laughter. There was hope for them yet.

Gabriel took one hand off the reins and laid it over hers. "You're good for me, Charity. I haven't laughed as much my whole life as I have the last couple of months with you."

No one had ever told her she was good for them, before. She liked it. She grinned and squeezed his hand. The sun shone brighter, the birds sang lovelier, and Charity's heart sailed with the wispy clouds in the cerulean sky.

*

Amos's horse reared when Gabe laughed. He fought with the reins in order to stay in the saddle. He didn't know why he followed them. Why he tortured himself so. His own farm was showing signs of neglect because of the time he spent spying.

But watching Gabe and Charity interact with each other and the children let Amos almost believe he was part of a family. He shouldn't do this. He turned his horse toward his own land. Shadowing the Williams' family was wrong and only made his heart ache more for what he didn't have.

Soon enough, they would all be snowed in. Amos had one more surprise up his sleeve before that happened. Then he would have plenty of time during winter to cook up another surprise for Gabe. Maybe one that would, this time, warrant Amos a pretty wife.

If those plans failed, maybe opportunity would toss something else in his lap. Something that would wound Gabe to the center of his being.

20

A wagon sat in front of their soddy with the horse already grazing in the corral beside the barn. Gabriel set the wagon and helped Charity down. She shaded her eyes with one hand. "It's Mabel and Hiram. What are they doing here?"

"Not sure." Gabriel lifted Meg down. "But Hiram is grinning like a hound, so it can't be bad news."

Charity rushed and enveloped Mabel in a hug. "It's so good to see you. We weren't expecting company." Lady and Prince bounded from the barn.

"Some watch dog you have there. Thought at first she was going to take my head off, but she settled down once she figured out I was up to no harm." Hiram shook Gabriel's hand. "It is a dog, isn't it?"

"So Charity says. Red Feather gave them to us. The young'uns are quite taken with the pup."

"They are dogs. Irish Wolfhounds." Charity

released Mabel and crouched to throw her arms around Lady' neck. Prince bounded toward the creek with Sam and Meg chasing after. "Did you miss us, girl? Did you keep the bad guys away?"

Hiram pulled Gabriel to the side and lowered his voice. Charity continued to scratch behind Lady's ears as she strained to hear while pretending not to.

"The dogs were locked up when I got here, and the cattle are loose again," Hiram said.

Charity peeked from beneath her bonnet. Gabriel frowned. "I'm at my wit's end, Hiram. How did he get here so fast? I just saw him. I went to the—" He caught Charity watching. "Meet me over by the barn."

Hiram glanced her way. "Sure thing."

"Guess it's up to us to unload the wagon." Charity planted her hands on her thighs and pushed to her feet. "The men will get the heavy stuff when they finish with their secrets."

Mabel grabbed a bag of flour. "Don't take it personal. They think they're protecting us. With all the years Hiram have I have been hitched, he still forgets sometimes that we're supposed to be a team. God created woman to be a help mate. Sometimes men seem to forget that."

Charity folded her arms on the wagon bed and rested her head on them. "It does hurt my feelings. We should be partners. We should share the good and the bad." She took a deep breath. "He kissed me last night."

"Do tell." Mabel's smile widened.

Charity turned and leaned against the buckboard,

the rough wood poking into her back. "I saw Amos Jenkins sneaking around like he was trying to waylay Gabriel, so I left the hotel room and went to warn him. Someone grabbed me and dragged me into the alley. I didn't get a look at my attacker, but I'm fairly certain it wasn't Amos." She shuddered at the remembrance of a stranger's hands on her. "I got away but Gabriel was furious I put myself in danger. It was the most brutal, most wonderful, kiss."

Mabel bumped her with her shoulder. "Sweetheart, you have that man aching for you in a bad way. Keep up the good work."

"But I'm not doing anything." Nothing she could put her finger on anyway.

"All the better. And remember, a bear is drawn to honey. You might want to sweeten things up. Watch your temper." Mabel hefted the flour sack. "Let's get these things unloaded. Hiram and I thought we'd visit for the day before we're all snowed in. I've missed having a woman neighbor in the worst way."

"I don't even have bread rising." Charity grabbed the bolts of fabric. "We just returned from purchasing our winter supplies, but we're glad to have you."

"Don't worry. Hiram and I brought the fixings for chili. Wouldn't be right to show up unannounced and expect you to feed us. Not when you got little ones." Mabel led the way into the house. "You just fix your mind on getting that man to ask you to stay. But he won't do that if you don't have your heart right with the Lord."

196

Charity was afraid of that. Why was it so hard for her to trust in God when it came easily for so many other people? How did one get the faith? Her ma tried instilling faith in her, despite her apparent unhappiness, but when she'd died, Charity stumbled. Pa stumbled right along with her, letting her know that a loving God wouldn't have taken a woman as good as her ma. Not if he cared. Charity believed him. What if they were wrong?

She needed time to ponder the questions in her heart. Dwell on them over the winter months while Gabriel read from the Word of God, and work slowed down. Maybe her questions would be answered then. She headed back to the wagon for more supplies.

By the time the smaller things were unpacked in the house, Gabriel and Hiram returned from their secret conversation and unloaded the feed for the livestock. Charity glared at Gabriel over the back of the wagon, and smirked when he avoided her eyes.

He looked as guilty as a fox caught in a hen house. She tilted her nose and sashayed away. Wouldn't hurt to let him know she was miffed. Maybe he'd come apologizing and tell her what was going on. She'd try the honey approach after he stewed for a while.

Gabe grunted as he carried in a box. "What's in here, books?"

"Never you mind. Just set it on the floor beside my bed." Heavens, the man was nosey, yet he didn't want to share a single secret of his own.

She followed him inside and nodded at Mabel.

197

"Let me hide these under my bed, and I'll be ready to help you with supper." Charity slid the purchased gifts under the bed.

"Are you excited about Christmas?" Mabel slung a dish towel over her shoulder. "You most likely haven't had one surrounded by the excitement of children, have you?"

"No, and I must confess to my own excitement. I think I'm worse than the children, and Christmas is three months away. It's Thanksgiving supper I'm concerned about." Charity tugged the quilt to make it hang lower on the side of the bed away from the wall. "I want it to be special and don't completely trust my cooking skills for such a holiday."

"You'll do fine. If the snow ain't bad, Hiram and I will join you for the meal. Chili's done, if you want to call the menfolk and children."

*

Hiram stuck a blade of straw between his teeth. Gabe propped a foot on the corral fence and waited for him to spill the rest of his news.

"As I was saying before your missus got all nosey, your cattle are gone again. The dogs were locked in the barn, so I figured someone came during the night while they was sleeping and slid the bolt." Hiram jerked his chin.

Gabe sighed. "I visited Sheriff Spraggins, and it's clear he's not going to question Amos." He pounded his thigh. "I know the man is behind all my setbacks. He spoke with Charity at the mercantile and threatened to take the children. I don't know what to do, Hiram. I really don't."

"Have you prayed about it?"

"I try, but the anger and guilt over the situation binds me up." Gabe shook his head and leaned his elbows on the fence. "I'm confused about what to do about the wager, about Charity, about..."

"Your wife?" Hiram raised his eyebrows. "Problems?"

"Definitely. I'm falling in love with her. Never felt this way about a woman before."

"That's good, ain't it, or am I missing something?"

"We have a marriage of convenience, Hiram. I expected Mabel to tell you." He sighed. "Once I meet the terms of my foolish bet, we'll have our marriage annulled." Saying the words out loud to a man he admired, made Gabe feel even more foolish. He peered at Hiram from beneath his hat brim. "I can't let her go come spring."

"Tell her."

"I don't know how."

"Supper!" Mabel hooted from the direction of the house.

"My woman sure was blessed with a set of lungs." Hiram clapped Gabe on the shoulder. "Don't fret. An opportunity will present itself. You've got all winter."

Hopefully. At least that's what he kept telling himself. Gabe shuffled behind his friend as they made their way to the horse trough to wash for their meal. He splashed his face with the icy water, ran his fingers through his hair, and prepared to face Charity across the table. She would spear him with glances until he told her about his visit with the sheriff. Not a conversation he wanted to have with the children or company around.

As clean as he could get without a dunk in the creek or a hot bath, Gabe headed inside and took his seat at the table. Charity tossed him a heart-stopping grin as she pranced to the table with a pan of cornpone. She had changed her clothes and now wore a wine red dress with black stripes that set off highlights in her hair.

Gabe returned her smile with a shaky one of his own. When she passed behind him to take her seat, she trailed her fingers along his back, sending spiders skittering up his spine, and gluing his tongue to the roof of his mouth.

"Should I say the blessing?" Hiram stuck his napkin in his shirt collar.

Gabe nodded, his gaze never leaving Charity's face. She blushed and placed her napkin in her lap. She peered from beneath her lashes, green eyes glittering. Then, she lowered her head. Gabe started as Hiram began praying, and then closed his eyes. How could he focus on Charity and forget to pray?

"Got meat stored up for the winter?" Hiram pulled him from his thoughts.

Gabriel jerked his head. "Pardon?"

"I just need me a big buck and my smokehouse will be full."

"Nope. Plan on heading out tomorrow. We've got a couple of pigs we can butcher, and some chickens, but I wouldn't mind a deer and some rabbits." Gabe dug his spoon into the chili.

He'd been kept so busy building the house and hunting down his cattle, he hadn't spent the time on winter preparations that he should have. A month away from being snowed in and his smokehouse wasn't full. He was a neglectful husband and father.

"Doesn't Charity look pretty today?" Mabel asked around the rim of her cup.

Gabe's hand shook as he reached for his mug, spilling his drink across the table.

Charity laid a hand on his. "Are you all right, dear? Do you need more water?" She stood. "Don't you worry about a thing. I'll get a rag and clean that right up."

Mabel giggled and dug into her chili.

Gabe shook his head, sliding his hand from under Charity's. He didn't need the distraction of her touch. What was she doing? She never voluntarily touched him. And what happened to her voice? Instead of low and husky as normal, it had risen to almost a girlish tone. Had he unleashed something when he kissed her? The thought scared him as much as knowing she'd been grabbed and pulled into the alley.

"Gotta feed the livestock." He pushed back his chair and raced outside, leaving Hiram sitting with the women and children.

*

Charity hadn't figured on being as affected by

touching Gabriel as she meant for him to be. Acting all sweet could be as dangerous for her as it was for him. Her hands trembled as she cleared the dishes from the table. She plunged them and the bowls into the washtub. Goodness, it was hot inside the soddy.

"I think he's being affected right fine." Mabel added spoons to the washtub. "That dress was the perfect touch. Is it new?"

Charity shook her head. "It was my mother's. It's rather dated, six years in fact, but it's still the nicest thing I own."

"I hope you bought yourself fabric for new clothes when you were in town."

"I did." She scrubbed the first bowl. "It's green like my eyes and I got some yellow like the sun." She set the bowl down hard enough to splash suds. "Are you sure this is the way to win his heart? Can't I just find gold and show him how valuable I am that way?"

Mabel shook her head. "Are you still set on discovering gold? Honey, there's no time. Snow is mere weeks away. Do you have winter clothing sewed for the children? Have you checked for holes in the soddy? There's no end to the work that needs done to prepare for winter. Not to mention setting up butter, soap, candles. Anything you might need. If you didn't purchase them in town, you have a lot of work to do."

Charity didn't purchase anything she could make herself. Mabel was right. There would barely be enough time to sleep at night. No wonder bears waited until winter to hibernate. There was too much to do during the warmer months and longer days.

"I feel as if I'm being deceitful." She handed the washed bowl to Mabel. "Gabriel looked at me as if he didn't know who I was."

"That's wonderful. Keep him surprised. Men like variety."

"I just don't feel right about it."

"I've been married over half my life. Trust me." Mabel watched Hiram move outside, ushering the children in front of him. "Even I throw in a surprise to my husband every blue moon. A new dress, a wink, a caress he isn't expecting."

"But your marriage was founded out of love."

"Yours will be too. Have faith."

Charity huffed. Faith again. Except this time, Mabel was not talking about a faith in God. She was talking about Charity having faith in herself. That was worse.

The ground vibrated under her feet, and Charity grabbed the edge of the counter to steady herself. From outside, shots rang out. She stared in horror at Mabel. Then she heard Meg screamed.

21

The ground over Charity's head rumbled. Dust and multi-legged varmints fell into her hair and eyes. She squealed and pawed at her head to knock the insects free. Was that a centipede? A millipede? Heavens it was a miracle they were all still alive!

Particles of dirt and grass filtered through the ceiling boards. Dust filled the room. The walls shook. She shrieked and rushed to the fireplace, grabbing Maggie's clock off the mantel before it could crash to the floor. Setting it safely in Gabriel's chair, she spun. Her gaze met Mabel's startled one. The children!

With her heart in her throat, Charity raced outside. "Meg! Sam!"

"They're here!" Gabriel had his arms wrapped around both children and flattened them against the barn. "Get back in the house. Someone started a stampede."

Charity drew back into the doorway. First one cow, then a couple more, then tens of cattle thundered past them, some leaping off the top of the soddy. Their hooves beat the ground with mighty thuds.

Charity threw out her arm to stop Mabel from dashing into the yard. "Lady! Prince!" *Please, God, spare the dogs.*

"Where's my Hiram?" Mabel clutched at her arm. "I don't see him. Lordy, he's trampled! God's taken him to heaven without letting me say goodbye!"

"Hush, Mabel, he's probably in the barn." Charity grabbed her friend around the waist and pulled her inside, out of harm's way. Lady and Prince skirted between the cattle's legs until the dogs stopped, trembling, in the doorway of the soddy. Charity threw her arms around them, not only giving love, but receiving comfort, and effectively blocking the door so Mabel couldn't escape.

"Lord, don't take my Hiram." Mabel sagged against the table. "He's all I've got." She covered her face with her hands and sobbed.

Tears sprang to Charity's eyes, and she went to her friend's side. She'd never seen Mabel exhibit anything but good nature and self-control, and she wasn't sure how to handle this new hysterical Mabel.

"God will take care of Hiram." Did she actually believe He would choose to save Hiram after taking her parents? What made him more special than they? Was he kinder, a better man? Sure her Da had gambled, her Ma bitter about her lot in life, but did that make them

205

unworthy of God's attention? God seemed choosey in regards to whom He decided to spare. At least the words would make Mabel feel better. If only they didn't taste like sawdust leaving Charity's tongue.

The thundering faded away, and Gabriel entered the house with Sam and Meg. Mabel bolted to his side and gripped his shirt. "Hiram? Where is he?"

Gabriel shook his head. "I'll look for him now. Last I saw, he was headed for my temporary corral." He grabbed the rifle from above the mantel. "All of you stay here. These cattle were stampeded on purpose. I don't want to have to worry about you while I'm searching for Hiram. Most likely, I'll meet him coming back this way. He's a smart man. He knows how to take care of himself."

"Be careful." Charity laid a hand on his arm. She wanted to tell him she couldn't live without him. Didn't want a world where he didn't exist. But she couldn't. She wasn't ready. Not until she knew with all certainty that he felt the same about her. She couldn't put her heart in someone else's hands only to have it shoved back at her.

"I will." He took a step toward her, then stopped and nodded, before whirling and heading back outside.

Charity gathered the children in her arms. "Are you two all right? You aren't hurt?"

"Nah, we're fine." Sam said. "We were in the barn when we heard the ruckus. As soon as we ran out, pa grabbed us."

Meg held up a finger. "I got a splinter from the

barn."

Charity closed her eyes and hugged them harder. "Let's get you two cleaned up, and that splinter removed. Mabel, would you like to help until the men return?"

She turned a shocked gaze on Charity. "I'll heat some water for a bath."

If Charity kept the other woman busy, maybe she wouldn't have time to worry about her husband. She eyed the other rifle over the mantel. Maybe Gabriel could use her help. Charity's hands tightened into fists. Most likely a good thing she didn't know how to shoot. If she did, she'd hunt down the man who started the stampede and put a bullet in him. Somebody could have been killed.

*

Gabe saddled Rogue and headed in the direction where he'd corralled his cattle. Hiram had offered to check things out earlier, and Gabriel appreciated the gesture. Now, his friend might be dead because of that neighborly offer. Gabe hadn't figured someone would cause a stampede. Not just someone. He clenched his jaw. Amos Jenkins. He would bet Sunday dinner that man was behind this.

His heart sat like a frozen boulder in his throat. *Lord, don't let me have to tell Mabel she's lost the love of her life.* What would it be like to consider someone that dear to your heart? He cared for Maggie, but didn't think he could call her the love of his life. More like a comfortable blanket after a hard day's work. Could he ever feel that way about Charity? Right now, she made his heart pound and his palms sweat. Did he really want the type of comfort he felt around Maggie? He leaned more on wanting to keep the excitement that Charity added to his life.

The closer he got to his destination, the more he relaxed. Unless the scoundrel who stampeded the cattle shot Hiram and dragged him into the bushes, the man wasn't lying in a trampled mess somewhere. Gabe figured if Hiram had been trampled, he would have found his body by now. He allowed Rogue free rein of his head and concentrated on the tree line.

After while he guessed was half an hour, he made out a tan shape through the green of a line of pine trees and low shrubs. Gabe slid from his horse, grabbed his rifle, and jogged the few feet. His heart stopped.

An Indian girl lay face down among the needles. Blood matted the side of her dark hair. He knelt and placed his face close to hers to check for signs of life. None.

Gabe straightened and studied the trees with an intensity born of fear. If caught by the woman's people, they'd assume he killed her. Some of the Indians believed a life for a life. Yet, he couldn't leave her here for the animals.

Rocks rattled to his right. Gabe leaped to his feet, rifle at the ready.

"Don't shoot." Hiram stepped from the trees. "I heard gunshots and went to investigate. Couldn't find the culprit. He must be long gone by now." He stopped and stared at the girl. "Is she one of Red Feather's people?"

"I don't know." Gabe lowered his rifle. "Your wife is worried sick about you. I promised to bring you back in one piece."

"Yep, she most likely is worried. Worrying is her favorite thing outside talking." Hiram squatted and smoothed the hair away from the woman's face. "A pretty little thing. That bullet crease on the side of her face wasn't what killed her. Looks like she fell and hit her head on that rock." He pointed to a three-foot boulder smeared with blood.

"Maybe. No telling how her people will look at it. Either way, the shooter is to blame for her death, accidental or not." Poor thing. She didn't look old enough to be a wife yet.

What if it were Charity lying here? The way she had come busting out of the house, it could very easily have been. Or one of the children. Gabe closed his eyes. Did he really want to be responsible for another human being? Maybe he should let his feelings go and allow Charity the annulment she wanted come spring. His heart couldn't take losing another wife to death.

"We can't leave her here," Gabe said. "Help me get her on my horse, and I'll see if I can't find Red Feather. Then, tomorrow I guess I'll pay another visit to the sheriff." One way or the other, the man who did this was going to pay for harassing Gabe, putting his family in danger, and murdering this young girl.

Gabe slid his rifle in its holster then scooped the

girl in his arms. If she didn't belong to Red Feather's tribe, he took a huge risk by moving her. But no one deserved to be left to the wolves.

He handed the body to Hiram, climbed into the saddle, then waited while Hiram helped him drape her over the saddle in front of him.

Hiram jogged out of sight then returned with Sam's pony. "Hope you don't mind me borrowing your son's horse. It was easier than getting mine ready."

"Don't mind at all. I appreciate you checking on my cows." Which he no longer had. It could take days to hunt them down. More time away from building the. "They *are* my cows, right?"

"Yep. I found the fence rails tossed to the side like firewood. Someone has it in for you real bad. How do you plan on finding Red Feather?" Hiram asked as they plodded home. "Ain't they gone to their winter grounds?"

"I'll check on the other side of the mountain. They usually winter on the other side of that pass." Gabe steered Rogue over a bumpy patch of ground. The girl might be dead, but it didn't seem right to give her a rough ride. "That's where they stayed last winter. Snows are less there."

"Are you expecting a harsh snowfall?"

"A few feet. Maybe a blizzard or two. Why? You still thinking on coming out for Thanksgiving?" Gabe knew what Hiram was doing. Keeping his mind off the dead girl in his lap. He'd been worthless for a few days after Maggie's death. This was different. The Indian girl was a stranger. Tragic, but it wasn't like losing a loved one.

"Mabel's got her heart set on it. She's been a bit lonesome since Maggie passed."

"We'll plan on you coming then. Charity will be thrilled." If Gabe could keep her safe that long.

*

Charity stared at her ruined garden, thankful she'd harvested and canned most of the produce. If they were careful, they ought to have enough put aside for the winter. It was meat they were low on, and since Gabriel was trying to build his herd, he didn't seem likely to butcher one.

"Sam!" She faced her son. "Come tomorrow, I need you to teach me how to shoot your pa's rifle. Can you do that?"

"Sure, Ma. But why don't you ask Pa?"

"I'm sure he'll be gone hunting his cattle tomorrow." If Charity learned to shoot, she could defend the homestead in her husband's absence and, with any luck, help put meat on the table. Besides, any time she asked Gabriel's help in matters of safety, he told her it was his job and not to worry.

"All you need is a steady hand and a good eye."

Charity laid an arm across Sam's shoulder and let him chatter as they headed toward the barn. Lady and Prince trotted beside them. Mabel and Meg chose to stay inside and prepare supper..

"Then, once I'm a good shot—" She figured a couple of hours of practice ought to do it, "you can show me the best hunting grounds, and we'll surprise your pa with a smokehouse full of meat."

"Have you ever shot before?" Sam frowned.

"No, but I'm a fast learner."

Sam shook his head. "It's nice to be optimistic and all, Ma, but you're talking about learning in a day what takes most folks a long time." He grinned and slid out from under her hand. "There's Pa, and he's got something on his horse. Maybe it's a deer, and we won't have to spend the time tomorrow."

Charity huffed and quickened her step. She would learn to shoot in a day if it killed her. After all, she learned to manage a house in just a week.

That wasn't a deer slung over Gabriel's horse. Raven-black hair swung against the saddle and slim legs hung over the opposite side. Charity clutched her throat and sped to the horse's side. "Is she dead?"

"I'm afraid so."

"Who is she?" Charity started to smooth back the girl's hair, and stopped, instead wiping her palm down her skirt.

"I have no idea." Gabriel glanced over his shoulder to where Hiram approached. "Let Mabel know her man is here. I'm going to try to find Red Feather. Maybe he'll know who she is."

"Do you want me to come with you?" Charity placed her hand on his knee. "It might help to have a woman. They might look at it as less threatening."

"They might at that, but it could be dangerous."

She scowled. "I will take that chance, Gabriel. If it

could make things easier, then I'm willing to attempt it."

After several tense, silent moments, he gave a slow nod, clearly not sure about the idea of her going.

Charity lifted her skirts and dashed to the house for her shawl before he could change his mind. Hiram wasn't far behind. When Mabel caught sight of her husband, she squealed loud enough to scare birds from the trees, then buried her face in her hands.

Charity smiled and reached for her shawl. "I'm going with Gabriel. Would you mind watching the children?"

Mabel shook her head then threw herself into Hiram's arms. "We'll be happy right here while we wait." She caressed her husband's face. "Where are they going, Hiram?"

Without waiting to hear his answer, Charity rushed back to Gabriel and mounted Sam's pony. She would have liked to ride Ruby, but Gabriel seemed to be chomping at the bit as it was. While she'd been in the soddy, he had tied bedrolls behind each saddle and remounted. Charity forced a swallow past her dry throat at the thought of spending the night in the dark, chilly woods. Maybe she should have grabbed her coat.

"Should we wait until morning?" She eyed the setting sun.

"I don't want her family to come looking for her and find her here. It wouldn't be safe for Sam and Meg. Not safe for any of us, most likely." He urged Rogue forward. "Better we find them, so as to take suspicion off ourselves. We'll have a hard enough time explaining her death as it is. Thankfully, very few of Red Feather's tribe own guns."

Charity gulped. What if the Indians attacked before Gabriel had the opportunity to tell his side of the story? What if having her along meant nothing more than that Gabriel had a woman to trade for the life of this one? Indians did that, didn't they? Oh, why hadn't she listened more when the miners spoke of such things? Read more books about the west?

Without speaking, Gabriel led the way from the homestead and toward a mountain pass. Despite the grievous circumstances, Charity couldn't help but scan her surroundings for caves that might yield gold. Gold, that in the right amounts, might make life easier for her and Gabriel.

Her stomach rumbled, reminding her of the savory stew at home simmering on the stove. She wished she had grabbed some biscuits or dried meat. Maybe the Indians would lend, or sell, them some food.

Who was the poor thing draped over Gabriel's saddle? Definitely someone's daughter or sister. Wife maybe? Were they even now searching for her?

She moved the pony to Rogue's side. Gabriel's lips moved in silent prayer, as his free hand rested on the deceased woman's shoulder. Charity let the pony fall back again. If her husband prayed, he must be more worried than she had originally thought. She closed her eyes. Because of her impetuous need to go where he went, to offer her services even though he obviously didn't need, or want them, she had put more worry on

Gabriel's shoulders. He had to consider her safety as well as his own. Why couldn't she curb her impulsiveness and think before acting? Why did she press matters when the answer was obviously no?

Because she was spoiled, plain and simple. Sure, she'd spent the last couple of years doing the laundry of miners, but she was spoiled all the same. When she wanted something, she went after it in total disregard of the circumstances. Her dear da had spent too much time and money on her. Until death took him away, she had not had to lift a finger if she didn't want to. She thought she'd left that behavior behind.

She opened her mouth to tell Gabriel she was sorry, but thought better of it. Now wasn't the time. She sighed. They had so much to talk about when things settled down.

When night fell, Gabriel halted in a stand of aspen. After sliding from his horse, he gently laid the dead girl under a tree. "We'll have to camp here and head into the village in the morning. I don't want to chance riding up on them in the dark."

Charity nodded and untied her bedroll with frozen fingers. Already, the night chill set her teeth to chattering and her bones to trembling.

While Gabriel built a fire, she wrapped her bedding around her shoulders and hunkered next to the fire pit. *Oh, hurry and light.* She peeked at her husband from beneath lowered lashes. What would he say if she asked to share his body warmth during the night?

Would he welcome her or push her away? She

stared into the flickering flames. Having so little experience with men, she had no idea how he would respond. They were married, he looked at her with admiration at times, but possibly he still loved his former wife. How could he not? He saw her in the faces of his children every day.

She stared at the dark night sky. A few stars twinkled between growing clouds. Maybe Charity should have asked her ma questions when she had the opportunity. Ma must have loved Da at one time. She must have looked at him with love rather than annoyance when they first wed.

Charity sighed. So many questions. She studied Gabriel hunkered down across from her. She was hitched to the finest man she had the privilege of ever knowing, and they were practically strangers.

.

22

Something sharp poked Charity in the ribcage. She swatted it away. "Stop it." A strange voice grunted and she opened her eyes.

A scowling Indian towered over her. She screamed, fought her bedroll to escape, and then scuttled backward until a tree trunk impeded her retreat. The Indian's menacing look deepened. He grabbed her arm and yanked her to her feet.

Gabriel stood imprisoned between two Indian. Blood dripped from his split lip. His face flushed as he gazed at Charity, sending her a silent warning to behave.

Another brave lifted the dead girl's body and lashed it to the back of an Indian pony. Other than Charity's scream, no one made a sound. Her skin prickled. Sweat broke out on her brow as her captor pulled her toward her horse. She wanted to pull away.

Everything in her screamed to know what their plans for her and Gabriel were.

Her captor ordered Charity to mount, and then tied her hands to the saddle horn. The Indians mounted and led her and Gabe in the opposite direction from where they had intended to go.

Gabriel sidled his horse closer to Charity. "These are not Red Feather's people. I think we've run into a rogue band," he whispered.

The tone of his voice told her that was very bad. "What are we going to do?" Her blood ran cold. "Does the girl belong to them?"

He shook his head. "I don't think so. We'll have to keep our wits about us and look for an opportunity to escape. If you see one, take it. Don't wait for me."

"I won't leave you." He couldn't ask her to.

"Please, for once, don't argue. The children can't be left alone. One of us has to make it back."

"They won't be alone. Mabel and Hiram would love to keep them."

"I'm begging you."

The lead Indian hissed and Charity and Gabriel pulled apart. She wanted nothing more than to kick Sam's pony in the side and gallop far away with Gabriel close behind her. Why hadn't she ventured forth and asked to share his bedroll last night? What if she never had another opportunity to steal a kiss? To feel his arms wrapped tight around her? See his eyes darken with desire? Even if he didn't love her as a husband loves his wife, she had noticed the way he looked at her when her hair was down.

Tears stung her eyes. She was a foolish woman, dwelling on dreams. They would die in these mountains. The children would be left to the likes of Amos Jenkins. She shook her head. Not if she could help it.

She took stock of where they were, wishing she had paid more attention yesterday. The tallest mountain peak was on her right. That meant home was to the left and back, right? She never was good at directions. She focused on Gabriel's strong back. With God's help, he would get them home safely. God seemed to listen to Gabriel.

Her stomach grumbled, reminding her of how long it had been since she'd eaten. Most likely, Gabriel figured they would be at Red Feather's camp and treated as guests by now.

She shifted in the saddle, trying to restore circulation to her numb bottom and chafed wrists. Not to mention her need to use the necessary. She cut a sideways glance at the Indian who woke her. He kept his gaze straight ahead, long braids hanging down his front.

"Excuse me? Could we stop for a moment?" She craned her neck to get his attention.

He remained as stoic as the pine trees around them.

"I don't think they speak English." Gabriel dropped back. "Besides, talking may only make them mad."

"But I need to …" She sighed, knowing she'd have to wait until they stopped. How did Gabriel manage to look every bit as strong as their captors, even with his swollen lip? Charity was terrified to within an inch of her life. She definitely didn't want to spend her last day on earth tied to the back of a pony. "What are they going to do with us?"

"Sell us, maybe? I'm not sure." Gabriel shrugged. "Don't worry. I'll think of something."

She hoped so. For a moment, she was almost tempted to pray, but was that would jinx them. Surely, Gabriel had them covered in the prayer department. She tightened her thighs and planted her feet in the stirrups to lift herself a bit off the saddle. A few more hours of this, and she'd wish the Indians had killed her in her sleep.

Were the children missing them by now? Had Mabel and Hiram taken them to their place? How long until someone contacted the sheriff? She shook her head. She could let the questions plague her, or she could think of a way out of their situation. The best she could figure, it all depended on their captors releasing her to use the necessary. Then, she could escape and think of a plan to rescue Gabriel.

The sun sat low in the sky. The wind had picked up, sending blasts of cold through her. Her bladder screamed, her legs burned, and her head pounded by the time the group stopped for the night. Thunder rumbled in the distance. Rain was exactly what Charity did not need. She didn't look forward to a cold drenching, or to being out in a storm at this elevation.

Gabriel slid from Rogue's back as if he were born to

the saddle. Charity had to be dragged off and left to crumple in a heap near the horse's hooves. None of her lessons had equipped her for hours on the back of a horse.

She glared and used the nearest tree to help get to her feet. Her mouth was as dry as a desert. Her stomach had given up on food hours ago.

She was lifted off the ground and deposited roughly next to Gabriel. Good. They could work together to get free. Work on each other's knots. Then, maybe if she danced around like Meg when she had to do her business, the Indians would get the hint and let her slide behind a bush.

"Help me up," she whispered to Gabriel.

"What do you have planned?" He took a quick glance to where the Indians worked at building a fire.

Charity would like to watch, interested in seeing how they expected to get a fire started in the rising wind, but more important things beckoned. "I need to use the necessary. While I do so, you make a distraction. I'll run so a couple of them chase me, and you take care of the rest. Then, we'll be free." She grinned.

"What if they catch you? Or what if I'm not able to 'take care of' the ones left behind?" He raised his eyebrows.

"That's the part you need to figure out. You work on distraction and getting away. I'll work on my part."

He shook his head. "Bear against me and use your legs to rise to your feet. I think it's a bad idea, but I don't have a better one."

She braced against him and "walked" to her feet. "Why did they take us and the girl?"

"I think they know who she is, even if she doesn't belong to their tribe. They probably want to use us to make some kind of deal."

"I refuse to be someone's pawn." She started crossing her legs and hopping back and forth.

Gabriel snorted. "You look ridiculous, but keep it up. You definitely have their attention."

The Indians pointed and guffawed before the leader waved Charity to a group of bushes off to their left. They jabbered in their language, laughed some more, and tossed a hunk of pemmican to Gabriel.

Charity paused for a moment and eyed the food. No, she needed to take care of business and escape. Food could wait. She hoped.

With her hands still tightly tied in front of her, Charity raced into the trees. She had told Gabe she would leave him, but she couldn't. If the situation were reversed, she could guarantee, Gabriel would not leave her behind.

First, she needed a place to hide. Somewhere she could work on her bindings and not be easily discovered.

She ran until her breath came in gasps. She tripped and slid across the forest floor, stopping against a hollow log. Could she force herself inside with the decaying leaves and insects? She swallowed back bile. It would be the perfect place to wait. Not too far from camp, but maybe far enough the Indians wouldn't look too hard.

A foul smell drifted from the log's interior. She recoiled and took a deep breath. She could do this. For Gabriel, she could crawl into the dark with the bugs and the stench. She dropped to her knees. Something sharp stabbed her from under a bed of leaves. She dug, finding a sharp rock. Grabbing it, she dropped to her knees and crawled inside the log, breathing through her mouth with small measured gasps. She never thought of herself as someone afraid of the dark before, but her skin chilled from more than the weather and bugs. Blackness engulfed her.

Her hand sunk into something mushy, and she shuddered. *God, if you could listen to me just this once, help me get through this and save Gabriel.* If He did, she promised to be a better person. Someone worthy of His attention.

*

Gabe eyed the pemmican lying in the dirt, and searched his brain for a way of distracting the Indians so Charity could get away. Even if he got hurt, it would be worth it for her to escape. He got a glimpse of her ducking behind a tree and wished he had said something. Anything. For her to stay safe. That he would see her later. Told her how he felt about her.

He closed his eyes, then struggled to his feet and leaned against the rough bark of a pine. He would give her a few minutes, and then, once the Indians turned restless wondering where she'd went, he'd make his

223

move and pray for God to protect him.

Minutes stretched like hours, pulling Gabe's nerves to the tearing point, before the Indians started talking and casting narrow looks in the direction Charity disappeared. She had been gone long enough to rouse suspicion.

"Hey!" Gabe kicked at the pemmican. "I'm not an animal you can toss food at."

The Indians ignored him. One stood and took a few steps toward the woods. Gabe kicked harder, sending dirt and dried leaves into the wind and over their heads. "Are you listening to me?" *Please, God, keep their attention on me.*

The Indian scowled and continued walking.

Gabe growled and kicked out his legs, taking the other man down. Before he could register his crazy act, the other three jumped him and planted punches and kicks of their own. Gabe smiled through the pain. At least his stupidity would give Charity the opportunity she needed.

A well-aimed kick filled his mouth with blood. Wonderful. Now his upper lip matched his lower one. He spit, spattering the beaded moccasin of one of his captors.

The man grabbed Gabe by the hair and yanked him to his feet, yelling something. One of these days, Gabe needed to learn to speak Crow. He didn't think the man's words boded well for him.

Another warrior grabbed his other arm and together they slammed him against a tree and tied him there. Gabe sighed, letting his head hang. Most likely they'd leave him for the animals morning. He prayed Charity would find her way back to the children and have a good life. It sure would be nice if he could have been a part of that life. He closed his eyes to the vision of tumbling red hair and sparkling eyes.

As the night darkened, one of the Indians pulled a bottle of whiskey from a bag. When they weren't taking swigs, they half-heartedly searched the surrounding area for Charity. Fools. If they had no intentions of keeping a tighter rein on their captives, then why bother capturing them in the first place?

He glanced to where the dead girl lay near the horses. Thankfully, the Indians had moved her from Rogue's back. Maybe someone put out a reward for the girl and the braves intended to collect.

He grunted as one of the braves bounced a rock off his head. If they were going to kill him, he wished they'd get it over with. He didn't relish being tormented all night by drunks.

It looked as if Amos would win after all. The papers Maggie signed said that should Gabe die before the land reverted to him, Amos would retain all rights. He jerked upright.

Was it possible the man hired the Indians to capture him and Charity? That the dead woman wasn't part of the plan? It would explain why the four braves weren't overly concerned about finding Charity. Of course, they could always sell her for a pretty profit, but leaving her alone wouldn't affect the overall goal if

Amos was behind things.

The desire to free himself rose up with the strength of the increasing storm. If he could escape, he would hunt Amos down and throttle him!

Gabe's arms ached from the pressure of the rope. The more he struggled, the more painful his wrists became as the rough fibers cut into his skin, and he bled. Yet, he continued to saw back and forth, stopping only when one of the Indians glanced his way.

The tallest, the one who initially tied up Charity, pulled a knife from a sheath at his waist, and strolled toward Gabe. He grinned and with the tip of his knife, popped Gabe's buttons one by one. So the time had come. Gabe prayed he would be able to stay brave until the end.

He hissed as the other man slowly drew the blade across his chest, barely cutting the skin. The next slash came a little deeper, as if he were a child at play. Gabe kept his gaze locked on the Indian's dark one, and forced his face to remain impassive.

Lightening slashed the sky, thunder rolled, the clouds unleashed their burden of rain, and the Indian head butted Gabe.

23

When she'd estimated an hour had gone by without hearing footsteps crunching outside her bug-ridden den of horror, Charity crawled free. She had spent the time cutting the rope that bound her wrists against a rock she'd found and took joy in tossing the frayed strands away.

Thankful for the whine of the wind and rumble of thunder to hide the sound of her footsteps, she made her way back to the camp and ducked behind a stand of thick bushes. She peered over the top in top to see Gabriel hit in the head and left slumped against the tree.

Was he dead? Was she too late? Tears welled and poured down her face, mixing with the rain. She slumped to the ground, unmindful of the cold. She had failed, again. Life dealt her one cruel blow after another. Still, she was needed, for a time. The children were waiting. Oh, how would she tell them their father was dead?

Swiping her hand across her eyes, she pushed to her feet. The least she could do was save his horse. Gabriel loved that animal. She sagged as sobs shook her body. She never had the opportunity to tell him her feelings. They rarely carried on a conversation that lasted longer than ten minutes, but Charity knew if they had the time, she would have found a kindred spirit in Gabriel. Oh, but she wanted to shoot every last one of those Indian braves, then curl up next to Gabriel and let fate win!

But she wouldn't. The children needed her. They must be worried sick by now.

She crouched and made her way to where the horses were tied, keeping a close eye on the Indians who covered the ground like snoring piles of deerskin. Rogue nickered when he spotted her, and she clamped a hand over his muzzle. Sam's pony, being the docile animal he was, stared with big eyes while Charity loosened his reins.

Lightning slashed the sky, illuminating the area. Gabriel groaned. Gabriel groaned! Charity scuttled to his side.

"You're alive." She smoothed his hair from his face and winced at the gash in his head. "I've got to get you out of here."

"I told you to leave me."

"Well, I was going to, but I know how much you love Rogue, and since I needed a way to get home—"

She worked at the knots around his wrist. "How do you feel?"

"Like I was beaten."

Finally, she released him from his bindings. "Can you mount?"

"Yes." He struggled to his feet, keeping one arm tight against his ribcage.

Charity helped him the best she could, then climbed on Sam's pony. Why couldn't her son actually give his horse a name? If they made it home, she'd suggest Paint.

Gabriel headed into the trees, the reins to Charity's pony clutched in one hand. They kept to a walk until a cry rang out behind them.

"Ya!" Gabriel whipped the reins. Rogue leaped ahead. Charity grabbed the saddle horn on the horse she rode and held on for dear life.

*

Gabe hadn't seen any guns in the hands of the Indians, but he wasn't taking any chances. He led Charity deeper into the thick underbrush and prayed the braves were too drunk to be much of a threat.

His side burned from the Indian's malicious slicing, and his head throbbed. He also didn't know whether he should shake Charity or kiss her. For once, he was mighty glad she chose not to follow directions, even though he thought his heart would stop for sure when he opened his eyes and saw her fumbling around the horses. She'd never seemed more beautiful, drenched hair, torn dress, and all.

Ducking beneath a low hanging-branch, he urged Rogue deeper into the forest. The rain would help hold back their followers. If Gabe made the search difficult enough, they might give up. He doubted Amos put too big a price on his head to warrant a search in a winter rain storm.

He shivered, and wished they had grabbed a couple of the furs loaded on one of the Indian ponies. He swiped his forearm across his eyes, clearing his vision of blood and water.

Charity cried out. Gabe turned in the saddle. She rubbed her cheek. "Just a branch. Gave me a nasty scratch."

They needed to remain quiet. Despite the increasing noise of the storm, if the Indians were close, they would hear. Gabe held a finger to his lips. His other hand brushed the back of the horse as he turned.

His rifle still hung in its scabbard. Why hadn't the braves removed it? Even with his hands tied, he might have been a small threat. Obviously, they didn't expect him to escape. *Thank you, God.* Their captors were definitely not the brightest. He pulled the gun free and motioned for Charity to move closer.

A thrashing in the woods to their right made him freeze. He aimed the rifle and held his breath. Lightning crashed, exposing the area ahead of them. Four figures rode past, ill-shaped under woven Indian blankets. It appeared they had given up their search, instead intent on taking the poor Indian girl wherever it was they planned to take her.

Gabe held up a hand to signal Charity to wait, then relaxed in the saddle. They might be hungry, frozen, and beaten, but they were alive, and it looked as if they would stay that way a while longer.

Charity shivered hard enough for Gabe to see the movement through the rain. He slid his gun back in its scabbard and dragged her over to sit in front of him. His breath hitched at the pain in his side, but sharing body warmth would benefit them both—not to mention how wonderful she felt in his arms.

"I didn't thank you for saving me." He laid his cheek against her hair and breathed deep.

She snuggled closer. "You're welcome. We're a team, Mr. Williams."

He chuckled. "Yes, we are, and a mighty fine one at that." With a flick of the reins, he set Rogue toward home, letting Sam's pony follow.

Gabe decided he wanted to court Charity. Never mind that they were already married. He wanted to stay hitched past the springtime. He wanted babies of his own with her. Surely a strong man such as himself could win the heart of an Irish girl. She had accepted his proposal readily enough. Even a blind man could see she cared for Meg and Sam, and had settled into life on the Montana prairie.

Now, he needed to make sure she fell in love with him.

24

By the time they trotted onto the homestead, Gabe's head wobbled as much as Charity's. Several times he caught himself before his chin connected with the top of her skull. Even the horses seemed to have barely enough energy make their way to the barn.

Charity barely stirred back to life when Lady and Prince barked a welcome. Light flared behind the window, and the front door swung open. Sam and Meg, followed by the Stoltzes rushed out.

"Oh, my heavens, she's dead." Mabel clapped a hand to her mouth. "And you look like you should be."

"We're both alive." Gabe swung his leg over and slid to the ground, keeping Charity tucked close. "We've had a bit of an ordeal, but we're home now."

"Come on in the house and let me take care of you." Mabel bustled back inside, followed closely by the others. "We'll get you cleaned up straight away and into bed. That gash on your head might need stitches."

Gabe gently laid Charity on his bed and slumped next to her. She might raise a fuss when she woke to find him next to her, but Gabe was too exhausted to worry about that now. He wanted her close in case she felt poorly in the morning. The Stoltzes most likely figured out he and Charity hadn't shared a bed up to this point, and Gabe didn't care. All he wanted was to stretch out and lose himself for several hours.

Before he could fully relax, Sam and Meg plastered themselves to each side of him. Meg smoothed back Charity's hair. "She ain't gonna die, is she, Pa?"

"No, sweetheart. She's plumb tuckered out. Your ma saved my life tonight." Gabe wrapped his arms around his children, thanking God he had the opportunity to lay eyes on them again.

"That's a story I've got to hear." Hiram handed him a cup of hot coffee. "I laced it with spirits." He held up a hand to ward off Gabe's protest. "My woman is about to poke your head with a needle. You'll need that drink. Once she scrubs your head wound, what little scabbing started is going to pull free and it's going to bleed something fierce and hurt like the dickens."

"Guess it won't harm me to imbibe this once." Gabe took a sip and grimaced. "Takes like medicine."

Hiram clapped him on the shoulder. "It is, my friend. Now, move into that kitchen chair and let my wife tend to you. When she finishes with you, she'll take care of your wife."

He wished they'd worry about Charity first, but was

smart enough to realize his injuries were more serious. Charity's problems were stress and exhaustion. Without Gabe feeling well, the ranch couldn't function, and the children wouldn't be safe. He pushed to his feet and moved gingerly to the chair by the table.

Now that he took the time to pay attention to his injuries, every move pained him. He'd bet his bottom dollar he had a broken rib or two, not to mention the gash in his head and the cut on his chest. If he looked in the mirror over the mantel, he'd most likely scare himself.

He allowed Hiram to pour more "medicine" in with his coffee, took a big gulp, and laid his head against the hard chair back. These weren't the first stitches he'd ever received so he knew they were going to hurt, and he didn't cotton to the youngsters watching. "Young'uns, y'all go to the barn. I'll call you when Mrs. Stoltz is done."

"I'll go with them. They can help me care for the horses." Hiram ushered them outside, rifle firmly clutched in one hand.

Grateful for the man's concern in realizing possible danger, Gabe closed his eyes and gave himself over to Mabel's torture.

*

Charity watched from the bed and tried not to cringe when Mabel poked the needle and thread through Gabriel's skin. The room reeked of liquor, and she pulled the closest blanket over her nose. It ought to be her stitching up Gabriel. He was her husband. She was the one who had saved him from the renegades.

He groaned at another thrust of the needle. A muscle twitched in his jaw, and his knuckles whitened as he gripped the armrest.

No longer able to lie idly back, Charity tossed aside her blanket and made her way to his side. She slipped her hand into his, and squeezed.

Mabel nodded and winked before pulling another stitch, then knotting the thread. She bent close and bit through the thread, before straightening. "There. Four stitches, Gabriel. Thank the good Lord, you've a hard head, for sure."

"I'm more for thanking the Lord for a stubborn wife." He returned Charity's squeeze and opened his eyes. "If not for her continuous disobeying of my orders, I wouldn't be here."

"Some orders are not meant to be followed." Charity stood and moved to the sink. "If you'll go to your bed, I'll have my turn to wash, thank you." His bed. Gracious! She'd been lying in it.

She leaned against the counter. Surely he placed her there. She hadn't gone of her own accord, had she? What must he think of her?

Taking a deep breath, she turned to lift a kettle of water from the stove and poured it into the wash basin. A sponge bath would have to suffice for now. Tomorrow, she'd lug water for a leisurely soak when Gabriel was away from the house.

"Let me help you." Mabel held out a rag. "You're a hero, I've heard."

"You would have done the same for Hiram."
Charity glanced behind them to see Gabe stretched out
on his bed and pulling the curtain across to shield him.

Mabel shook her head. "I'm not so sure." She
dipped the rag into the water, then dabbed at Charity's
face. "I was at a complete loss when I thought Hiram
was gone. A hysterical mess."

"You were distraught."

"That I was." She dunked the rag again. "What
happened out there? You both look like death warmed
over."

Charity swallowed against the tears clogging her
throat. "We had stopped for the night. When we woke,
we were the captives of a small band of Indians." She
dropped onto the bench beside the table. "They tied us
up. I don't know where they were taking us. I escaped
and hid until they passed out drunk. I thought Gabriel
was dead. Oh, Mabel, they beat him so." She took a
deep breath. "Thinking he was dead, I was intent on
saving his horse. When I discovered I wasn't a widow, I
freed him, and here we are."

Mabel sat down next to her. "That's some tale.
What happened to the girl?"

"I don't know." Charity propped her elbow on the
table and rested her chin in her hand. "Funny thing is,
they didn't seem all that determined to pursue me.
They were more focused on Gabriel."

"Do you think they were following you with the
intentions of capture?" Mabel's eyes widened. "As if
they were following you from the beginning?"

"I think so." Charity lowered her voice. "I intend to keep a close watch on my husband, and a gun at hand. Sam promised to teach me to shoot, and I plan to start right away."

"Why don't you ask Gabe to teach you?"

"Ha. He wouldn't want me in harm's way. But sometimes, his heavy-handed ways of protecting me are more dangerous." Charity went back to the sink and began washing her arms. If she had known how to shoot, she could have picked the Indians off one by one while she hid in the bushes.

Could she actually shoot someone? If they meant harm to her family, she definitely could.

She planted both hands on the counter and hung her head. Exhaustion warred with her desire to clean up and care for Gabriel.

"Come here." Mabel put an arm around her shoulder and turned her toward her cot. "Let me help you undress, and get you tucked in. Hiram and I will bed down by the fire tonight and see how you feel in the morning. Our livestock can last one more night without us. They've plenty of hay and water. Our milk cow dried up last year."

"Bless you, Mabel. You're a dear friend." Charity allowed herself to be babied and enjoyed the feeling. It had been so long since someone tenderly cared for her. Once she lay on her back, a thick quilt pulled to her chin, her eyes drifted shut.

She couldn't help but wish she still lay in Gabriel's bed.

*

Stupid savages! Amos yanked his horse's reins. He had hired them to do one simple thing; take care of Gabe Williams. Not only did they let him escape, but that fiery wife of his, too. Now, they would be more wary, and Gabriel and Charity were back at home. Sure they looked a little worse for wear, but nothing that wouldn't heal.

Amos hadn't meant to kill anyone. The death of the Indian maiden could cause problems in the long run. He needed to think on a solution to that problem. Who knew she would be picking berries in the woods so close to the Williamses's homestead, or would be frightened by a little gunfire? Where had she come from anyway? Most of the Indians were long gone to their winter campgrounds.

He shrugged. Maybe she was part of a hunting party. He didn't believe in killing women. No matter what race they were and didn't much like killing men either, but sometimes a man had to do what he needed in order to get what belonged to him.

Hopefully, her people would blame Gabe and not go looking for someone else. The Crow could be violent enough when riled, and he didn't cotton to an all out war because of an accident.

Why couldn't anything go as planned? He kicked his horse, spurring it faster as sight of his barn came into view. He had wasted an entire day and night watching the Williamses's homestead. If he wanted something done right, he would have to do it himself, and he was running out of ideas.

*

Charity stretched. Cold air brushed her bare arms, alerting her to the crisp dawn. Sunlight streamed through the window and low murmurs came from the other side of the curtain. She'd overslept, resulting in the others doing her chores. She grinned. Almost like her first morning beneath this sod roof. Except Meg didn't stare down at her today.

Tossing back the quilt, she donned a clean dress, then slid her feet into her boots. Her body protested. When she heard Gabriel's familiar rumble from the direction of the kitchen table, she hurried, forcing a bounce into her step that her body did not feel. .

"Good morning." She skipped around the curtain, forcing back a wince at her back's protest.

Gabriel glanced up from his bowl of oatmeal. "You're chipper this morning. Feeling all right after yesterday?"

"Rarely better." She kept the smile on her face as she fairly skipped to the stove. Her body hated her for the chipper movement. Mabel and the children gazed wide-eyed at her, then Mabel's eyes narrowed. "What?" Charity demanded.

"Nothing." Mabel turned to the sink.

Charity figured Mabel saw through her ruse, and they would have a conversation about it later. She plopped a heaping spoonful of oatmeal into a bowl and sat at the table. She didn't want the others to know how much her body ached. How every breath was agony. She couldn't tell, but if she had a full length mirror she'd guess more than a few bruises painted her skin.

Would she do it all again? To save Gabriel or one of the children she would. There would be time for rest and recuperation after she learned to shoot, and when Gabriel left the house to work. She had no broken bones, no stitches. There was no sense in lying around like a ninny whining about her pains. Sure, her feet and back ached from her romp through the woods, she had a scratch on her face that she didn't believe would leave a scar, and she doubted she would ever get the tangles out of her hair, but she'd survived hours inside a dead tree with a multitude of bugs. She could survive anything.

She grinned at Gabriel and stuck a spoonful of breakfast in her mouth. He shook his head, clearly befuddled at her behavior, and returned his attention to his food.

Her smile faded. He looked awful. The black thread of his stitches provided a dark contrast against skin paler than normal. Purple and blue bruises dotted his face like dabs from a paintbrush. A goose egg rose from his temple. He very well could have died the day before. Where would that have left Charity and the children? She definitely needed to keep a closer eye on him.

Her hand paused on its upward travel to her mouth. How was it possible she hadn't thought of gold in days? Her situation hadn't changed. There was still the impending annulment. She had six, maybe seven months left to convince Gabriel she was worth keeping around, and if the chill making its way under the door was any indication, winter was fast approaching and gold mining inadvisable.

Gabriel stood and grabbed his hat. "I'll be back by supper."

"Where are you going?" Surely he didn't intend to follow through on riding to town?

"I need to see the sheriff." He patted Charity's head as if she were a child. "Don't worry. Hiram is going with me. We'll stop by and tend his stock first."

She swatted his hand away. The man could turn her mood faster than a striking snake. "As if I'm worried that you're a fool headed off to do more damage to yourself."

He chuckled. "Stay out of trouble." After planting kisses on the cheeks of both children, he tossed Charity a wink and left.

"That is the most infuriating man." She carried her bowl to the sink. "A knot on his head the size of Ireland, and he's bent on riding half a day's journey into town to report the rowdy behavior of some Indians. Me dead ma would have clobbered him with a skillet."

"As if you're any different." Mabel shooed the children outside to do their chores. "Pretending everything is fine when every move you make pains you."

"Somebody has to take care of my husband. It's obvious he is incapable of doing so himself."

"What really has your dander up?" Mabel turned

her to face her.

Charity took a deep breath. "I'm falling in love with my husband and the thought of losing him is comparable to losing a limb."

"Have you told him how you feel?"

"Oh, I couldn't! What if he doesn't feel the same?" She hung her head. "You saw how he said goodbye. A pat on the head, as if I were nothing but his wee sister." She sniffed against approaching tears. "I'm nothing but a nanny for his children and someone to help him win a bet."

"Oh, I think you're worth more than that to him." Mabel grabbed a dishtowel. "Don't forget. The long winter months are coming. You'll be thrust together twenty-four hours a day."

And that thought terrified Charity. There would be no way of hiding her insecurities. Her tendency toward snappishness. The real Charity O'Connell would be right in front of Gabriel Williams.

25

Gabe regretted his decision to ride to town by the time he'd made it halfway to Virginia City. If he had taken time to think things through, he would have waited a day or two, instead of heading out like a man without busted ribs.

Spots swam before his eyes and sweat beaded his upper lip. He uncorked his canteen and took a large swig of water. Maybe if he ignored the pain it would go away. He refused to let Charity know she was right. He would keep his head up, inform the sheriff of yesterday's happenings, then slump his way home, only to lift his head again before walking through the door.

As if he could tell what Gabe was thinking, Hiram laughed. "You're a stubborn man, Gabe Williams."

"Can't disagree." He slung the canteen back over his saddle horn. "And I've got a wife that has me beat in the stubborn department."

"It really sticks in your craw that Charity rescued you yesterday and not the other way around, doesn't it?" Hiram handed him a slice of jerky.

Gabe smirked and accepted the food. "A bit. A man is supposed to take care of his woman. Those Indians had me trussed up like a turkey, and she managed to get them to allow her to use the necessary. Even savages aren't immune to her charms, it seems."

"Marriage is a partnership, Gabe. That's the way the good Lord created it." Hiram tore off a bite of the dried meat with his teeth, then continued talking with his mouth full. "Take me and Mabel for example. Cooped up all winter long with a woman who talks more than a mockingbird is not an easy task. Yet, I nod and grunt and she's happy to bustle around me like a momma chicken. Let Charity fuss. You're still the man, and I'd say it's a mite harder to sit quiet and let the womenfolk go on and on than it is to strut our stuff." He took another bite of jerky.

Gabe couldn't remember a time when Hiram talked so much. But, the man made a good point. Charity was so different from Maggie, he really hadn't known what to expect.

He shook his head. That wasn't entirely true. He had expected her to be just as quiet and submissive as his first wife, but he thanked God she wasn't. Life took an interesting turn the day he married Charity.

He rolled his shoulders and focused on the road into Virginia City. Townsfolk darted here and there in a rush to purchase supplies to get them through the winter. Dust hovered about a foot off the ground. With the dark clouds overhead, it gave the scene a warm sepia-tone.

He sighed. He still hadn't filled his smokehouse. What, with one thing or another, if he weren't careful, they wouldn't have enough meat to last, unless he butchered a cow. He didn't want to do that until his herd was bigger. And, there was the looming reminder that it would take a miracle for him to complete the house on time.

Maybe God was trying to tell Gabe something. When was the last time the family sat together for a Bible reading? Maybe once since Charity arrived. How was he going to convince her of God's love if he didn't subject her to The Word? Sure, they did most of their reading during the long winter months, but why? Couldn't they start a new tradition of spending relaxing time together *every* evening? He vowed to start as soon as he returned home.

Before he reached the sheriff's office, Amos Jenkins stepped off the sidewalk and headed in the direction of the saloon. Gabe gritted his teeth at the desire to run the other man down in the street like the dog he was.

"Easy, Gabe." Hiram stopped beside him. "Let the law handle things."

"The law ain't doing anything."

"We don't have enough proof. With proof even Sheriff Spraggins would have to act."

"How am I supposed to have proof Amos coerced a

handful of renegade Indians into kidnapping me and Charity? It isn't as though I had them sign a note or anything." Had the man gone loco? "It won't hurt to let the sheriff know I'm on to Amos, and that I know he's in Amos's back pocket."

"Nope. Won't hurt to tell the sheriff what happened."

They pulled in front of the sheriff's office and dismounted to hitch the horses to the nearby railing. Gabe knew he wasted his time. Sheriff Spraggins wouldn't do a blamed thing, but Gabe would feel better telling him he knew what Amos was doing.

With Hiram close behind, Gabe shoved through the door and clomped across the plank floor to where the sheriff leaned back in his chair, napping. Gabe gripped the chair leg and pulled it back to all fours.

Spraggins sputtered and leaped to her feet. "What do you think you're doing?"

"Filing a complaint. A man can still do that around here, can't he?"

"Against who? What happened to you?" Spraggins narrowed his eyes. "You look like you were in a fight."

"I was." Gabe crossed his arms. "With some renegade Indians. I want you to go after them."

Spraggins plopped back in his chair. "Nope. I ain't interfering with Injuns. They are unpredictable. Stay out of their way, and they'll leave you alone."

Heat rose up Gabe's neck, and he slapped both palms flat on the top of the sheriff's scarred desk. "My wife and I could've died, sheriff! Not to mention, I found a dead girl up on my property. It's up to you to do something. Besides, my gut tells me they were hired."

"By who? Are you trying to tell me that your paranoia about Amos Jenkins leads you to believe…"

"Paranoia!" If not for Hiram's restraining hand, Gabe might very well have launched himself over the top of the desk and strangled Spraggins.

The man sneered. "I suggest you leave before I arrest you for something. I have work to do."

"Yeah, work as important as staring at the back of your eyelids." Gabe shoved away and stormed outside. His gaze landed on Amos exiting the saloon. In twenty long strides, Gabe reached the man and landed a sharp uppercut on his jaw. Amos crumpled like a felled tree and blinked up at him.

"You want to tangle with me, fine." Gabe bent over him. "But you leave Charity out of it. She's done nothing to you."

Amos rubbed his jaw. "You're plumb loco. You can't accost a man with no reason."

"I have plenty of reason, and you know it." Yet, the man was right. Gabe shouldn't have punched him. If Amos wanted to, he could press charges against him, and Gabe would spend a night or two in jail.

What kind of a spiritual witness did he leave knocking even his enemy to the ground? Didn't God ask that man love his enemies? Although it galled him, Gabe held out his hand. "My apologies. I should not have hit you."

Amos stared at the offered hand for a moment,

then slapped it away. "Apology not accepted. I know you Bible thumpers expect folks to forgive you, but not this time. You have no proof I had anything to do with them Indians. The sheriff and half this town are on my side. "

Gabe slowly lowered his hand. "What makes you think I'm here about Indians? I never said anything to you about that."

*

Shooting was harder than she thought. Charity lifted the heavy rifle again and took aim at the stump in front of her. Learning to load the gun was easy, but actually hitting her target was something else. Sam had given up on her an hour ago, choosing instead to wrestle in the dirt with Prince.

Occasionally Mabel would stick her head out of the house and yell something about a waste of good ammunition, and that Charity should have her husband teach her. Still, Charity persevered. She would learn to shoot and do it well. Even if her shoulder did feel as if it had been kicked by a mule.

"Come on, Ma." Sam tapped her shoulder. "You've been at it all day. It's almost suppertime, and Pa will be home soon. Besides, you're going through his ammo like it's water poured out of a glass."

Charity sighed. They were right. She shouldn't waste something they would need for providing food. "I'm coming."

She glanced at the heavy clouds. Snow would fall within a day or two. Maybe not a lot at first, but soon, they'd be stuck in the soddy. Charity shrugged. She had plenty of quilt scraps and yarn to keep her hands busy, clothes to sew for two growing children, and a husband who seemed to split his at the seams. Maybe she ought to make his next shirt a mite bigger.

She smiled at the sight of the dogs romping across the yard. Their little home would be busting at the seams during the winter months, and she wouldn't have it any other way.

The sound of horse hooves drifted on the afternoon breeze. Charity shielded her eyes. Gabe and Hiram trotted toward the barn. Hitching her skirt, Charity hurried to the house. The men would be hungry.

"Men are here." She grabbed an apron from a nearby hook. The tantalizing, rich aroma of chicken stew filled the soddy. She took great satisfaction in knowing the vegetables came from a garden she tended.

While Meg set plates on the table, Charity gave the stew a stir and checked the biscuits in the oven. She enjoyed having Mabel around, but it would be nice when she and Hiram headed home in the morning. The kitchen wasn't big enough for two cooks.

By the time the men came in—Gabe favoring his side, the stubborn man—the table was set and the children's faces washed. Gabe took his seat at the head of the table and motioned for Hiram to sit opposite him.

Charity looked long and hard at Gabe's scowling face. He caught her looking and shook his head, signaling they would talk later. Sure they would. Just like all the other conversations waiting to be had.

"I'm taking Sam hunting tomorrow," Gabe said. "Snow is coming, and the smokehouse is low. I don't want to eat only pigs and chickens all winter."

"A deer would be nice." Charity reached for the serving spoon. "Maybe a turkey and a goose for the holidays."

"If you're hard up for food," Hiram said, grabbing a biscuit. "Just come on by. We've plenty, and we know you've been set back a bit what with all that's been happening."

"Ma's been target shooting," Sam offered. "Used a lot of ammo. Still can't hit the side of a barn, though."

"What?" Gabe's frown deepened. "And we will have plenty of food, Hiram."

"Well, I, uh, thought I should learn to shoot and help gather meat." Charity carefully ladled stew onto her plate. "And, I can help guard the homestead when you're away."

"What is it with everyone?" Gabe tossed his spoon in his food. "I am perfectly capable of taking care of my family."

"No one is saying otherwise," Hiram said. "Mabel knows how to shoot and often brings home a squirrel or two. Makes things easier on me."

"That's right, Gabe. Especially when a rabbit or something gets into my garden." Mabel nodded. "Then I'm more than happy to take care of the situation and not have to wait on Hiram."

"That isn't why Charity wants to learn."

"It isn't?" Charity's spoon paused half-way to her mouth.

Gabriel shook his head. "Nope. You think you need to learn how to shoot in order to protect this family. You saved me from the Indians, and now, I'm incapable of keeping the rest of you from harm."

Charity took a deep breath and rested the utensil on her plate. It was a good thing they had company because it kept her from losing her tongue on her mulish husband. "You must be in pain, Gabriel, because you are speaking nonsense."

Mabel's eyes widened, and she ducked her head. Hiram cleared his throat and ate as if someone were going to steal his supper.

"Nonsense!" Gabriel shoved to his feet.

Charity did the same. "Yes. If I had listened to you yesterday, you would be dead right now." She spoke each word distinctly, with special emphasis on dead. "There is nothing wrong with a woman knowing how to shoot or any other supposed 'manly' type pursuits." She lifted her chin. "I intend to teach Meg to be self-sufficient, also."

"My wife will be submissive."

"My husband will be objective."

Charity took a deep breath and closed her eyes. Clearly something happened in town that set Gabriel over the edge of reason. She needed to defuse the situation before something was said that couldn't be taken back. "If it's any consolation, I am not a good shot."

Gabriel growled and marched to his bed, drawing the curtain.

*

Gabe scrubbed both hands down his face and sat on the edge of his bed. Yes, he was in pain, but that did not excuse his actions. His pride had been wounded, and he had acted like a young boy. He owed everyone an apology. Especially his wife.

There was no reason to get angry over her learning to shoot, except maybe the loss of ammo, but he had plenty stashed in the trunk at the foot of his bed. One of the things he purchased plenty of when times were good. With two rifles, and two people capable of using them, they would never go hungry or left helpless when he was away.

He was the king of fools. Many more evenings like this one and he wouldn't have to worry whether Charity would want to stay. She'd run back to town like a cat with its tail on fire.

Tomorrow, when he returned from hunting, they would start their Bible readings, and he would find something about repentance and being sorry for wronging others. Then, he'd explain to his family about punching Amos and let the children know that what he had done was very wrong. Jesus did not punch the ones who crucified him, and Gabe should not retaliate against his enemies that way either. Right attitude or not, the notion left a bad taste in his mouth.

Standing and pulling aside the curtain, Gabe squared his shoulders and walked back to the table. "I apologize for my behavior. Charity, you may learn to shoot if you so please. Sam, I need your help with chores. Hiram and Mabel, I'm sorry for being an ungracious host." With as much pride as he could muster, Gabe spun on his heel and moved outside.

He didn't stop until he got to the corral where he penned his cattle. The poor beasts were crowded and looked miserable. But, they were home, and not scattered across the territory. He checked the hay he had left the day before, satisfied there was plenty for a few more days.

Lady leaned against his leg and he reached down to scratch behind her ear. When Sam joined them, Gabe sent him into the barn to fork hay to the horses. He needed to be alone with his thoughts for a few minutes.

Maybe he should walk away. Leave the house, leave the land. Take his family and head to California. Adopt Charity's attitude of mining for gold. If there was gold there years ago, there was bound to be more. They just needed to look in the right place. They could strike it rich and start over.

He laughed. Might as well mine right here. But the last time he heard of a big strike was over by Grasshopper Creek near Bannock. He shook his head, not believing he would even entertain the notion of mining for gold that probably panned out four years ago.

He crossed his arms on the top rail of the corral and let the cattle's lowing soothe him. He glanced at the darkening sky, and shivered. The temperature was dropping fast, and the cloud cover had thickened. Within minutes, he'd be thrust into total darkness. Early in the morning, he would most likely be heading out to hunt with the season's first snowfall. With Thanksgiving only two weeks away, he prayed he could bag a turkey for Charity. He knew the Irish favored goose on Christmas, so he would also try to take a trip to the mountain lake.

With his mood lightened, Gabe went to the barn to help his son prepare the animals for night. Yep, it was going to be a wonderful winter. One where he would win Charity's heart and show her that nights where he lost his temper and acted like a child were few and far between.

26

Gabe and Sam left to go hunting before Charity and Meg crawled out of bed the next morning. Charity stared at the ceiling, thankful it was finally cold enough that bugs no longer dropped on them during the night. With a low fire burning in the fireplace, the room was comfortable. The dogs and cat lay curled around each other on the small rag rug in front of the hearth. Charity smiled at the cozy picture, glad to be a part of it.

Tossing back her blankets, she tugged on long socks then reached for her dress. A peek outside showed still no snow. Maybe her and Meg could head into the woods and harvest the last of the crab apples. The apples would make a pleasant jam for their holiday dinner.

She patted Meg awake. "Come on. Let's go pick apples while we still can."

"It's cold."

"Bundle up. We'll be snowbound soon enough, and the berries will be gone." Charity slipped her dress over her nightgown, taking her own advice. "We'll pack a lunch and make a day of it. Your Pa and Sam will be gone until supper, unless they stay out all night."

"Can we take the dogs?" Meg crawled out of bed.

"Sure. I doubt they would stay behind anyway." Not to mention the safety they would provide. Two dogs would give ample warning if a wild animal ventured too close.

Charity rushed through her morning chores, scrambled some eggs for breakfast, wrapped Meg warmly in a scarf and coat, then headed out the door with the dogs gamboling around them.

She remembered seeing some crab apple trees when she and Gabriel had ventured out to take the Indian girl to her people and set off in that direction. Her skin prickled at the thought the Indians might be close by. Surely not. They must have headed on their way shortly after she escaped. Nevertheless, she'd keep her eyes peeled and pay attention to the dogs' behavior.

About a fifteen minute march up the mountain led them to trees still containing a few berries. Wrinkled, but edible. Charity set her pail at her feet and started picking the few left on the lower branches. "Do you think you can safely climb these branches, Meg? There are more apples farther up."

"Yes, Ma." Meg tucked the hem of her dress into the waistband of her bloomers.

With her heart in her throat, Charity watched Meg scrambled up the tree like a little squirrel. Soon, apples rained down on her head and shoulders. She laughed and started plucking them into the buckets. They weren't in as good of a condition as she would have preferred, but she was bound to get enough good ones for a jar or two or jam. Not to mention how pleased the children would be.

Over the summer months and into fall, she'd witnessed Meg and Sam growing more lighthearted. The kitten had been only the beginning. The dogs helped the children learn to play, too, and Charity couldn't wait until Christmas when they opened the few toys she had splurged on.

"Meg, I'm stepping behind that clump of bushes for the necessary. You stay right where you are."

Meg nodded and plopped in a pile of dried leaves.

While Charity did her business, her gaze fell on a dark spot farther in the bushes. She stood and pushed through. A cave! Her heart stuttered. Could there be gold inside? A bear? She glanced around for something to throw. She couldn't tell, but she didn't think the cave deep enough to house a wild animal. She found a good-sized rock and tossed it inside.

It clattered against stone. The cave wasn't deep at all. Nothing growled, and nothing charged at her.

"Meg! Come here."

"Why are you in the dark, Ma?" Meg took one step inside the cave and stopped. "I don't like it in here. It scares me."

"Your eyes will adjust. It really isn't that dark. I just want to look around for a minute. That's all. Stay right by the entrance." Charity hadn't seen the dogs in a while, but knew the loyal animals wouldn't have gone far from her and Meg. Oh, she wished she had a lantern.

She ran her hands over the rough walls of the cave until the pads of her fingers were sore. She didn't feel anything that felt like veins of gold. Who was she kidding? She didn't know what veins of gold felt like. Without the proper tools, she would never know what lay under the soil.

Tears stung her eyes, and she plopped to the cave floor in a puddle of dejection and dirty calico. That was it. No more silly dreams of striking it rich. She would be content with the life God gave her, whether it was with Gabe and the children or not. She scoffed. Most likely, considering how God didn't seem to care much about bestowing blessings on Charity, He would choose to send her away in a few months to struggle through life alone.

Having spent more than enough time and energy on foolish pursuits, she got to her feet and joined Meg. There would be no more time for chilly wading in the creeks or scouring caves for veins of gold. Winter was upon them. Even someone as stubborn as Charity knew when something was not meant to be.

"What's wrong?" Meg slipped her hand into Charity's. "You look sad."

"I'm fine, sweetheart. I just got my eyes opened

today."

The sound of a bullet shattered the day's stillness.

*

Gabe lined up his sight and pulled the trigger. "Look at that, Sam. Bulls eye!" He had just bagged the biggest turkey he had ever shot. Charity would be thrilled. And, praise the Lord, he had shot not one, but two, geese that morning. Since the odds seemed to be in his favor, he prayed for a deer. He strolled forward to claim his prize. Almost certainly Charity could make a hat for Sam adorned with one of the turkey's tail feathers, and they'd have quills for pens.

His joy over the success of the hunt was diminished by his lack of progress in building the house. He glanced at the sky. If the snows held, or weren't as severe as he feared, he could possibly get the walls up this winter. All Amos's and Maggie's agreement said was a finished house. It didn't say anyone had to be living in it by the set time limit. Well, the floors and roof were on. It just lacked walls and a door. He could still win the wager.

"Let's go find that deer, son." Gabe grabbed the turkey by the spindly legs and stuffed it in a burlap sack.

"Hello, friend." Red Feather materialized from the brush like a vapor.

"Red Feather." Gabe smiled and nodded. "What brings you out this way?"

"I am searching for my brother's daughter."

Gabe's heart fell. It was worse than he imagined. The girl was most likely from Red Feather's tribe, and a family member at that. "I believe I have seen her.

Come. Share our lunch, and I will tell you what I know."

Gabe clutched his bag and led the way to a clearing. He doubted he would kill a deer that day, but he could relieve a friend's worries. If only he didn't have to do so while breaking the man's heart. He sat on a stump and motioned for Red Feather to do the same.

"You do not have good news for me." Red Feather could have been chiseled from stone, so hard was his features. He sat across from Gabe and stared with dark eyes.

"Someone stampeded my cattle two days ago." Gabe folded his hands, hanging them between his knees. "They fired off a few shots and sent the cattle toward my place. When I went looking for the culprit, I found a young girl. She had hit her head on a rock and died. I'm so sorry."

"Where is the girl?"

"My wife and I were headed to your camp with her body when we were accosted by five braves. I did not recognize them. I think they were hired by an enemy of mine who wanted me disposed of. We escaped, and they kept the girl."

Red Feather took a deep breath. "They will sell her body back to us. Who is this enemy of yours?"

Telling Red Feather about Amos would solve a lot of Gabe's problems. But he did not want the other man's death on his conscience. "I am not at liberty to tell you. Forgive me, my friend."

"This wounds me deeply." Red Feather's face darkened. "We are friends. Like brothers."

"I'm sorry. I can't have the man's death on my conscience. What can I do to lessen the pain of your niece's death?" Gabe met his stare.

Red Feather glanced at Sam. "The man who was to wed her believes in a life for a life."

Please, don't let him ask for my son.

"But, I cannot let you do that. You have a family that needs you." He waved a hand at Gabe's face. "It looks like you already paid a price with a beating." He stood. "I will discover the truth and make amends myself."

Gabe held out his hand. "You understand?"

Red Feather nodded and accepted the shake. "The Mighty God would not want you to tell me. But I do not plan to kill the man. Just to receive payment in the form of another sister, or a slave."

"What was she doing to so close to my home?" Gabe asked. "Surely she wasn't alone."

Red Feather shook his head. "She went with a small hunting party. They parted ways after she argued with her soon to be husband. They expected her to go home. When they went back for her, they could not find her. So, I am here." He turned and melted back into the tree line.

Gabe breathed deeply to steady his nerves. He had been friends with Red Feather for many years, but never knew exactly how the Indian would react when wronged. The death of a family member was a serious thing. Gabe said a prayer for the dead girl's relatives, and wondered, exactly, what form of payment was suitable for a woman's life. His friend's words about a new sister gave him pause, and he hoped Red Feather wouldn't set his sights on Charity.

*

Charity fought tears all the way home and felt like an idiot for doing so. Why should it feel like the end of the world because she wouldn't be spending time chipping away at cave walls or wading in icy creeks? Gold wouldn't buy Gabriel's love anyway. It might get him to keep her around, but after a while he would be frustrated and feel as if she had trapped him.

Even the cat's antics failed to cheer her when she opened the door to the soddy. Thanksgiving loomed, and a cloud of despair hung over her. Her life's aspirations amounted to nothing.

She halted mid-step. Her life aspirations or her father's? Charity collapsed into the nearest chair. Being rich was her father's dream. What was hers? To be loved. She was. If not by Gabriel, then by his children. Sam and Meg adored her as much as she did them. The thought of leaving ripped her heart out. She could refuse, she supposed, but who wanted a husband who didn't want her?

She supposed she could choose one of the other miners. Most of them had proposed to her at one time or another, and with women being as scarce as they were, she doubted many had gotten hitched in the last few months. Ugh. She was putting the cart before the horse. God might finally have mercy on her and convince Gabriel to ask her to stay. To ask her to be his wife in all ways. Could she even ask that he profess love for her?

Lady set up a fierce barking from the yard. Charity rushed to the door, blocking Meg inside. "Stay here, Meg." Charity glanced at the empty mantel. Of course Sam would have taken the second rifle. She bolted the door and parted the curtains at the window.

Amos Jenkins sat on his horse and stared at the house. He wore two pistols low on his hips.

Charity opened the window. "What do you want? You are not welcome here." She waved at Meg. "Get out of sight."

"Where is your husband?"

"In the barn. You should leave before he comes out." She put a hand to her chest to still her pounding heart, certain it could be heard from the yard.

"You lie." Amos glanced that way then back toward the house. "I'm tired of playing games, Mrs. Williams. When your husband returns, tell him it is time to settle this."

"Settle what? It isn't springtime yet. There are months left for him to win that silly bet."

"So, he has told you about our wager."

"Of course he has. I'm his wife." No need to tell the scoundrel she only knew the bare bones about their bet. Or that the subject touched a raw spot deep inside her. "Go away and come back in the spring."

Amos laughed. "Why don't we make a wager of our own, Mrs. Williams? If your husband fails to meet the terms, then you marry me."

27

Charity parted the curtains and looked into the yard as the first snowflakes fell. Hiram and Mabel climbed from their wagon, arms loaded with their contributions to the Thanksgiving meal. The aroma of baking turkey, basted with butter, filled the soddy. Life couldn't be better, or Charity any happier.

She and Gabriel still hadn't had any deep conversations, but they were coming. Both were subdued since his day of hunting, and her realization that finding gold wasn't in her future. Although the discovery had set her back mentally and emotionally, she felt a surprising freedom from a drive that was her father's, not her's.

"Happy Thanksgiving!" She threw open the door and ushered in her friends. "Your pies smell wonderful."

Gabe shook Hiram's hand. "Getting nasty outside. You going to be able to make it home all right?"

"Sure. Got the sled runners in the back of the wagon, but I doubt it'll snow enough today for those. Maybe in a few more weeks." Hiram freed Mabel of her coat and hung both of theirs on hooks by the door. He eyed the animals. "Going to be a bit snug in here, isn't it?"

"Yep." Gabe sighed. "Can't get Charity or the young'uns to banish the dogs to the barn."

"It's too cold. They would freeze." Charity opened the oven to baste the turkey, and smiled at the golden brown skin. Her first turkey dinner and it promised to be wonderful.

While the men sat in front of the fireplace and discussed winter coping skills, Mabel joined Charity in the kitchen corner. Sam and Meg tussled on the beds with the dogs, while Patches watched from under the table.

Mabel watched for a moment, then wiped a tear from her eye. "I would have liked to have children. But God had other plans."

Charity understood God having other plans. "I've always wanted a family, too." She grabbed a knife and chopped potatoes. "And for a while, at least, I do."

"You and Gabe still not had that talk?" Mabel opened a jar of beans and dumped them in a pan. "You ain't any closer to letting him know you want to stay?"

Charity glanced in the men's direction. "I want him to want me to stay. I don't want to ask."

Mabel shook her head. "Pride is the downfall of many a man, or woman."

"I don't know what I'm going to do if Gabriel doesn't want me." She whacked through a potato. "Accept a proposal from one of the other men in town, I suppose. Or maybe head farther west and see what trouble I can get into. I've heard opportunities abound, for men and women."

"Marriage vows should be taken more seriously than that, Charity." Mabel checked the water on the stove. "After all, it's a commitment set in place by God."

"My vow to Gabriel is very serious." Charity eyed her. "But, God hasn't seen fit to make my circumstances solid and binding. I have to do the best I can."

Mabel shrugged. "We should cheer up. It's Thanksgiving after all." She grinned. "We have much to be thankful for."

Charity glanced back at the men and children, the animals, the snug soddy over her head. Months ago, she had been shocked to discover she would live in a hole in the ground. Now, it was home. What would Gabriel do with it once he moved into the big house? "We do."

*

Once everyone sat around the table, Gabe carried his Bible from where he kept it on the mantel. "As I did on the Fourth of July, I found verses dealing with Thanksgiving." He took his seat at the head of the table. "Today, is a day we give thanks for God's provision. I'd like to read the verses, then possibly, we can each say one thing we are thankful for."

Charity paled and ducked her head. Mabel and Hiram nodded. The children grinned.

"I've been lax on reading God's Word, and I would like to rectify that starting today. Let us bow our heads for the blessing." Gabe cleared his throat. "Father, we come before You with Thanksgiving in our hearts. Thank You for the abundance of food before us, the roof over our heads, and the blessing of friends and family. Amen."

A chorus of amens rang out. Gabe opened his Bible. "*O give thanks unto the Lord; for he is good: because his mercy endureth forever.* That's in Psalms. In Ephesians, it says, *Giving thanks always for all things unto God and the Father in the name of our Lord Jesus Christ*, and finally in 1 Thessalonians, it says, *In every thing give thanks: for this is the will of God in Christ Jesus concerning you.*" Gabe closed the Bible. "Sam, what do these verses mean to you?"

"That I should be thankful for my food even though it's growing cold." He eyed a biscuit.

Charity snorted and covered her mouth with her napkin.

Gabe bit back a grin. "Yes, and I apologize. We can eat while we discuss God's reasons for us being thankful in all things."

Everyone dug into their meal except for Charity, who stared at her empty plate. Gabe laid his hand over hers. "Is something bothering you?"

She took a deep breath and met his gaze, her eyes as hard as emeralds. "Give thanks? I can understand giving thanks on a day like today when there's plenty of food and we are warm and snug in our home, but what about the other times? What about when me Ma and Da died? Ma died sick and in pain. Da died and left me with debts from his gambling. You tell me I'm to be thankful?" She pulled her hand free and slapped the table. "That those things were God's will for me?"

"God has a reason for everything He does." Gabe so wanted to comfort her, to give her the words that would soothe the pain in her heart. "We don't always know the reason right away." What could he say to show her God's love? He hadn't done a good job of being an example, although he had tried.

"I don't want to hear His reasons if it means losing someone I love." She stood. "I'm sorry for raising the issue. Continue eating without me." She grabbed her wool coat and stormed outside.

The room remained silent for a moment. Heat rose in Gabe's neck and face. His children looked stunned, then shrugged and went to eating.

"I'm sorry." Gabe hurried to follow Charity.

He found her sitting on a hay bale in the barn, staring at the two barn cats who tussled over a mouse. The horses snuffled a welcome. Without saying anything, he sat beside her and wrapped his arms around her. "I'm sorry about your parents."

She sniffed. "I'm sorry for ruining everyone's day."

"You didn't. They understand. Do you want to talk about it?"

"No. This is between me and God."

"So you do believe in God."

She pulled back and looked at him. "Of course I

believe. Only a fool wouldn't. My mother didn't raise a heathen."

He chuckled. "Well, God can handle your anger." He gave her a squeeze. She felt good in his arms. Her hair smelled like sunshine and lavender. A few strands pulled free of her bun and tickled his chin with silky fingers. If it weren't freezing, he would be tempted to stay a while. "Are you ready to come back in?"

She shook her head. "I'm embarrassed."

"Everyone was eating when I followed you, and I can hear your stomach growling. I'm mighty hungry myself."

"Fine." She pulled her coat tighter around herself. "I need to think of an explanation for the children."

"Not unless they ask. Sam and Meg will come to their own conclusion based on the fact your parents are dead, and you're sad. They lost their mother, too, remember?"

She nodded. "All right. I'm ready."

*

Charity followed him outside. The snow fell heavier, lending a strange hush to the property. Their footsteps crunched on the way to the house. When would she take control of her pain and her temper? She hadn't liked it that her mother to had lived in pain, taking laudanum every day. She had no control over her da's gambling. He had made his choices, and now Charity needed to make hers. She would have to deal with the past—and the future.

After hanging up her coat, she squared her

269

shoulders and faced the others at the table. "I apologize. Sometimes my grief overwhelms me." She marched to her seat and sat down before reaching for the platter of turkey.

Mabel patted her shoulder. "We understand."

At that moment, surrounded by her friends and family, Charity felt more loved than she had in a very long time, and for this she was very thankful. When they continued the discussion around the table, listing the things they were thankful for, having these special people with her was at the top of her list.

Later that night, after the Stoltzes left and everyone was in bed, she sat and stared into the fire. Gabriel's gentle snores filled the room. Outside, the snow continued to fall. At her feet, lay the two dogs, their heads keeping her feet warm.

Give thanks in all things. She could easily give thanks for this moment, this day, even, but the death of her parents, and the uncertainty of her future, gave her pause. She reached up and removed Gabriel's Bible from the mantel. Caressing the worn leather cover, she wondered what treasures were hidden in the pages.

She'd never owned one for herself, and rarely opened her ma's. The thought of reading the book so precious to her ma had seemed sacrilegious almost. Maybe it was time. Tomorrow, she'd dig it out of her trunk and read some of the notations written in her mother's sweet hand.

Ma would have been shocked at Charity's behavior at the supper table. She clutched the Bible to her chest.

One look from Ma's blue eyes would have had Charity straightening her attitude right away. Oh, she missed her so much. Da, too. He had been funny and accommodating, given to moments of drink, but how he had loved Charity. Ma had held the family together.

Charity glanced at the curtain dividing the males from the females. She had no healthy father to compare to her husband, or to God for that matter. Except for his wager, Gabriel was the complete opposite of Patrick O'Connell. Another thing for Charity to give thanks for. She smiled. Now, she thought of a long list of thanks. She replaced the Bible in its favored spot and headed to bed. Maybe she would take a few minutes to speak with God for the first time in two years.

*

Amos should never have approached the house two weeks ago. Now, he'd spent the afternoon staring at the Williams homestead, occasionally catching glimpses of the happy holiday supper whenever someone opened the door. Why did he torment himself so?

He rubbed his jaw. The bruise had long ago disappeared, but not the power behind Gabriel's rage. Amos was almost tempted to tell Gabe to forget the wager. That he had had enough of the bitterness between them. Maggie was most likely spinning in her grave at the way the two men she cared the most about were acting. Not to mention how far away from God Amos had wandered.

Bitterness ate away at his soul, leaving no room for

love or forgiveness. What would he have done had Charity said yes to his ridiculous proposal? He would definitely have married the woman. A man didn't see many as beautiful as her, but what kind of life would they have had? Would she marry him because she felt she had no choice? Maggie's children would want to stay with Gabe. After all, they knew no other father.

Amos stared into his fire. His life was a lonely existence. Maybe, instead of lusting after something that didn't belong to him, he should look for a wife of his own. Maybe one of them mail order brides some of the miners were sending off for. He could specify a woman with yellow hair and black-eyed Susan eyes like Maggie's.

Wouldn't much matter what the rest of her looked like, as long as she was able to fill some of the loneliness in his life. It gave him something to think about. He had a choice to make. Continue his feud with Gabe, or settle down with a woman of his own.

28

After her uncomfortable conversation the night before with God, Charity was determined to make this day the best one yet. A deeper chill than in the previous days filled the soddy. She pulled the quilts higher around her chin and glanced at the body beside her. Only the top of Meg's curly head showed.

Charity would fix oatmeal for breakfast. Something hot that would stick to their ribs on the coldest day they had had so far. She patted Meg's hip. "Time to get up. Dress warm to fetch the eggs." She glanced at the window. It was hard to tell through the oil cloth, but she thought it might still be snowing.

The other bed lay empty, telling her that Gabriel and Sam were already at work on their morning chores. Her late night conversation with God caused her to sleep in. How early had Hiram and Mabel woke and headed home? "Come on, sleepyhead. The men are ahead of us."

Meg groaned and rolled over. "It's too cold."

"We have a lot to do today." Charity threw back the covers and grabbed her dress. "Laundry." Which would not be fun in this cold.

She would need to string a line across the room, and she definitely did not relish hauling water from the frigid outdoors onto her new wood floors. "Not to mention reading and figuring. We don't want you and Sam to get behind. I need to make bread and have Sam bring in more firewood. We have a full day of work ahead of us."

She leaped from bed and hurriedly dressed. One glance out the window showed that snow did indeed still fall. She grinned. Maybe it was deep enough for bowls of snow dribbled with honey. A treat the children would love.

By the time the rest of the family returned, Charity had breakfast ready and hot coffee made. She set out the bowls, and poured two mugs of coffee. She greeted her family with a smile, but pulled back when Gabriel stepped to her side and leaned in close.

"Is it bad?" She asked, taking a step back.

"The storm?" Gabriel shook his head. "No. We won't get a bad one for a few more weeks."

"Good." Charity turned back to the stove with a lighter heart. Her skin prickled when Gabriel followed. She had nowhere else to go, and he stood way too close smelling of shaving cream and wood smoke. And there she stood in a stained apron and her hair not even put up yet.

"I've given the young'uns chores to do after breakfast," he whispered. "So you and I can sit and have a serious conversation."

"Oh?" Her spine tingled. She knew they needed to talk. Had needed to for some time, but why now? Why today?

He grinned and tugged at a curl. "Don't worry. You didn't do anything wrong. I love your hair down."

Mercy. The man could make her legs go weak.

Her appetite fled. He was right, of course, but the thought of sitting across the table with just Gabriel staring back at her was enough to make her ill. "I've a list of chores of me own to do."

"They can wait." He laid a hand on her shoulder. "This talk is way over due, Charity."

She nodded and removed the pan from the stove. "You're right, of course." What had he and Hiram talked about in front of the fire yesterday while she and Mabel cleaned up after Thanksgiving supper? Had Hiram given him pointers on dealing with a strong-willed woman or had he shown Gabriel how to turn Charity into a submissive wife, like Mabel?

She forced herself to eat, knowing she would need the energy for the conversation and chores afterwards, but the motion was mechanical. The children chattered, excited about the snowfall. Obviously the cold in the barn wouldn't bother them overly much.

By the time everyone finished, the dishes were cleared away, and the children outside, Charity's hands trembled. She smoothed them down the front of her apron and took her seat beside Gabriel.

He smiled. "Don't be so frightened. I won't bite you, and you've done nothing wrong. Am I so fearsome?"

She shook her head and exhaled forcibly. She had worried a mite that she had angered him. "What's on your mind, Gabriel?"

*

Gabe fiddled with the floppy brim of his hat, working the fabric between his fingers. Why should a conversation with a little bit of a woman make him so nervous?

Hiram had mentioned the day before that Charity had a problem with gambling because of her father losing everything they owned. Gabe wasn't a gambler. Not really. He made one stupid wager, but was indeed in danger of losing everything he owned, just like Charity's father. Must he pay the price for the rest of his life? He was doing the best he could do with a bad situation. Regardless, Charity deserved an explanation that should have been given to her months ago.

He took a deep breath and stared into her green eyes. "As you know, Sam and Meg are not my biological children." She nodded. "Maggie's husband died in the War Between the States. After his death, Maggie came to Montana with Amos Jenkins."

Charity's eyes widened. "He's her cousin, correct?"

"Distant cousin. Anyway, Amos has loved Maggie for years, ever since we were kids, so of course he

276

wouldn't allow her to travel to Montana alone." He didn't want to dwell on the ramifications of those actions. Maggie's reputation had suffered for quite a while. Folks didn't relent on their suspicions until Maggie married Gabe. Even Gabe wasn't totally convinced about nothing improper going on during their trip across country, but had chosen not to dwell on what he couldn't change.

"Why did she come?" Charity stood and fetched the pot of coffee and refilled their mugs. "A widow with two children? Couldn't have been an easy task."

"Most likely not. Maggie's first husband was her soul mate. She said she couldn't bear staying in the place they had lived together."

"She didn't love you?" Charity frowned.

"Sure, she did. But I knew I wasn't the one she would have chosen had John still been alive. Anyway, Once they got here, Maggie needed a co-signer for the land. Her husband left her money, and she got more from the sale of their place in Missouri, but it wasn't enough. Amos proposed, telling her that if they married, he would purchase the land for her. Maggie refused. She cared for Amos, just not as a husband." Gabe took a drink. Amazing how dry one's throat got while talking. Or maybe it was nerves about how Charity would react to his story.

"So, he cosigned. Then when Maggie married me, he got a bit angry." An understatement for sure. The man was madder than a rabid wolf. "Said I stole Maggie from him."

"Did you know Maggie before she moved here?"

"Sure, I did. We grew up together. Attended the same school. I didn't intentionally follow her out here, but was pretty pleased when I discovered she was widowed and living in Montana. I came out here after the war with hopes of being a rancher and found a wife with ample land to make that dream a reality. Having that woman be someone I'd cared about most of my life was an added bonus." Gabe studied Charity's face. She gazed at him with the utmost attention. Encouraged, he continued.

"Amos wanted to go back on his word about the land when Maggie refused to marry him. This was before I got here. So, she made an addendum that she would have a "real" house built by the end of five years. One with wood walls and a roof. Amos said a soddy wasn't a real house.

"She was living in her wagon with the children when I arrived, but I'm rambling." He leaned back in his chair, concentrating on his line of thought. "Let me backtrack a minute. Maggie's husband died in 1864. She moved out here almost immediately. The following spring I arrived, and she was busy digging out this place and not making a lot of progress.

"I offered her marriage, she accepted, and I finished the soddy. Then Maggie got bit by a snake, and Amos showed up one day, even angrier than before, claiming I didn't know how to care for a woman. I told him the house he claimed should be here would be built by spring of 1869 or he could have everything. The land, the creek, the barn. I was foolish enough to put the terms to paper. I was suffering grief and guilt on my own without him spouting nonsense. That was a big mistake, and I should never have said it. But, I did. Well, spring is fast approaching, and I'm in danger of losing everything but the horse I rode in on."

Charity gnawed her bottom lip while Gabe waited nervously for her to say something. He didn't think she would leave him. Not this close to winter. She had known a little of the circumstances that led him to marry her, but it was way past time for her to know it all.

"So, you see, I'm not really a gambling man, you can rest assured in that area."

She stared at him for a moment before answering. "Yet, you not being a gambling man as you say, wagered all that you have, in a weak moment, with your enemy. That's a pretty big gamble, don't you think? For a non-gambling man, of course."

*

Charity moved away from the table and began measuring coffee for a fresh pot. Anything to keep Gabriel from staring into her face. He was right. They needed the conversation. She just didn't know how to respond to what he told her.

She understood the reason behind what Gabriel did, but couldn't give her approval. He stood to lose everything. Even, possibly, his children, since Amos was a blood relation. She bowed her head. What could she possibly do to help that she hadn't already done? She could not control the weather or circumstances that arose. She turned to face her husband.

"What do you want me to do?" She held the coffee-pot like a shield.

"Understand."

"I do, but I can't condone it. Not after what me da put me and Ma through." She set the pot back on the stove. "We had a good life in Ireland, or so we thought. We had no idea Da was making most of his money gambling. We thought his employer overly generous and blessed our good fortune. We had a fine stone cottage. Then, we came to America. Ma took sick with a fever and died. Da gambled even more and lost everything. Then, he decided to mine for gold and was killed when a cave collapsed. I took to doing laundry, and you know the rest."

She poured a pan of hot water into the washbasin and swished her hand to make suds. She loved him, she could admit that to herself now, and that pained her, too. Loving a gambling man was dangerous. Sure, he said he had only bet the once, but how could she be certain? No, it was best she guard her heart against the type of betrayal her Ma suffered through.

"Has life with me and the children been so bad?" The sad tone in his voice caused her to look back. The vulnerable look on his face was almost her undoing.

"No, it's a fine life." One that contained memories she would cherish forever.

"But you will allow one mistake to keep us from pursuing something ... more?"

What was he saying?

"Pa!" Sam burst through the door. "That man you don't like is here, and he's got guns."

"Wait." Charity held up a hand to stop Gabriel from charging outside. "Amos Jenkins came by the day you went hunting. Said he wanted to settle things. I'm sorry I didn't tell you."

Gabriel gave her a stern look and grabbed his rifle. "You should have told me. We'll settle things for sure alright. I won't have him bothering my family."

Charity grabbed her coat and raced after him. "Don't do anything foolish, Gabriel Williams."

"Stay in the house." Gabriel glared. "The children, too."

Charity wrapped her arms around Meg and Sam and stood in the doorway. Amos Jenkins sat on his chestnut mustang, his lips stretched into a thin line under his moustache. His two pistols were holstered on his hips.

"Did your woman tell you I was here asking for you a while back?"

Gabriel stepped forward, his rifle cradled in his arms. Charity left the children in the house and stood beside him. She wouldn't let him face his nemesis alone.

"She told me," Gabe said.

Amos nodded toward the new house. "Not finished, and the snow is falling. Looks like I'm going to win, unless you want to make another wager. Winner takes all?"

"I don't care to wager again." A muscle ticked in Gabriel's jaw. "We'll leave things as they stand. The house will be finished."

"We'll see. If not, I get everything you have. Including your family. Did your wife tell you I asked her to wed me if you fail?"

29

"Let's cut down a tree!" Gabriel called from outside.

Charity put down the scarf she knitted and grabbed her coat. Already the children raced to join their father. When she had mentioned getting a tree the day before, Gabriel had seemed to shrug it off, calling it a silly waste of time. Now, here they were, heading into the woods. She motioned for the dogs to follow.

Gabriel waited outside, an axe rested on his shoulder. "Ready to get that tree?"

Charity grinned and nodded. After her conversation with Gabriel and the subsequent visit from Amos, things were tense again around the Williams homestead. When Amos rode away, Gabriel had stalked to the barn, not to return until supper time. Then, he made it clear he was unhappy that Charity hadn't told him about Amos's visit around Thanksgiving. She sighed.

She should have told him, yes, but the damage was done. No sense in acting as if the world had ended.

Maybe it was the fact Amos wanted to wed Charity if Gabriel lost the wager that had his long johns in a bind. Not that she had any intention of agreeing to such a preposterous proposal. She had told Gabriel that, but the silly man wouldn't listen. Pride was a powerful thing. She doubted she would ever understand its mighty hold on men.

Clouds pregnant with snow filled the sky. A breeze, cold enough to set Charity's eyes to tearing, flew across them, singing through the branches of pine trees. She buttoned her coat, wiped her sleeve across her eyes, and followed her family.

Gabriel led them at a steady pace down the creek before veering up the mountain. As they traveled, the trees thickened, casting them into a twilight darkness. "Where are we going?"

"There's a meadow farther on," Gabe shouted over his shoulder. "That I promise will have the perfect tree."

Charity exchanged a skeptical glance with Meg and continued, her leg muscles burning with the effort. Gabriel and Sam climbed with barely a struggled breath. Despite the cold and rugged terrain, pleasure filled Charity at the simple tradition of chopping down a tree for Christmas. For as long as she could remember, her da had always gotten her one, even if it was only small enough to sit on a table.

"We've never had a tree in the house before," Meg said, slipping her mittened hand into Charity's.

"Then you're in for a wonderful surprise. Once we get home we'll make garland. Keep your eyes open for lush green swags to hang above the fireplace." Charity smiled down. "A tree is a wonderful tradition passed down from generation to generation in Europe."

"Here we are." Gabriel stepped back and ushered them into a meadow covered with an unspoiled carpet of snow. A small clusters of young firs clustered in the center of the meadow, highlighted by a break in the clouds.

Charity clapped her hands. What a gift they'd been given. Her gaze lit on the perfect tree.

*

Charity set the last wrapped gift under the Christmas tree and stepped back. Paper garlands and fabric bows made the small pine festive. Swags of greenery adorned the mantel.

The children had finally fallen asleep an hour ago. Gabriel labored on something in the barn. Charity lowered herself into his leather chair and prepared to enjoy the quiet for just a little while.

Tonight was Christmas Eve and her husband was holed up in the barn. What would it be like to snuggle with him in front of the fire? To know they would share a bed that night and rejoice, together, at the glee on the children's faces come morning when they opened their gifts? Would he like the books she had purchased for him? The shirt she had sewed?

She sighed and rubbed her hands over the worn

leather chair arms. She should be sitting in the rocker. This chair was Gabriel's domain, but sitting here made her feel closer to him, despite her wanting to remain at a distance. Oh, life and the emotions that went with it were too complicated to dwell on so late at night.

She lowered the wick on the lamp and headed to bed. The children would wake them early.

*

Gabe sanded the last piece of the pine nativity he had carved for Charity, then laid the baby Jesus in the manger. He hoped she had finally gone to bed so he could have the nativity set up under the tree when she woke in the morning. He glanced at the carved doll cradle for Meg, and the new rifle for Sam. He had worked late many nights out in the barn, but the looks on his family's faces would be worth the lack of sleep.

He hefted the items in his arms and trudged through the falling snow to the house. Charity had left the lamp lit and more packages sat under the tree. The scent of pine filled the room, and Gabe smiled at the decorating. The tree sat in a corner, taking up more space than they could afford to lose. He had definitely missed a woman's touch in the place over the last couple of years.

The nativity looked great under the tree, Mary and Joseph watching over the baby Jesus while shepherds looked on. He had even had time to carve the wisemen and some sheep. The nativity wasn't the only gift he had for his wife. He prayed he had done well in choosing something feminine.

He wrapped Sam's rifle in an old blanket and leaned it against the wall. Satisfied he had done everything he could to make tomorrow perfect, he shucked his clothes and crawled into bed.

The next morning, Meg and Sam jumped on him while Charity smiled. "Merry Christmas," they called.

"Merry Christmas." He waited for Charity to turn around before pulling on his pants.

She had donned a ratty robe over her flannel nightclothes and tied her hair back in a green ribbon. "Should we have breakfast or do presents first?"

"Presents!" The children dashed to the tree. The dogs barked, joining in the frivolity.

"Wait." Gabriel removed his Bible from the mantel. "We read from Luke first. Same as every year."

"Someone hung up our stockings!" Meg pulled hers free from a nail, ripping Charity's careful stitching. Gabe glanced at her, eyebrows raised.

She blushed and nodded. "A nativity? It's beautiful, Gabriel."

"There's an orange and nuts inside our stockings. And a peppermint stick!" Sam dumped his on the floor and shoved Prince away.

Gabe stepped closer to Charity. "Thank you. I hadn't thought of stockings."

She shrugged, and took a seat in the rocker. "It's what a mother does, I'm sure."

"Maybe so." He laughed and placed a kiss on the top of her curly head. The fact she didn't pull away, gave him hope. Hope that someday, she would accept a declaration of love from him.

It also pleased him that she didn't seem as reluctant to hear him read from the Good Word as she once was. By the time he finished reading of the first Christmas, Sam and Meg were fairly bursting out of their skin. Charity seemed rather excited, too, and the first scents of roasting goose began to fill their home.

"Sam, why don't hand out the gifts?" Gabe replaced his Bible.

"Yours is heavy, Pa!" Sam pushed a two-foot high package toward him. "I know what it is. Open it."

"Let's let Meg go first. She's the youngest."

"Yippee." Meg unwrapped a new rag doll and hugged it to her chin. Wrapped with the toy was a dress for Meg that matched the emerald one the doll wore. Gabe recognized the fabric and was glad to see something of Maggie's benefit the children. "Thanks, Ma. I will love her forever. Is that cradle for my doll?"

Gabe nodded. "Yep. Made it myself. Sam, take a look in the corner." He thought his grin would split his face when tears welled in his son's eyes at sight of the gun.

"It's mine?"

"All yours. Respect it, now." Gabe turned to Charity.

With her cheeks still pink, she unwrapped a thick present. Inside were yards of scarlet velvet and pearl studded hair combs. "Oh, Gabriel." Her eyes shimmered in the firelight. "I can make a beautiful cloak with this. I've never had anything so fine as this fabric and these combs."

"You're welcome." He unwrapped his gift, and gawked at the stack of books. "Where in heaven's name did you find this many? We could start a library." He lifted the top one. "Great Expectations? Uncle Tom's Cabin?"

She beamed. "A miner turned them in to the mercantile for credit. Do you like them?"

"I've books to read all winter. Books the children can read. Books to stock shelves in our new home." The gesture was almost more than Gabe could bear. She couldn't have gotten him a better gift if he had told her what to purchase.

"It's a gift we can all enjoy, for sure. Open your others."

He unwrapped a blue chambray shirt from Meg and thick, store-bought socks from Sam. Where had they gotten the money for the gifts and books? He studied Charity's face, not willing to ask a question that would wipe the happiness from it. He would accept her gracious gifts and keep his mouth shut.

*

The children dressed in their Christmas finery. Charity wore her best dress, a deep blue wool skirt and white blouse. She protected her clothes with a ruffled red apron she had made special for the occasion. Lighting candles on the table for breakfast, she called the others to eat and wished the day could go on forever.

"You look beautiful, Charity." Gabriel took his seat

at the head of the table.

She flushed. He had brought the goose in from the smoke house earlier and she had put it in the stove before presents. The mouth-watering aroma of roasting meat filled the house and reminded her of Christmas with her ma and da.

After breakfast, they would sit in front of the fire while the children played. Meg with her doll, and Sam with the tin soldiers he'd discovered stashed behind the tree. Gabriel would read, and Charity would crochet a new afghan to adorn their home. They would make a picture of the perfect loving family. A picture she would hold in her heart, much as Jesus's mother, Mary, had pondered words after the visit from the angel.

Not that she compared herself to the Virgin Mary. Far from it, but she would treasure, and wonder, about the day's perfectness her entire life. Long after she left this place and headed only God knew where.

Despite Gabriel's reluctance to get out his former wife's good dishes, she had dug them out of a crate in the barn and set the table with the white china adorned with blue roses. Today's meals deserved to be served on something pretty, even if that something once belonged to someone else.

She knew Gabriel wondered where the money for the gifts came from, and she admired his restraint in not asking. Once spring came, if she left, she would take in laundry again and build up her nest egg again. For now, she counted the money well spent.

Gabriel looked down at the dishes. "I'll have to buy

you your own someday. These were Maggie's when she was married to her first husband."

"And we'll keep them for Meg to use in her home someday." Charity set a plate of flapjakes in front of him.

"You don't want your own things?" He studied her face.

She sat. "Of course. Every woman does."

"You're avoiding the subject, Mrs. Williams." He waved his fork at her.

Must he tease her so? She didn't want to dwell on what would happen in a few months. She wanted to enjoy the day. Fine. She would play along. "Next Christmas you can buy me the finest set of china in Montana."

"It's a deal."

She smiled. She definitely enjoyed the light-hearted, happy Gabriel to the sullen one focused primarily on winning a bet. There was still hope that over the long winter months, her husband would fall in love with her. "The snow is coming down harder."

"Won't be pleasant taking care of the animals later, but at least it ain't a blizzard. When we get one of those, you can hear the wind howl down the chimney. Even a sod house doesn't stay completely warm in a blizzard." He cut into his pancakes. "I remember once, we all had to sleep in the same bed to stay warm. It wasn't safe to have a fire. Thankfully, that isn't common, though."

Gracious, she hoped not. She wouldn't get a lick of

sleep if she shared a bed with Gabriel.

The day unfolded just as she had envisioned. The dogs lay under the table, Meg and Sam played in front of the fire, and Gabriel and Charity sat in their favorite chairs while he read and she crocheted with rose-colored yarn. If Charity were an artist, she would sketch the image to keep forever. Maybe even frame it to adorn a future wall.

She laughed at her fanciful thoughts, and wondered whether she would ever have a permanent family of her own.

30

The year 1869 came on the skirts of a snowstorm. Not the slight flurries that ushered in the end of 1868, but a bone-chilling blizzard.

Charity wrapped her sweater tighter around her and untacked the oil cloth from the window in order to see exactly what the storm was doing outside. Despite the blazing fire in the fireplace, the room was chilled by a wind that sneaked under the door and blew hard enough to find its way through the window covering. She tacked it back in place.

The warm glow of Christmas seemed months past. Tempers flared from the four humans and three animals confined in the small space. Many times Gabriel threatened to banish the animals to the barn. Charity shivered. How could anything stay warm out there?

"The weather is only going to get worse. I thought as the day progressed, maybe the storm would lessen. I suppose it won't." Gabriel tugged on his boots. "I'd best care for the livestock now before it's pitch dark."

"A body can't see out there as it is." Charity faced him. "Will the lantern work?"

"I'll keep a good hold of the rope. I've done this many times before. I've a lantern in the barn." He planted a kiss on the top of her head. "Keep the children and dogs indoors."

She nodded. A few times since Christmas, Gabriel had given her small tokens of affection, like now. The gestures gave her hope that maybe he would love her enough to ask her to stay. "Be careful." She wrapped a scarf she had made him tightly around his neck, mouth, and nose.

"I will," he mumbled through the yarn. "I'll be as hungry as a bear when I'm done."

"Supper will be waiting. Venison stew with vegetables from our garden." She watched him go, then swept away the snow that had flown in when he opened the door. She sat at the kitchen table and called the children away from their toys. They could squeeze in time to practice their sums. She turned up the lamp and slid a slate and slate pencil to each child.

"One hour, that's all I ask." She grabbed her mending to keep her hands occupied while they worked, and to keep her mind off the storm raging outside.

Time passed. Slate pencils scratched across slates. Charity's knitting needles clacked a steady rhythm as she worked on a new shawl, having set her mending aside over an hour ago.

A crack ricocheted. Possibly a tree branch breaking.

Charity jumped and met the frightened gazes of Meg and Sam. Enough was enough. Over an hour and there was no sign of Gabriel. She would have to go look for him. What if he were lying in the snow somewhere, freezing to death? The sun would set soon and the temperature would drop fast. She could not sit back and do nothing.

"All right, children. I'm going to the barn to help your father so he finishes the chores quicker. It's taking much longer is this horrible weather." She stood and buttoned her sweater, then slid her arms into her coat, feet into boots, and covered her head with a wool scarf. "If we're not back within—a" She glanced at the mantel clock and pulled on a pair of gloves. "Thirty minutes, eat without us. We'll be back soon."

Meg grabbed her sleeve. "No, Ma. Pa said to stay here."

"It does take longer to do chores in the winter," Sam added. "Wait just a little longer."

Charity peeked out the door. The wind had increased, filling the world with whirling white. Staying put just a while longer sounded like a wonderful idea, except for the nagging feeling that something was horribly wrong.

*

Gabe removed his gloves and stuck his hands under his arms in a futile attempt to warm them. His breath plumed. He couldn't remember the last time he had been this cold, or been in a blizzard this severe. Sure, it snowed in the Montana mountains, but this seemed excessive.

"Well, boy, hopefully, this will keep you warm enough." He tossed an extra saddle blanket over Rogue's back then moved to do the same to Charity's and Sam's horses. There wasn't anything he could do for the cattle. They were grouped by a thick stand of trees that he prayed would be enough to cut the worst of the wind. He certainly did not want to brave the weather to check on them again. Once was more than enough. He had thought the wind would blow him right out of his boots, and the hike to the corral, battling the fierce wind, had taken over an hour.

He opened the barn door and stared into the increasing snow. Visibility was nil. The howl of the wind rivaled a pack of wolves.

It would be foolish to go outside right now, even using the rope to guide him back to the house. Not with the strength of the wind. He settled on a hay bale as close to Rogue as the horse would let him, in order to use the animal's body heat, and prepared to wait.

Charity and the children would be frantic, but not as worried as they would be if he were lost in the storm. Maybe he could signal them somehow. Would they be able to see a lantern's light through the swirling snow? It was worth a try.

After several attempts to get his frozen fingers to work, he managed to light the lantern and hung it on a hook outside the door. The glass dome protected the flame from the wind, but for how long, Gabe didn't know. He settled back on his hay bale and leaned against Rogue.

The animal was so warm. Gabe was tempted to hunt down the barn cats and stick them in his coat. Their bodies would put off heat, but the things were so feral, they'd most likely claw him to death. They weren't anything like their cuddly sibling Patches.

He shivered and second guessed his idea of remaining in the barn. Supper should be waiting on the stove for him. A thick venison stew that would stick to a man's ribs and warm him all the way to his toes. Yep, Charity had turned into a right fine cook. She didn't seem to spurn his affectionate gestures either. Yep, things were looking up for them.

Lord, don't let her do anything foolish. Like come to look for him.

*

This was the craziest thing Charity had ever done. But after another hour without Gabriel, even the children were worried. She couldn't take another minute of their puppy dog glances.

Her eyes watered from the cold. The wind found its way through her layers of clothing and bit at her skin with razor teeth. She could barely feel the guide rope through her gloves. Maybe she should go back. She had to be at least half way to the barn by now. It made more sense to continue forward where she could find Gabriel, warm up, then make the trek back with him. Was that the glow of a lantern? Surely,

Gabriel wasn't still outside in this.

Oh, what if he was out with the cattle? Charity stopped and glanced around her. In this world of all-encompassing white, she had no idea which direction the corral was.

She was so cold, her bones rattled. She glanced behind her and in front of her, torn about which direction she should go. Fetch Gabriel, or go back and sit by the fire?

A wolf howled, or was it the wind? The storm seemed to increase with each passing minute. Charity drowned in a sea of white, blind to the world around her.

A sharp gust tangled her skirts around her legs. She slid and fell. The rope! She would never find it now. She climbed to her feet and, with hands outstretched in front of her, she shuffled to where she thought she had seen the lantern light.

She was going the wrong way. Surely she should have reached the barn by now. Charity switched directions. She stumbled and fell again. The wet snow dampened her skirts causing her to shiver harder. Would she die mere feet from her own home? Frozen to death in a snowstorm? Oh, how that would devastate the children.

She had to make it. For their sakes. They couldn't stand to lose another mother.

Something crunched under her boots. Ice covering the creek? She turned around again, hoping she headed toward the house this time. Surely, a person could only go in circles so much before running into something familiar, right?

She blinked back tears before they could fall and soak into her scarf or leave ice tracks on her cheeks. There had not been a time when Charity could remember being this frightened. "Hello! Can anyone hear me?"

If nothing else, walking kept the blood flowing. She ducked her head against the wind and continued, increasing her pace, occasionally shouting out a cry for help.

*

Gabe jerked awake. Was that a cry for help? He leaped to his feet and made his way to the door. Struggling against the wind, he finally got it open, and strained to hear the sound again. "Hello? Is there someone out there? Charity?"

Please, God, don't let it be her. Snow had a way of playing tricks on a man, leading him to believe he saw and heard something that wasn't there.

The lantern had blown off the hook. Gabe took a deep breath, grabbed the rope in his left hand, and slowly began to make his way to the house. He should never have fallen asleep, but Rogue's body warmth and soft snuffles had been as effective as a lullaby.

There it was again. The cry for help. Or was it a trick of the wind? Gabe was close enough to the house that he could detect the warm lantern glow through the window. There was mere minutes before he could sit in front of the fire.

He stood still for a moment and listened. Nothing but the wind. He decided the cry had been nothing but his imagination. He increased his pace to the house, his stomach growling in anticipation of a hot meal.

A wolf howl sliced through the late afternoon. Was the wind lessening? Did he dare hope the storm was blowing itself out? Visibility still wasn't good, but he could make out the outline of the barn behind him and the white mound of the soddy in the other direction. The lamp's glow was brighter.

Another wolf howled. He turned back to make sure the latch on the barn was secure. The cattle would have to fend for themselves. He prayed he wouldn't lose any to the storm or to predators.

By the time he reached his front door, he wondered whether he would ever be warm again. He shoved his way inside and stomped the snow from his boots.

"Pa!" Meg and Sam launched themselves at him.

Gabe braced himself against their onslaught and glanced around the room while loosening his scarf. His heart sank. "Where's your Ma?"

31

Charity sagged against a tree. The fierce wind had finally slowed, and she could make out her surroundings. Unfortunately, nothing looked familiar. How could she have passed the soddy *and* the barn? She should have run into one of them; stumbled past the corral; heard the lowing of cattle. She was going to die out here. Night was falling. She was going to freeze and some unfortunate hunter would find her come spring.

She wiped her eyes and nose with the end of her scarf and pushed onward. Maybe she headed toward Mabel and Hiram's homestead. But, she didn't remember this many trees or such a steep incline. She headed up the mountain.

A wolf's howl sent shivers up her spine. She whipped around trying to locate where the chilling sound came from. Would a wolf attack an adult? Would they be hungry enough after only the first blizzard to want to eat her?

Her heart pounded loud enough to drown out the sounds around her. She needed to find shelter before it grew completely dark and she was at the mercy of wild animals. Was Gabriel looking for her? Surely by now, he was. She must have been wandering for well over an hour.

The temptation to sit and wait came over her. But, if she did, she would definitely freeze before being found. Already she struggled to keep her eyes open. Continuing in the direction that led only God knew where could also result in her death, but moving meant keeping warmer. She hunched farther in her coat and put one foot in front of the other. The fact she might die before telling Gabriel she loved him, ripped at her heart.

*

"How long ago did she leave?" Gabe retied his scarf.

"More than an hour," Sam answered. "You didn't see her? You must have passed her."

"No." Gabe's heart stopped. Charity had done the unthinkable. Gone out into the storm. Thank God, it was waning. "You two stay here. Keep warm. I'll go looking for her. Hold onto Prince because I'm taking Lady, and I don't want to worry about a pup with the wolves." Maybe the dog could find Charity, even with the falling snow.

"Here, Pa." Meg thrust a chunk of bread in his

hands. "It ain't stew, but you gotta eat."

"Thanks, sweetheart. I'm much obliged." He cupped her cheek and stared into brown eyes shimmering with tears. "Don't fret. I'll find your Ma." Or die trying. *God protect her from the cold.*

"Come on, girl." He motioned for Lady to follow him. He felt a moment's remorse at coaxing the dog out into the weather, but finding Charity was more important than the dog's comfort. He grabbed a knapsack from a nail by the door, giving him the tools he would need to start a fire, and Charity's red cloak. The color would help her feel better while she warmed up from the cold. Her old jacket was so worn.

Sam thrust a bedroll at him. "You taking Rogue?"

"Yes. I'm hoping it won't be too difficult for him. It will be faster than going on foot." Charity left over an hour ago. With the way the wolves seemed to be on the move, he might already be too late.

*

Charity found a stout stick to help her walk. Her feet ached. Her mind went numb an hour ago. Sleep sounded very good. Instead of leaving the woods for open ground, she seemed to be moving into thicker trees and upward. Everything looked so different covered in snow.

A wolf howled closer than before. She wanted to join her cries with the animal's. Instead, she forced herself to move faster. Eventually she would have to hit some sign of civilization, right? An Indian village or a homestead? How many neighbors did Gabriel have? She should have asked.

After what she judged to be an hour, the wind died, the snow stopped, and stars winked between the dissolving clouds. Footfalls padded around her, and Charity caught glimpses of dark shadows darting among the trees. The howls had stopped to be replaced by snarls. Instead, the moon and stars glittered off yellow eyes fixed on her.

She clutched her stick tighter. She wouldn't go down without a fight. The snarling grew closer. She glimpsed a fire through the trees, and ran. She burst into a clearing, turned, and brandished her stick.

"Mrs. Williams?"

Charity glanced over her shoulder. Amos Jenkins grabbed his rifle and fired three shots into the air, scattering the wolves.

"Mr. Jenkins." Charity sagged with relief. A fire blazed from the center of the clearing. Next to it was a lean-to thick with pine branches. She dropped her stick and rushed toward the fire. Pain pricked her fingers as they warmed. Was that coffee in the pot? "I am so thankful to see you. How did you weather the storm out here alone?"

"I managed." Amos hunkered down opposite her. "How long have your been out here? *Why* are you out here? If I hadn't gotten stranded myself, you could have wandered for days, if you didn't freeze to death first."

"That thought did occur to me. May I?" She reached for the pot and the mug next to him

He nodded. "Help yourself. There are beans in the

pan, if you're hungry."

She wrapped her fingers around the hot mug. Heaven. She met Amos's hard gaze. Though his words were cordial, his manner was colder than the snow. It seemed as if she inconvenienced him. "I do appreciate the coffee, Mr. Jenkins. Very much. I'm sure Gabriel will also appreciate any aid you give me. If it is a problem for you to take me home, could you point me in the right direction?"

"I'm afraid that won't be possible." Amos poked at the wood in the fire pit with a stick. "I am headed to the Crow village. Seems I am responsible for the death of one of their young women, and they are dreadfully unhappy. You are the solution to my problem. If I give them you, maybe they will stop hunting me." He grinned.

"What were you going to do if I had not stumbled upon you?"

Amos shrugged. "I was hoping to barter several some horses," He motioned to a couple of horses over his shoulder. "For the girl's death. I no longer need to do so."

Charity dropped the mug, turned, and ran. A breath later, Amos tackled her to the ground. Her face froze from contact with the ground.

"I really was hoping you would cooperate." He got to his feet and yanked her to hers. "Now, I'll have to tie you up and hope you don't freeze."

"You won't get away with this." Charity struggled. "Gabriel will have your head."

"I won't need my head if the Indians take my scalp. Circumstances are more promising now." He pushed her down as close to the fire as he could, and bound her hands and feet. "If I were you, I would pray the wolves don't come investigating during the night."

"I didn't have the opportunity to eat, Mr. Jenkins. Or finish my coffee. Please untie my hands."

"You should have thought of that before you tried to run."

Charity glared. Amos wasn't as smart as he thought he was. He obviously didn't know Red Feather was Gabriel's good friend, but she wouldn't be the one to give him that information. She scooted to where she had dropped the mug, wrapped her hands around it, and managed to wedge it between two rocks so she could pour in more coffee. When she had finished, she tossed Amos a confident grin.

He frowned and grabbed a bedroll from the back of his piebald horse. Wrapping a wool blanket around his shoulders, he stretched out in front of the fire. "If you're still alive in the morning, we'll head out."

"Hmmph." Oh, she would be alive all right! She wouldn't give the scoundrel the satisfaction of finding her dead come morning. Wouldn't she love to bash him over the head with a rock? She sighed, knowing she wouldn't, but the thought kept her from drifting to sleep. She wanted to stay awake as long as possible and plan her escape. Would she ever be warm again?

She lay as close to the fire as she dared and rolled into a ball. At least one side of her would be warm.

Gabriel and the children must be so worried. If nothing
had happened to Gabriel, that is. He could very well
have gotten lost in the storm as she had.

She gave herself a mental shake. Most likely he had
stayed in the barn. Only she was foolish enough to
venture out in a storm. But she had been genuinely
afraid something had happened to him. She never
thought she would lose hold of the rope. Closing her
eyes, she squirmed to get more comfortable and waited
for tomorrow and Red Feather or Gabriel. Whichever,
or whoever, came first.

*

How far could one small woman have gone?
Gabe's legs hurt from tromping through a foot of snow.
Maybe he went in the wrong direction? He headed in
the direction that made the most sense to him—where
Charity might have gone; toward the creek.

Then, she would have noticed where she was and
reversed direction. Had she gone straight up the
mountain or veered to the left or the right? His
shoulders slumped. She could be anywhere. Choosing
the right direction would require a miracle, but his God
was a God of miracles. He paused for a moment to pray,
then set off up the mountain.

He whistled for Lady to follow. She darted, nose to
the ground, from tree to bush and back to Gabe. He
didn't know if Irish Wolfhounds were hunters or not,
but the dog did seem to care a great deal for Charity. He
prayed it was enough for the dog to pick up her trail.

If it didn't snow again, maybe they would see

307

footprints soon. Most lost folks tended to wander in circles. Without fresh snow falling, any new tracks would remain visible.

When he found her, he would tell her he loved her. No more wasting time. No more waiting for the 'right' moment to have a serious conversation. He, of all people, should know that nothing was for certain on the Montana prairie. Not your next day, not your next breath.

It hadn't occurred to him or Maggie that her simple trek to the creek would result in her death. That was one thing these dogs would be good for—alerting the family to the whereabouts of snakes. He shuddered.

Occasionally, he cupped his mouth and called out Charity's name. His spirits sank each time he didn't hear a response. Night fell. He desperately needed to get warm and rest. Just for a moment. He got a fire started, pulled the dog close, and then munched on dry bread.

He prayed the children would be all right during the night and into tomorrow. His chance of running across Charity as soon as the sun came out was slim. Nope, looked like he was going to have to work hard to find his woman.

His woman. The words sounded wonderful. When he found her, he would grab her, kiss her hard enough to take her breath away, and declare his love. He would beg her to stay, promising whatever she desired. There was absolutely no way Charity O'Connell Williams was getting away from him.

Sleep tempted him, but if he succumbed the fire

would go out and there would be nothing left of him and the dog in the morning but a couple of icicles. He needed to get back on his feet and continue his search. He kicked snow over the fire until it was out and grabbed his knapsack.

The knapsack he had brought with him contained the bare essentials: a few cups worth of coffee, some dried meat, and flint for a fire. *Lord, please let Charity need the food and drink.* The alternative didn't bear dwelling on.

32

Every joint in Charity's body ached when she woke. Her front side stayed warm, while her back felt as though it wore a thin crust of ice. She struggled to get her bound feet under her without pitching headfirst into the fire.

Amos watched her, a smirk on his face. "Sleep well?"

"Please at least remove the ropes from my feet. I'm in danger of falling."

He shook his head. "I don't think so. Somehow, you and Gabe managed to escape from the Indians. I'm thinking it was because they untied you for some reason."

The man was smarter than he looked. "Please. I can't travel like this."

"True." He untied the rope from around her ankles, then tied one end to a nearby tree. He pulled a pistol out of its holster and advanced toward her. "Please remain still. I wouldn't want the bullet to go somewhere I didn't intend."

Charity's eyes widened, and she withdrew as far as the rope would allow. Amos stuck the barrel of the gun to her leg, and pulled the trigger.

Fire shot across Charity's thigh, bringing her to her knees. Tears poured down her face. "You shot me?"

"You won't be able to run very well, but you'll be able to walk, it's only a flesh wound." He withdrew a knife from its, sheath, lifted her skirt high enough to cut a swatch of her petticoat, then roughly bound her leg with the muslin. "There. You shouldn't bleed to death."

He was crazy with hatred. How could he shoot a defenseless woman? "What kind of a man are you?"

"One who believes in justice." He yanked her to her feet, then untied the rope again and retied to his horse's saddle horn. He did intend for her to walk while he rode the horse.

"Justice for what?" Charity limped after him toward his mount. Agony shot through her leg.

"Your husband stole the only woman I've ever loved. You live on land that should have been mine."

"Maggie made her choice, Mr. Jenkins. You should accept that fact."

He yanked the rope hard enough to bring her again to her knees. Blood ran down her leg, soaking her clothes. Her head swam with pain and tears clouded her vision. "I've done nothing wrong to you. You are a scoundrel." Despite her agony, she squared her

311

shoulders and lifted her chin. "If you're a praying man, I suggest you pray Gabriel doesn't find you."

"He will have no idea I had anything to do with your disappearance." Amos swung his leg over the saddle. "He'll believe you perished in the wilderness."

The man was delusional. Charity was too stubborn to die in the snow, despite her fear from the day before. That had been exhaustion and cold talking.

He spurred the horse to move, almost yanking Charity's arms from their sockets. If she had a gun, the man would not need to worry about Gabriel. She would take care of him herself! Her leg burned, and her knee buckled. How could he be so cruel?

The act of lifting her foot clear of the snow for each step caused unbelievable agony. "Just leave me here. I can't go on like this. You're a horrible man."

"Shut up." He slowed his horse. "Walk in the horse's tracks, and you'll be fine. Use your head for something other than a hat rack, woman."

She glowered, deciding she would not complain again, even if she found herself dragged, which might not be a bad idea considering how much her leg pained her. "How far is the Indian village?"

"Half a day's ride. You should be glad that the savages have no qualms about taking white women. I would hate to have to kill you myself."

"We can't have that, can we?" The coward.

She would never make it. She almost gave into the sobs threatening to burst free. Instead, she focused on bringing to mind Gabriel's strong jaw and hazel eyes.

The children's dark curls. She hung her head, and for the first time in over two years, prayed for God to help her. If He chose not to, then she prayed He would comfort the children and ease their sorrow at losing another mother.

After what she thought was a couple of hours, maybe less, she trudged mindlessly behind the horse, often losing her footing and being dragged until Amos noticed and stopped long enough for her to gain her footing.

This time, he glared at her until she wanted to smash her fist into his nose. Instead, she struggled upright and returned his glare. She wanted to scream at him, tell him that if he would let her ride they would reach their destination faster. But, she wouldn't. She would not say another word to him. When they reached Red Feather's village, she would not speak.

When she could go no farther, she collapsed and refused to move. Let him shoot her. She would welcome the end to her misery. With what little strength she could muster, she lifted her head and stabbed him with her gaze.

*

Gabe jerked as a gunshot rang out. He forced his stiff joints to move faster and called to the dog. "Come on, girl."

Who could be shooting way up here? He was pretty sure Charity hadn't taken one of the rifles with her. He should have checked the mantel. There weren't any homesteaders this far up the mountain that Gabe

313

knew about, but he supposed it was possible someone could have put in stakes without him knowing. Maybe Charity found her way to them. He faltered. Maybe they weren't the type of folks for a woman alone to stumble upon.

Gabe increased his pace, lifting one leg, then plunging, then lifting until he got into a rhythm of making his way through the snow. In some areas, the wind had swept the ground almost clear amongst the trees, something Gabe expressed great thanks to God for.

He stopped in a clearing and eyed the fire pit. He held his hand over it. Still warm. "What's this?" He squatted next to a dark stain on the snow. Blood? He stood and looked around, his rifle held ready.

Lady sniffed around the blood and a packed down spot in the snow where a body had obviously lain. She whined and looked up at Gabe.

"Was Charity here? Is this her blood?" He patted the dog, even while his heart thundered. Had the shot he'd heard wounded, or killed, Charity? If she was dead, where was her body? He quickly checked the surrounding area, his movements frantic.

Wait. Slow down and think. Somebody had lain there, and somebody, or something, was shot there. He studied the ground, noting hoof prints and what was clearly a set of human tracks following behind. He placed his foot next to the track. The prints were too small for a grown man.

He set his jaw. Clearly Charity, or another small

person, followed somebody on a horse. "Come on, Lady. Let's follow these tracks."

The farther he walked, the clearer it became that someone was following and falling several times in the snow. Blood stained each scuffed spot that marked a fall, and spots of it could be found in between. Was an injured person being taken against their will? What if he wasn't following his wife at all? What if he wasted valuable time following the wrong person? He stopped for a moment and studied the tracks once more.

He couldn't be wrong. There weren't that many people up here. He glanced at the dog. Lady whined and continued down the trail ahead of him as snow began to fall. Gabe raised his rifle and fired off a shot.

*

"Get up." Amos yanked on the rope.

Charity's head drooped, and she stared at the ground. Snow fell and dusted her head and shoulders. She had read somewhere that a thick blanket of snow could actually keep a body warm. Maybe she would try it.

"I said, get up!" He yanked harder.

She yanked back, barely affecting him on the horse. His face darkened.

He dismounted and stomped over to her. "Do you want to die out here?"

She speared him with as icy a gaze as she could muster.

He growled and grabbed her elbow. "Get on the horse. We're almost there anyway."

Pain screamed through Charity's thigh as he hauled her to her feet and shoved her toward his horse. He half helped her and half threw her into the saddle, then swung up behind her.

"Of all the women in Montana, you must be the most stubborn. I don't care if you talk or not. Doesn't affect me any."

Obviously her silence did bother him, since he rattled on like a magpie. Charity clamped her lips together to keep from smiling. It wouldn't do to let him know she played him like a fiddle.

A gunshot sounded about a mile behind them. Charity screamed. Gabriel was coming for her! Amos clamped his hand over her mouth and kicked his horse into a trot.

Within the hour they arrived in an Indian village. Teepees sat in a circle. Villagers in buckskin and furs stared as Amos steered the horse toward the largest tent.

A massive Indian that Charity didn't know, parted a flap and emerged with Red Feather. Red Feather's eyes widened at the sight of Charity. She shook her head, hoping he would read her unspoken message and pretend he didn't know her.

"Do you speak English?" Amos demanded.

"I do. I translate to chief." Red Feather gave a nod. "Why you here?"

Amos took a deep breath. "It has come to my attention that a young girl was killed. I did not shoot her, but she died as a result of my gun being fired. I have come to offer this woman in trade." He slid Charity from the horse. She cried out as she landed on her wounded leg and crumpled in the snow.

Red Feather frowned and translated. "She is wounded."

"Well," Amos shrugged. "This one I did shoot when she tried to escape. Once healed, she will make a fine slave or wife."

Red Feather motioned to a woman to assist Charity to her feet. He said something else to the chief, then returned his attention to Amos. "We accept your trade." He cocked his head. "Where are her people?"

Amos met Charity's gaze, and grinned. "I found her wandering in the storm yesterday." He glanced at the rapidly increasing snowfall. "Now, that we have reached an agreement, I must head home myself before I am snowed in. It was a pleasure doing business with you." He tipped his hat and turned his horse.

Charity slumped to the ground.

Red Feather stood over her. "Stand. Do not let the enemy see you weak."

She grabbed the woman's arm and struggled to her feet.

"He will look back. Walk to that teepee on own two feet."

Charity followed the direction he pointed, trying not to lean too heavily on the woman helping her. "Thank you for not letting him know we are acquainted."

"Babbling Brook will tend to your wound. I will get

317

word to your husband as soon as possible." He gave another nod and ducked back into the teepee with the chief, but not before Charity saw him motion to a young brave who immediately melted into the trees.

Despite his evil, Charity's heart constricted at the thought that Amos would have to pay for his crime after all. She sincerely doubted the brave followed to make sure the man made it home safely.

33

The Indian woman didn't speak a word of English, but spoke a mile a minute in her own tongue. Her smile seemed like a permanent fixture on her face, helping to set Charity at ease. She had only ever had experience with one Indian, Red Feather, yet she didn't believe any of his tribe intended her harm. They had stared as she walked to the teepee, but they looked more curious than hostile.

She sat on top of a bundle of furs and watched while Babbling Brook dumped some type of powder into a gourd of water. She stirred the concoction with a stick, then motioned for Charity to drink.

It smelled foul, and Charity wrinkled her nose. Babbling Brook waved harder. Ugh. She didn't think she could drink the liquid that was now a putrid shade of green. But if she didn't, she risked hurting the feelings of someone who seemed to want to help her. Charity closed her eyes and took a sip of the most rancid tasting thing she had ever put in her mouth. Heavens, the woman was trying to poison her.

Babbling Brook upended the gourd until Charity had no choice but to swallow or drown. Her stomach churned, and her eyelids grew heavy almost immediately, whether from the drink or sheer exhaustion, she didn't know. She only knew that rest suddenly became the most important thing to her.

The smoke from the fire rose toward a hole in the tanned hides that made the teepee's walls. The tendrils danced a joyful jig on their way. Charity smiled and wanted to reachout a hand to touch it, but her arm wouldn't move. What was in the drink? If she had the energy to do so, she would ask for more, terrible taste or not.

The other woman gently nudged her back onto the furs then lifted Charity's skirt. Charity ought to be embarrassed, but she couldn't even muster the energy for that.

Babbling Brook clicked her tongue and shook her head, then picked up a knife from a rock in the fire ring. Charity hoped the other woman intended no harm. Too weak to stop her, she let the drowsiness overtake her and prayed for God to save her.

*

Gabe whipped around as a shot rang out. A deep rumbling high on the mountaintop filled the air. Amos Jenkins rode hard through a narrow mountain pass toward him, a look of determination on his face.

So this is how it would end. Gabe pulled his rifle free, prepared to put an end to the silly feud. He didn't want to shoot him, only to make the man stop long enough to listen to reason.

The rumbling grew louder, and the ground shook under him. Rogue tossed his head and neighed in fear.

Gabe looked up. The mountainside barreled toward the mountain pass like a freight train. He kicked Rogue into action to get further away, yelling over his shoulder. "Ride hard, Amos! Avalanche. Hurry, man." Amos might be Gabe's enemy, but Gabe didn't want him dead, and the other man's location didn't bode well. Amos rode directly in the avalanche's path, and most likely couldn't hear Gabe's warning over the noise.

Amos's eyes widened. His horse reared. Amos's mouth opened in a scream as the wall of snow swept over him, taking him and the horse over a cliff. His heart sank. There was no way the man could survive a fall of that magnitude.

Gabe reined Rogue to a stop, his heart pounding in his throat. He made out the silhouette of an Indian high on the ridge. Had he been the target of Amos's bullet and not Gabe? Nevertheless, the gunshot must have started the avalanche.

Gabe dismounted and stared at the wall of white in front of him. There was no way he could take Rogue over something so high and soft, and they were too far from home to send the horse back alone. He couldn't leave Meg and Sam alone any longer. Could he get Miriam to stay with them and then return with Hiram?

Or had Charity found the Indian camp and sought shelter there?

He fell to his knees. What was Amos doing out here? Had he taken Charity? Was she still lost in the wilderness? He buried his face in his hands. The myriad of questions for which he had no answers tormented him.

His heart told him to continue, his head told him he could search no longer. The children were alone. Forcing himself to his feet, he climbed back in the saddle, *God, please protect her.* He turned Rogue toward home.

*

Charity woke to the quiet murmurs of two people speaking in a foreign tongue. Her leg throbbed, and she reached down to inspect the damage. Someone had bandaged her wound and dressed her from head to toe in soft doeskin. Her hair spread free across the furs she lay on. She wanted nothing more than to drift back to sleep, but her rumbling stomach wouldn't allow her to.

"Food." Red Feather thrust a bowl of meat and vegetables at her.

She pushed to a sitting position. "Thank you. How long was I sleeping?"

He shrugged. "Few hours. Long enough for Babbling Brook to close wound in leg."

"Gabriel hasn't come for me?" She thought he would have by now. What if Amos had gotten to him before the Indian brave got to Amos? "Where did you send that young man?"

Red Feather squatted in front of her. "After the man who shot you. The one who killed the young brave's woman. They were to be ...wed ... in the spring. She was my niece."

"I'm sorry." Charity tipped the bowl and slurped some of the stew. "I'm pretty sure he's the one who shot Gabriel, too. But, Red Feather, killing is wrong."

"I am not the one killing him." He poked at the fire with a stick and avoided Charity's gaze.

"You sent someone to do so, therefore you are also at fault." Charity didn't want to argue with the man who most likely saved her life. "I apologize. I mean no disrespect."

"Not all my people believe in the white man's God. My nephew is such a one." Red Feather tossed the stick into the fire and sat cross-legged in front of her. "Most do, but not him. He believes in a life for a life. Chief tried to talk him out of going after the white man, but he insisted. It is his decision."

Charity nodded and ate more of the simple stew. "The Old Testament speaks of a'n eye-for-an-eye,' but Jesus abolished that when he died on the cross." She smiled, remembering some of the things her Ma had taught her. Things Charity had chosen to forget.

"God has seen fit to give you to us, and take Amos Jenkins."

Charity stared at him in surprise. He couldn't be serious.

"Yes, I know who he is. I know his name. God used my nephew as a tool to rid the world of a bad man."

Red Feather took Charity's empty bowl from her hands.

"Used? He's dead?"

Red Feather nodded. "Nephew returned while you were sleeping. Jenkins fired a shot at him and the noise caused an avalanche. You may go home when the pass is cleared."

"I don't want to stay here." Tears welled in Charity's eyes. "I want to go home. Not when the pass clears." Her heart sank. That could be months.

"Snow piled high. You must rest now. God has sent you here for healing. He told me this. That you have much to ponder in your heart." Red Feather nodded a few times, his feather bobbing.

The notion that God might use an uneducated Indian to get Charity's attention was not lost on her. As the Bible stories her mother told her came back to her, she realized that God used such methods many times. He intended to use the ill deeds contrived by Amos for something good for Charity.

Amos intended for the Indians to do harm toward her, yet they healed her, dressed her, and gave her food as if she were a worthy guest. A worthy guest. Tears spilled over. How could she ever have thought herself unloved? God loved her more than any mortal man ever could. He could give her a contentment gold never could. The cross made her worthy of God's love, and therefore Gabriel's.

Red Feather stood. "You are sad. Time for you to pray." With those words, he turned and left her. Babbling Brook sat in a corner mending a piece of deerskin. For the moment, she was so quiet it was easy to forget she was there.

Charity lay on her back. Tears overflowed and ran down her cheeks to soak her hair and the furs under her. God was a God of hope. A God of promise.

If not today, maybe not tomorrow, but Charity would be reunited with Gabriel. Of that she had no doubt. She prayed it would be on earth rather than in heaven.

She had so much to tell him. Of her re-acquaintance with God who had never given up on her; of her love for Gabriel; of her desire to stay as long as he would have her. More than anything, she hoped she would have that opportunity. Her heart told her that Gabriel was looking for her. How long until he gave up? Would he be able to make it over the avalanche?

Two more days. She would give him that long, then she would go to him. Not even a fallen mountain would be able to keep her from doing so. She rolled over, snuggling deeper In the furs. She would go over the blocked pass or tunnel through it, but go she would.

There would be no question of what bed she would sleep in when she returned home. She would ask Mabel to watch the children for a few days, and she would show Gabriel what it was like to be truly married to Charity O'Connell. Her face heated, she smiled, and closed her eyes.

*

Amos lay under the suffocating blanket of snow. After being swept from his horse, he had tumbled and slid, finally landing, broken and bleeding somewhere at the foot of the mountain. He knew his moments were numbered. No man could survive being buried under several feet of snow. Already, he labored for breath. His heart beat slowed.

Bitterness and anger made poor bedfellows, and Amos had spent too long with each of them. Gabe Williams was the better man. He could have rejoiced over the sight of Amos being swept away, instead he had cried out a warning. Had he not been in danger himself, Gabe most likely would have rushed to Amos's side. Amos doubted he would have done the same.

He struggled to move his pinned arm and gave up when pain shot through his shoulder and back. He was in bad shape. His breath came in gasps now. It wouldn't be much longer before he met His Maker. He might have ridiculed some folks about their faith, but now Amos pulled from the faith his dear mother had instilled in him. Thank the Good Lord, that small amount was all he needed.

He smiled, knowing Maggie's children would be set for life by the provision in his will. Now, he could spend eternity with the one he loved.

Forgive me, God. Welcome me, despite my bitterness, into your arms.

*

Gabe wasn't much of a man for tears, but his shoulders shook with the sobs he couldn't hold back. The sight of Amos being buried alive brought to mind Maggie's death, and the fact that Charity might be stranded, or dead, and alone. He pulled her cloak to his lap and stroked the plush velvet as Rogue plodded his way home.

She had yet to wear the gift, stating it too fine for every day. What if she never got the opportunity? Why did women insist on holding onto nice things for those "special" times?

The sun began its descent over the mountain. It would be well past dark by the time Gabe made it home. He reached into his pouch and pulled out the dried. ⸻

He glanced back. Could he make it through the pass on foot? He thought again of taking the children to Hiram's and Mabel's then continue looking for Charity. Was she even on the other side of the pile of snow? *Lord, show me what to do!*

He couldn't remember the last time he felt this helpless. Every instinct told him to brave the pass and find the woman he loved, but responsibility told him to head home and care for the children. God would watch out for Charity or choose to take her home. Either way, Gabe needed to accept His will.

The thought brought him up short. It wasn't that Gabe couldn't keep his wives safe, it was that God decided it was time to bring them home.

Still his heart sat heavy. Charity was the love of his life. He would never find another woman to affect him, or claim his heart, the way she did. He would spend the rest of his life alone, caring for his children and the homestead that was now fully his. Yet, knowing he no longer needed to meet a deadline in regards to building the house left him empty.

The wind picked up, sending chills down his spine. He pulled his collar up to his ears and hunched in his coat. He wrapped the scarlet red cloak around his shoulders, feeling a bit like Charity was with him.

There was no way of knowing whether Charity was in heaven, but Gabe would do everything he could to find out as soon as possible. He would have faith in God's mercy in the meantime, and have hope.

34

Charity could not wait another day. Her leg still throbbed, despite her four days at the village, but the burning in her heart to be home and at Gabriel's side overshadowed everything else. She wanted to hug the children, pet the dogs, and laugh at the kitten's antics. She yearned to cook on the stove in the crowded soddy. She wanted to profess her love and tell her husband of her renewed relationship with their Heavenly Father.

She was willing to forget his lapse of judgment in making a wager with Amos. A wager that was now null and void.

Wrapping herself in furs, she marched out of the teepee, determined to state her intentions to leave to Red Feather. The morning sun warmed her face. Perhaps the pass wouldn't be too difficult to travel. She would leave today.

After she begged Babbling Brook for a bit of food

and water, she would make her way over the blocked pass and into the arms of her family. She had come to learn that Red Feather's nephew wasn't his nephew, at least not in the sense Charity would consider him to be. Pledging to wed Red Feather's niece gave him the title, and since his return after the avalanche, the young Indian's gaze followed Charity around the village like a dog slobbering after a bone. If she stayed much longer, she feared she would be forced to take the dead girl's place as his intended. Just as the cowardly Amos had planned.

The young brave, Straight Arrow, strolled past, adorned with intricate beadwork on his chest and feet. His dark gaze roamed over Charity, sizing her up for his future bride, no doubt. She forced her features to remain impassive and wished she had asked Babbling Brook for something with which to tie back her hair. The young man did not seem to understand that Charity was already married. He took Amos's word that she was in exchange for the dead girl. Several times, the young man reached out and ran his fingers through her red strands, making guttural sound in his throat and sending prickles of unease up her spine.

Way too forward, if he asked her, which he didn't. She complained to Red Feather, but he just stared, perplexed, and moved on about his business. Enough was enough. Charity whirled back to the teepee, and paused inside the flap.

She had nothing to pack. Her clothes were thrown away the first day, too dirty and torn to be repaired. She took a deep breath and approached Bubbling Brook who sewed beads onto a new pair of moccasins.

"I will be leaving today." Charity wrapped the robe tighter around her. "And I would like to thank you for helping me. I would also like to ask for a little food and water for my journey."

"No. I get Red Feather. You stay." Babbling Brook set aside her work and bustled outside.

She spoke English? Why hadn't she said anything? Communication over the last few days would have been much easier.

A few minutes after leaving, Babbling Brook rushed back inside and started bundling furs. "We leave now. Talk later."

"We're leaving to take me home?" Hope lit in Charity.

"No. Men come. Take furs." Babbling Brook ushered her outside, thrust several furs into her arms, then stepped back as others began to dismantle the teepee.

The usually organized and calm village had erupted into what looked like chaos. Women screamed, babies cried, dogs barked, and villagers ran here and there dismantling homes and tossing possessions onto the backs of horses.

"Wait." Charity turned, her gaze raking the village in search of Red Feather. What if the men thought she was an Indian captive? What if they captured her themselves? They could take her farther away from Gabriel. She spotted Red Feather by the chief's teepee.

She set the furs down and made her way through the milling villagers, dodging small children and dogs. "Who are these men?"

"Bad men. They take our furs and try to take our women." Red Feather clapped a hand on her shoulder. "Hide."

She shook her head. "I must leave. I cannot be taken by these men. Please, understand. I only want to go home. If they catch me, they will only detain me," Or worse. "My heart already aches more than I can bear."

He nodded. "Good luck. May God go with you."

"He will." She placed a hand on his arm. "Will you be all right?"

He nodded. "Red Feather will be fine."

"I will keep you and your people in my prayers." Lifting the hem of her fringed skirt, Charity limped ran into the woods.

A shot echoed across the snow-covered village. Charity increased her pace. Her leg screamed. Behind her, someone yelled for her to stop. Hooves pounded.

She dodged fallen trees and boulders. If she didn't find a place to hide soon, the man would capture her. *Lord, help me!*

*

Gabe stood beside the corral and stared in the direction of the mountain pass as he had done for the past two days. Each morning he climbed out of bed, fixed breakfast for the children, and went about his chores. All the while his heart yearned to search for Charity.

If she were still alive, did she think he had abandoned her? How could she possibly survive in the wilderness this long? She had no food or water. Did she know how to obtain any?

He forked more hay to the cattle. The children moped around the house worse than when Maggie had died. Of course, they were awfully young then. They most likely didn't remember their first ma very much.

Cattle taken care of, Gabe headed to the barn, thanking God the snowed had stopped and the sun shone bright, its rays glancing off the pristine whiteness. Normally, he enjoyed the view. Today, all he could focus on was the possibility of Charity being lost in nature's harshness. Again, he had failed to take care of his wife. To keep her safe.

When he had woke that morning and caught a glimpse of her dress hanging on a nail and her apron slung over a chair, he'd choked back a sob. Married less than a year and the loss of her left his life empty.

After checking that the horses were cared for, Gabe headed back to the house. Meg and Sam sat working on their numbers. Charity's scarlet velvet cloak lay draped across the foot of his bed where he laid it each morning when he woke. Having it near him and being able to touch it, brought a small measure of comfort to his aching heart.

He probably shouldn't keep it so close. Most likely, it wasn't healthy. He sat in his chair and stared into the flames.

"Pa?" Sam put a hand on Gabe's shoulder, pulling

333

him from his thoughts. "Have you given up on Ma coming home?"

"I can't leave you to make it over the pass."

"Don't you trust God to take care of her?" Sam knelt beside him. "He chose to take our other ma home, He might want to take this one, but until we know for sure, we shouldn't give up hope."

Gabe ruffled his hair. "You're right, son. When did you become so wise?"

"You taught me. In the Bible stories you read." Sam flashed a grin, warming Gabe's heart.

Gabe had a mighty high opinion of himself to think he could do better than God at keeping people safe. It wasn't Gabe's decision when it was a person's time to be called home. Sure, he could be sad about losing Maggie, and possibly Charity, but it wasn't because he didn't do his part to keep them safe.

"Son, you've lifted my spirits. There is still hope, and I think the situation deserves something special." He had done nothing but mope around for two days, and that type of behavior was no good for the children. "I believe there is enough cocoa powder left for some hot chocolate."

Sam and Meg cheered. Meg grabbed the kettle off the top of the stove while Sam took mugs off the shelves. Charity's blue tin mugs. If he had to do so every minute, Gabe would continue to remind himself that God was in control. Each time sorrow reared its ugly head, Gabe would need to hand the situation back over to God.

"I'm right proud of the way the two of you kept things going while I was gone the other day," he said, taking his customary place at the head of the table. "I pray I never have to be gone that long again, but if I ever should, and you feel the need, go to Hiram and Mabel."

Sam measured the cocoa powder into their mugs. "We were thinking on that the other day. If you hadn't come by daybreak, we would have rode my pony over. Don't worry, Pa. We can handle things around here. You worry about fetching Ma once the pass clears."

Gabe poured hot water into the mugs. "You really think she's on the other side, do you?"

Sam nodded. "Yep, saw it in a dream. She's making her way back to us."

That night, before Gabe crawled into bed, he hung Charity's cloak back on its peg where it belonged. He stroked the fabric, then turned down the lamp. God would take care of Charity. Gabe had to only trust him. For the first time in two nights, he closed his eyes, rolled over, and slept.

35

Charity peered from her hiding place beneath a mound of leaves and debris as two soldiers rode slowly past. Tobacco smoke whirled around them. She held her breath to ward off a sneeze and prayed they would hurry past.

"She couldn't have gone far," one of them said. "You would think a white captive would want to go back to her people."

"Maybe she's been with the Injuns for too long. Doesn't know she isn't one of them."

"Reckon you're right. Some captives forget how to act white. I ain't gonna ride around in this cold all day. Let's head back to the village and help round the others up. That's more fun anyway. Did you see them run?" He laughed, the noise startling birds from the trees.

They turned, leaving Charity alone. She expelled her breath and closed her eyes, laying her head on her folded hands. Her leg hurt so much she wanted to cry, and she was so close to having her plans to return home thwarted. She would not be captured! If she were, she would lie down and die.

She could hear screams from the village and the occasional cry of a child. She would need to remain hidden until the sounds quieted. Her heart ached for her new friends, and she prayed their rounding up would not result in any injuries or deaths. She wondered why Gabriel never mentioned Red Feather's tribe was destined for the reservation.

What would it be like to have someone dictate where she should live? There were times in her life when she felt as if she had no freedom, but never to the extent of being rounded up like cattle and shuffled off to a land that didn't belong to her.

When sounds from the village ceased, and no hoof beats pounded the forest trails, Charity climbed from her sanctuary. Her few hours of rest calmed the ache in her leg to a degree she felt ready to commence her journey. As a precaution, she searched for a stout stick to aide her progress. Finding one that her hand comfortably wrapped around, she set off with a smile on her face. By evening, she would gaze again upon Gabriel's and the children's faces and warm herself in front of her own fire.

The sun sat high in the sky by the time she reached the blocked pass. With the temperature warming a bit during the day, and freezing at night, she hoped the snow was packed hard enough for her to travel across.

She tested the firmness with her stick. The crust seemed strong, and if she jammed her stick in enough, she could make steps to climb to the top. She lifted a prayer of thanks, and placing her stick before her foot, set off across the expanse of white.

A few times, she sank to her knee or her hip, but she kept going despite the bone-numbing chill and increasing pain from her recent wound. Her mouth dried and her stomach rumbled, yet she still moved forward. Determination fueled her steps. The desire to see her family warmed her from the inside out.

She pushed aside the thought that she might, at that moment, be walking across Amos's grave. Instead of rejoicing, she prayed for God's mercy for a man so eaten up with bitterness that he had resorted to violence and evil intentions. It surprised her to realize she actually felt sorry for him.

A rabbit darted past her. Charity stifled a scream, then gave a nervous giggle. If only she had a rifle. Her stomach growled louder.

The creek would most likely be at the bottom of the mountain. She switched directions, sliding a few feet until she reached a small waterfall cascading into a brook. She cupped her hands and drank her fill of the icy water, and wished she had a container to carry some with. God had provided the water, He would see her home safely.

Straightening, she studied her surroundings, deciding which direction she should go. Down the mountain, for sure. The creek that ran in front of the soddy would take her home if she found it and followed it in the correct direction. Standing around wouldn't get her home and faster. Slipping and sliding, she made her way down to level ground.

She prayed she would find it soon before frost bite set in her fingers and toes. Moccasins were not the warmest footwear she had ever had, and her trip down the small cliff to the water had not done her leg any good.

There! She increased her limping gait at the sight of a frozen silver ribbon, winding its way home.

*

Gabe sank the axe into a chunk of wood. Two pieces of wood fell to the side. They most likely had enough stacked against the soddy to last the winter, but his hands needed to be kept busy. His gaze, despite last night's revelation that God would take care of Charity, still roamed too often to the tree line.

The sun had begun its descent. Another night fell with Charity gone. He plunked the axe into the tree stump and popped the kinks from his back. It would take self-discipline not to grab Charity's cloak and wrap himself in it when he slept. Last night, he had promised himself he wouldn't do that again. Doing so was admitting defeat. That she was gone for good.

Lady plopped on the ground next to him. She rarely left his side since they had returned from their search. She lay to his right, her soulful eyes trained on him. Her ears pricked, and a low woof sounded deep in her throat. The bark quickly turned to a whine, and she dashed toward the creek. Gabe turned and squinted through the dusk.

His heart stopped at the sight of a fiery-haired woman limping toward him. She lifted a hand, then fell to her knees. Gabe sprinted toward her.

"Charity." He pushed the excited dog away, then gathered Charity in his arms and rushed to the house, bursting inside.

"Meg! Heat water for coffee." He placed Charity on top of the quilt, then tugged the smelly buffalo robe off her. Indian garb. How had she gotten there? A blood stain covered her right thigh. "Down, Lady." The dogs, ecstatic to see their mistress, kept poking their massive heads in his way. "Sam, control the dogs, please."

Sam wrapped an arm around each of their necks and pulled them aside.

Modesty forgotten, he pulled the deer skin dress higher, and took in the sight of stitches, dark against her pale skin. A couple of them had pulled open. It *was* her blood he had found in the snow. His heart fell to his knees.

Who injured her? His hands formed into fists.

"Gabriel, I'm home," she whispered hoarsely, keeping her eyes closed. Her tongue flicked out across her chapped lips. "I made it."

He smoothed the hair away from her face. "Yes, you did. Rest, sweetheart. Coffee is coming. We'll have you warm in no time."

"Will she be all right?" Sam ordered the dogs to stay and approached the bed with Meg at his side. Tears shimmered in their eyes.

"I think so." Gabe took another quilt from the foot of his bed and laid it over Charity. "She's exhausted and cold. Nothing we can't fix."

Meg rushed to make the coffee. Gabe propped pillows behind Charity and helped her sit up.

"Can you manage to drink by yourself?" he asked her.

"I may need a little help, at first. Also, I'm starving. I've been walking since morning." Her eyes flicked open. "I'll drink the coffee and try to stay awake."

"I searched for you." He took the cup from Meg. "Thank you, Meg. Could you and Sam go to the barn for a few minutes while Ma and I talk?" He couldn't wait any longer to find out what happened to her. He held the mug for Charity to sip from while the children left. "I search until the avalanche almost buried me, then I headed home to care for the children. I couldn't leave them any longer than I already had."

She nodded. "I understand. I was with Red Feather's people. Amos thought he was trading me to them in exchange for forgiveness for the girl's death. Red Feather played along like he didn't know me. He arranged for a woman to care for me." She took the cup from him. "Oh, that feels so good.

"Anyway, a young Indian brave went after Amos in retribution, but the avalanche took Amos before the brave could." She took a deep breath. "The morning I left, the soldiers arrived and started rounding the tribe together for the reservation. I escaped in the confusion."

Gabe swallowed back his anger and forced his voice to remain calm. He wanted to ask how Red Feather was, but Amos's actions stayed in the forefront of his mind. He would worry about Red Feather later. "Did Amos hurt you?"

"I tried to escape the night we camped, so he gave me a flesh wound." She tossed out the words like they meant nothing. "Minor enough that I could still walk, serious enough I couldn't run."

"He shot you!" Gabe lunged to his feet. "If the man weren't already dead…"

She placed a hand on his arm. "What Amos intended for evil, God turned for good. I made my peace, Gabriel." Her eyes pleaded for him to understand. "God used this circumstance to open my eyes and show me what really mattered; what is really important. You should be pleased for me. For us."

He knelt beside her and took her hand in his. "I could have lost you, Charity." He rested his forehead in her lap. "I've been out of my head with grief and worry until Sam reminded me that God carried you in His hands. It's been a struggle every minute for me to leave you in the best place you could be—God's hands.

"I don't want you to leave come spring." He lifted his head and stared into eyes the color of summer grass. "I should be sorry that I wagered and tricked you into marrying me, but I'm not. If I hadn't made that stupid bet with Amos, I would not have had a need for a wife. I owe him for giving me you.

"I love you more than I could possibly express in a lifetime. You mean everything to me. Please say you'll stay with me. If not me, then the children. I'll take whatever you want to give me."

*

The words she had waited for years to hear from a man pierced her heart. Now, she was loved by a wonderful, godly man and by her Heavenly Father. Together they could improve this land and raise a passel of children.

"I don't want to leave. I've never wanted to leave." She ran the fingers of her free hand through his hair. "You are the sun that rises in the morning to me. If I didn't have but this moment, it would be enough."

He took the cup from her and set it on the floor, then cradled her face in his hands. Slowly, he brushed his lips across hers before finally claiming them as a husband should claim his wife. When he had left her totally breathless, he pulled back an inch, his breath tickling her skin. "You have made me the happiest man in Montana, Charity O'Connell Williams."

Her heart leaped. "Knowing you love me has made me the happiest woman on earth. Kiss me again."

He chuckled and leaned down.

The End

ABOUT THE AUTHOR

Multi published and Best-Selling author Cynthia Hickey had three cozy mysteries and two novellas published through Barbour Publishing. Her first mystery, Fudge-Laced Felonies, won first place in the inspirational category of the Great Expectations contest in 2007. Her third cozy, Chocolate-Covered Crime, received a four-star review from Romantic Times. All three cozies have been re-released as ebooks through the MacGregor Literary Agency, along with a new cozy series, all of which stay in the top 50 of Amazon's ebooks for their genre. She has several historical romances releasing in 2013 and 2014 through Harlequin's Heartsong Presents. She is active on FB, twitter, and Goodreads. She lives in Arizona with her husband, one of their seven children, two dogs and two cats. She has five grandchildren who keep her busy and tell everyone they know that "Nana is a writer". Visit her website at www.cynthiahickey.com